WRATH OF THE FORGOTTEN

Descendants of the Fall Book II

AARON HODGES

Edited by Genevieve Lerner
Proofread by Sara Houston
Illustration by Eva Urbanikova
Map by Michael Hodges

ABOUT THE AUTHOR

Aaron Hodges was born in 1989 in the small town of Whakatane, New Zealand. He studied for five years at the University of Auckland, completing a Bachelors of Science in Biology and Geography, and a Masters of Environmental Engineering. After working as an environmental consultant for two years, he grew tired of office work and decided to quit his job in 2014 and see the world. One year later, he published his first novel - Stormwielder.

FOLLOW AARON HODGES...

And receive TWO FREE novels and a short story!
www.aaronhodges.co.nz/newsletter-signup/

Only in the darkest of times,
Can we see the light of heroes.

Thanks to all the essential workers.
You're life savers.

THE KINGDOMS OF HUMANITY

PROLOGUE

THE SOLDIER

Lukys stumbled through the night, his feet catching on unseen obstructions, eyes straining to pierce the gloom. His chest ached from the blow he'd taken just hours earlier and the chainmail vest weighed heavily on his shoulders, but he kept on. He had no choice. Cords bound his hands tight behind his back, and another was looped around his neck, constricting whenever he slowed, his captors urging him on. Grunts came from behind as his fellow captive, Dale, struggled to keep pace.

Briefly, light shone from overhead and Lukys's eyes were drawn to a gap in the canopy. A sliver of the moon appeared between the branches. Then it was gone, the forest returning to darkness—but not before he glimpsed the movement all around them. Their captors. The Tangata.

Lukys shuddered at being surrounded by the creatures. Cruel and inhuman, they had no problem seeing in the dark. It was one of their many powers, stolen from the Gods in ages past and inherited down through the generations. For decades the Tangata had waged war against humanity, destroying all who came against them. And now he was their prisoner.

He still struggled to understand how it had come to pass. He'd arrived on the frontier with his fellow Perfugians, thinking he was to become a soldier. Reality had crushed those aspirations. Untrained and terrified, the Perfugian recruits had been ordered into battle that first day. Against the superhuman strength of the Tangata, they'd never stood a chance.

Yet Lukys had survived. Survived because of Romaine, the ferocious warrior of Calafe. Even amongst other soldiers, the man was an enigma. Wielding a great battle axe, he had stood alone against one of the creatures, and won. Lukys had never heard of such a feat—the professors of his academy learning asserted that just one Tangata possessed the strength of three human soldiers.

After the battle, Lukys had sought out the warrior and begged for his help. Reluctantly, Romaine had agreed to train him—and eventually over half the surviving Perfugian recruits had joined them. They'd fought together, learned together, had almost thought themselves true soldiers.

Until this disastrous expedition. Now his fellow Perfugians were dead, all except he and Dale. The two of them should have been slaughtered as well, cut down on the banks of the Illmoor River, but something had given the creatures pause. Something had changed their minds.

Something about Lukys.

A tremor slid down Lukys's spine as his eyes fixed on the creature that led them. Long, curly brown hair suggested it was one of the females of the species, though they were just as strong as the males. Lukys had no doubt she could tear him in half should the desire take her. She had not said a word through the night. The Tangata did not speak. Or so they'd thought…

Move…further east…catch them…

Around him, the forest was silent, the movements of the Tangata abnormally quiet. But in Lukys's mind…words whispered, mixing and churning against one another like the rumblings of a packed crowd. Unintelligible, yet unmistakable for what they were:

The thoughts of the Tangata.

Lukys didn't know why he could hear them—he hadn't even recognised the voices for what they were until that confrontation on the banks of Illmoor. Not until one of the creatures had spoken directly into his mind.

Who are you?

Ice filled Lukys's belly at the memory. The Tangata had seemed as confused as Lukys about his ability. That alone had saved them. But how long could this deferment of their execution last? How long before the beasts grew tired of their human captors, and put them down? Lukys had no illusions as to what awaited them.

Unless they could escape. Cautiously, he glanced back, seeking out Dale in the darkness. Until recently the two had been rivals, but they'd formed a mutual respect during this fateful expedition. Fighting together, they had slain several of the Tangata, in itself a miracle. Perhaps they could—

A flicker of moonlight sliced through the night, momentarily revealing Dale's face. Bruises purpled his cheek and had almost swollen his eyes closed, while a trail of blood ran from his mouth. The creatures had beaten them both before discovering Lukys's talent, but Dale had received the worst of their anger.

A soft wheezing came from Dale's throat and with his eyes on the ground, he didn't notice the attention. Quickly, Lukys returned his gaze to the way ahead, all thoughts of escape fleeing his mind. Dale could barely walk, there was no way they could outrun the Tangata, even if they somehow managed to break free.

Despair wrapped its thorny tendrils around his heart and began to squeeze. In his mind he heard new whispers, not of the Tangata now but his own, commanding him to give up, to sit down and surrender to his fate.

Yet he stumbled on, legs burning, chest screaming, driven by some tiny, determined part of him to reach the morning, to survive the night. The Tangata were not immortal; they *could* be defeated. All Lukys could do was wait, and hope.

Almost imperceptibly, the light began to grow, the sounds of the night retreating. Focused on the rhythm of the march, Lukys didn't notice at first. Eventually though, he began to make out shapes on the ground before him, tree roots and fallen branches, rocks and the footprints of creatures that walked before him.

Blinking, he lifted his head and felt a tingle of triumph. The red light of dawn now filtered through the winter forest. The Tangata had kept to the lowlands—that much he knew from the gentle terrain they had traversed—and the canopy was low above their heads, empty branches reaching for them like claws. The sky was clearly visible, though grey clouds stretched out as far as the eye could see.

Lukys was no woodsman, but there was only one direction the creatures could be taking them—south, towards those unknown regions beyond the broken Agzor Fortress, to the ancestral homeland of the Tangata.

The thought twisted his bowels into knots. They were passing now through the fallen kingdom of Calafe. Just six months ago, with their armies broken, the last of its people had fled north into Flumeer. Only the Tangata roamed these lands now. But at least they still bore the echoes of that lost civilisation. What would they find in the Tangatan homeland, unknown to humanity for centuries?

Their captors did not stop with the emergence of the day, and though the light made the going easier, Lukys could feel his final reserves of strength dwindling. The last weeks had taken their toll and now he desperately needed rest. Dale could hardly be any better. Yet still the female who led them continued, her brethren slipping through the forest in their silent manner.

"How much farther?"

The words slipped from Lukys in a desperate gasp. Even as he spoke them, he stumbled, his weakened legs tripping on a rock that protruded from the hard ground. With his hands bound he was unable to steady himself, and he slumped to one knee. The rope tightened around his neck, but thankfully the Tangata had stopped at the sound.

Slowly she turned, and Lukys felt a bolt of fear as solid grey eyes fell upon him. Those eyes were the mark of the Tangata, the only outward difference to a human. Yet they meant everything. In those eyes, Lukys could see his death.

Not long now, human.

Lukys's skin crawled as the voice whispered directly into his mind. The whispers around them remained indistinct, but this creature's words were crisp, clear. Their presence in his innermost thoughts felt like a violation, and he wondered what else the Tangata might be capable of. Could the monster before him read his mind? Was she doing it even now? He swallowed, staring into those cold eyes, but seeing no signs of emotion.

Finally he nodded and carefully pulled himself back to his feet. The Tangata regarded him for a long moment, then turned and started off again. A tug on the rope urged Lukys to follow.

"It's useless," a voice gasped from behind him, "I…can't keep up…sorry, Lukys."

"Don't give up," Lukys hissed, glancing back at Dale. "We're almost there."

A frown touched his friend's forehead. "What?" he rasped. "How…do you know?"

"I…" Lukys hesitated.

He hadn't told the other recruit about the whispers. What would Dale think if he discovered Lukys could *hear* the enemy? It seemed…treacherous, blasphemous even. No, better he keep it a secret for now, until he learnt more about this new ability.

"They can't run forever," he said instead. "Even the Tangata have to rest."

Despair shone from Dale's eyes, but after a long moment, he nodded and lowered his head. Lukys breathed a sigh of relief as the man continued walking. He didn't know what the creatures had in store for them, but the thought of being left alone with the beasts…it didn't bear thinking about.

Lukys stumbled as the rope around his neck suddenly went slack. He looked up, surprised to find that the female Tangata had come to a stop. Her silver eyes were watching him again, and he quickly looked away, unable to hold that eerie gaze. Movement came from nearby as the others emerged from the trees.

Rest. The voice seemed cold in his mind, like a ghostly breath upon his neck. *We will stay here a time.*

He forced himself to meet the female's gaze. No more words were forthcoming, and after a drawn-out moment, Lukys turned to Dale.

"I think we're stopping here."

The recruit didn't wait for confirmation. He slumped to the ground and leaned against a nearby tree trunk, a moan slipping from his mouth. Lukys longed to join him, but instead he turned to inspect their surroundings.

The forest had thinned here, the canopy opening to grant them a view of the nearby hills. What Lukys saw confirmed his suspicions from the night. They were moving through one of the southern passageways—long, flat valleys that ran for hundreds of miles, so straight that some claimed they'd been carved from the earth by the Gods themselves. There were some in Flumeer as well—Lukys and his fellow Perfugians had taken one on their journey to the frontier. But that passageway had ended some fifty miles from the town of Fogmore, forcing them to climb the foothills to reach their destination.

There was no sign of an end to this passageway, though. Stark cliffs stretched away into the distance, their tops covered by a scattering of deciduous forest. Standing amidst the grandeur of that landscape, Lukys could understand how some had come to associate them with the Gods. Many were the legends of the Divine beings that had brought about The Fall, that terrible darkness that had almost destroyed humanity centuries ago. The Gods had vanished during that time, retreating into the forbidden mountains, it was said. Never to be seen again.

Until now. Until the battle for the Illmoor.

A smile crossed Lukys's lips as he pictured his friend Cara soaring above the river, wings spread wide, auburn feathers shining in the dying light of day.

A Goddess, hidden amongst them.

She had fallen upon the Tangata with vengeance, tearing through their ranks, hurling them aside with wing and fist and boot. More than a few of Lukys's captors sported bruises from that encounter, and he wondered what they thought of the Divine being that had appeared amongst them. Did the Tangata know what Cara was, what it was they had fought?

The whispers continued in Lukys's mind and he tried to focus, to draw sense from the chorus, but the words remained a jumbled puzzle, nonsensical.

He shook his head, spirits deflating once more. In the end, not even a Goddess had been enough to save them. Cara had been driven back by sheer numbers, and while she'd managed to rescue the Archivist, she could not save them all.

Dale and Lukys had been left behind.

His gaze fell to Dale again. Bruised and broken, the man had slipped into a doze. Watching him sleep, Lukys could hardly imagine this was the same arrogant noble born who had mocked Lukys on the journey south from Mildeth. The weeks of strife had changed him—had changed them both. Blood and dirt stained their uniforms to the point where the Perfugian blue was barely recognisable, yet Lukys felt more a soldier now than he ever had north of the River Illmoor.

A shame those new skills hadn't mattered, in the end. They had been defeated all the same.

Come, human.

Lukys started as their captor's voice spoke into his mind once more. Swinging around, he was surprised to find the female standing directly behind him. Somehow, he managed not to shrink away.

"Already?" he hissed softly, struggling to contain his anger. He gestured at Dale. "He can barely stand."

The Tangata's grey eyes flickered toward Dale, then returned to Lukys. *He can stay,* came her reply.

"Stay?" Lukys muttered. Suspicion touched him and clenching his fists, he stood his ground. "I won't let you harm him."

The female crooked her head to the side, eyes unchanged, unreadable. *The other…will not be harmed,* she said finally. *You are wanted.*

"Wanted by who?" Lukys asked, his voice trembling despite himself.

A face burst into Lukys's mind in response: of himself lying on the shores of the Illmoor, a Tangata raising a blade above his head. In that instant, he sensed this was their leader. Lukys didn't need to question further to know who wanted him.

"What does he want?" he whispered finally.

A knife appeared in his captor's hands. He flinched at the sight of it—though of course, she needed no weapon to kill him. Before he could pull away, the blade flashed out, severing the rope that had connected him to Dale. He staggered, but a firm tug on the cord around his neck prevented him from falling. His breath was stolen away as she hauled him back up, bringing his eyes level with hers.

Come!

Lukys went.

❦ I ❧

THE FALLEN

Consciousness came slowly to Romaine. It began as an ember on the forest floor, slowly growing brighter, greater, until suddenly it burst asunder, pressing back the darkness. He fought to stay, but the pull was irresistible, and slowly he was drawn back into the cold, unforgiving light. Back to the pain.

An ache radiated through his chest as he opened his eyes, revealing a rough wooden ceiling above. He quickly closed them again as a pounding began in his skull and stifled a groan, though none of those aches compared to the searing heat that engulfed his left hand.

Or rather, his missing left hand.

Images flickered through his mind and he saw again the creature as it attacked, the terrible grey eyes staring out from an all-too-human face. The thing might even have *been* human once, but there was nothing natural about the way it had moved in those caverns beneath the earth. Nothing normal about the strength it had wielded, about the way it had broken him.

Shuddering, Romaine pushed aside the memories and

drew another breath. It hurt a little less this time. The scent of burning coal carried to his nostrils and he realised someone had lit the brazier. Exhaling, he forced his eyes open once more and struggled to sit up. The ache in his chest turned to a lancing pain, but if he didn't move too quickly it seemed manageable.

He gritted his teeth as his head swam and stars flashed across his eyes. When his vision finally cleared, Romaine was surprised to find himself in his own cabin. His wounds couldn't be as bad as he'd feared if they hadn't kept him in the infirmary. Then again, he supposed a medic could do little for broken ribs or severed hands.

His gaze passed over the cabin, though the space was hardly worthy of the name. His bed was pressed up against the wall opposite the entrance, and there were few furnishings besides the brazier in the corner and the clothes chest tucked against the wall. He didn't need anything more than that, between taking his meals in the soldiers' mess hall and the occasional visit to the communal bathhouse. Indeed, the cabin was more than a simple soldier could normally expect. While those of other nations were bunked in barracks of fifty, the last soldier of Calafe slept alone.

Grief washed over him like a wave, threatening to overwhelm him. He had set off on an expedition in search of hidden ruins, of a place abandoned by the Gods. Tunnels dug beneath the earth, sealed away for millennium, their secrets with them. But the site was in enemy territory, in lands that had once belonged to his people. Romaine hadn't expected to return. He had gone to protect the men and women he had mentored, Perfugian recruits who had stood little chance of surviving without his guidance.

How fitting, then, that he should now find himself back here. Alone.

Romaine scrunched his eyes closed, struggling to

contain the pain, the sorrow. He had failed them all—
Lukys, Travis, Dale and so many others—failed to protect
them, to save them. Now they were all gone, slain by the
Tangata, their corpses left for the scavengers.

Was he cursed to forever suffer this grief, to watch
everyone he cared for perish, while he lived on? Even his
family had been taken from him, so long ago now, yet the
wound still felt fresh. The memory of his son lying dead in
the snow, of his wife's silent corpse, haunted him to this day.
They too he had lost to the Tangata, the first of many he
had loved. After a decade of war, Romaine was tired of
counting the bodies.

At least there was still Cara.

Regret touched him as he thought of the young woman.
She might have saved the others, might have saved them all,
if only he had not been so blinded by his hatred. He'd
thought her a spy, one of the Tangata that had learned to
camouflage itself amongst humanity. They'd all seen her
eyes in those awful tunnels, seen the grey madness of the
enemy lurking there.

But they'd been wrong.

Cara wasn't Tangata at all, nor even human. She was
a God.

Driven by desperation, she had revealed herself on the
banks of the Illmoor River. The sight of her soaring across
the muddied waters, auburn wings spread wide, was one
Romaine would remember until his dying days.

He could hardly believe it now, that one of the Divine
had hidden amongst them, had spoken with them,
befriended them. The Gods were mythical beings, their true
nature long since hidden beneath rumour and legend. To
think of one living amongst humanity…it changed
everything.

Yet even Cara's power was limited. Alone, she had

fought to rescue their friends. But it had not been enough to stem the tide of Tangata that had swarmed across the banks of the Illmoor. In the end she had been forced to retreat, able only to save the Queen's Archivist, Erika. The others…

Romaine scrunched his eyes closed and levered himself to his feet. The agony returned to his chest, but it seemed preferable now to the pain of his loss. He staggered to the trunk at the foot of his bed and retrieved a fresh tunic—the one he still wore was stained with blood. It was a struggle to pull it over his broad shoulders with only one hand. So strange, how he could feel it still. If he closed his eyes, he could swear his fingers were there…

But no, better he face reality. There was only the ruined stump now. The thought filled him with dread, and his gaze was drawn to the great-axe that had been left propped against the head of his bed. He reached for it, then paused.

The axe was a two-handed weapon. Desperation had allowed him to wield it against the Tangata in defence of his friends, but even then, only by luck had he survived the encounter. No, it would be the height of arrogance to continue carrying it into battle. His hand returned to his side and he clenched it into a fist. He would need to find a new weapon.

In the meantime, Romaine turned his attention back to dressing himself, pulling on a fresh pair of pants and a belt. The simple manoeuvre left him panting, the pain in his chest robbing him of strength. But he managed it before slumping back to the bed, gasping.

The murmur of voices came from outside as the citizens of Fogmore woke to begin their days, and the squeak of boards from overhead announced that his neighbours had risen. Romaine let out a sigh, struggling to beat back the despair. What was the point of leaving his bed? If not for Erika, he would have lain down and died back on the banks of the Illmoor. He would have finally been free. Now he wondered what madness had taken him, that he had listened to the woman.

She had claimed to be the daughter of his fallen king. Even now, the thought made his stomach flutter. The Calafe king had been slain in the first battle against the Tangata, when he'd led an allied army deep into enemy territory. It was said the enemy had taken him by surprise, decimating the Calafe forces before the Flumeeren warrior queen had come to their aid. That had been the beginning of the end for his people.

Maybe that was why, through the pain and fatigue, he had accepted Erika's claim so readily. But in the cold light of day, her assertion seemed farcical.

The voices in the street were growing louder, and letting out a sigh, Romaine rose from the bed. He took a moment to gather his strength, then staggered to the door and slipped into his boots. Deciding the laces were beyond him, he pushed out into the street instead. A cold breeze greeted him, a reminder that winter had not yet released its grip on the land. Ducking his head beneath the doorway, Romaine stepped outside.

A light snow was falling, though the passage of people had already crushed it into the muddy streets. Clouds hid the sun above, but from the faintness of the light Romaine knew it still to be early. He pulled the door closed and started down the three wooden steps that led to street level, taking care not to slip on any ice and injure himself further.

"Romaine!"

He had just placed his boot into the puddle at the bottom of the stairs when a voice cut through the crowd. A moment later, he glimpsed the scout Lorene moving towards him down the street. The man had not accompanied the Perfugians south with Romaine, but he was probably one of the few Flumeeren soldiers he knew beyond a casual acquaintance.

Relieved for an excuse to rest, Romaine sat on the bottom stair. More than a few of the passersby flashed him strange looks as they went about their business, but Romaine ignored them, his attention instead on the approaching scout. There was a sense of controlled urgency about the man. He was puffing by the time he stopped in front of Romaine and his cheeks were a bright red, as though he'd run the entire way. Even so, he still had time to frown as he looked Romaine up and down.

"The medics said you'd be in bed for a week," Lorene commented.

"Fast healer, lad," Romaine grunted, though his head was swimming. "Something you came to tell me?"

Lorene hesitated, seeming to doubt himself for a moment. He swallowed, jaw tight. It obviously wasn't good news. Romaine wondered what fresh agony the world had in store for him.

"It's Cara…ah, the Goddess," Lorene croaked. "She's gone. We think the Archivist took her."

𝕏 2 𝕏

THE FUGITIVE

E rika sat in the front of the sailboat, watching how the mist curled around the bow, how it clung to the swirling waters. The white tendrils hid the night sky, concealed everything but for a sparse foot around them. It also hid them. Just as well—with their pursuers out in force, the fugitives needed every advantage they could get. Even now she could hear the voices on the river, the distant calls of the Flumeeren hunters, seeking their prize.

They would not have her.

It was the second night since she had fled the town of Fogmore, aided by the mysterious Gemaho spy. Her gaze was drawn to where the woman sat at the back of the boat, hand on the tiller. Erika didn't even know the woman's name—only that she'd been sent by the King of Gemaho. Why the man would want to help her, Erika couldn't under-stand, though...

Her eyes fell to the vessel's third occupant: the woman lying chained at Erika's feet. At first glance, Cara might have been mistaken for human. Copper hair hung across her shoulders and the amber eyes that looked out from her narrow face were far from the Tangatan grey. Her clothes were plain, grey and red, borrowed from their Flumeeren hosts.

But even in the darkness, there was one stark difference between Cara and a human, one that marked her as one of the Divine.

Wings.

Swathed in auburn feathers, they sprouted from somewhere near the middle of Cara's back. At this moment they were furled around the young Goddess and bound in chains for good measure—along with her arms and legs. Thankfully, they seemed to be enough to hold her. Erika didn't want to find out what the Goddess would do to them if she ever got free.

Shivering, Erika's gaze returned to the mists, and she found herself wondering what she was doing there. She was an Archivist, a student of history, of the Gods that had vanished after casting down the world. She should be asking Cara questions, seeking answers to the mysteries that had plagued humanity for centuries. Not locking her up, not making her their enemy.

Yet, what choice did she have?

She had lost everything in that disastrous venture south: her reputation, her position in the Flumeeren court, her chance to stand side by side with the nobility. All because of General Curtis's betrayal, because he had sent her Perfugian recruits instead of real soldiers. The queen had promised penance should she fail. Erika wasn't about to allow the general's incompetence to cost her life. So when the King of Gemaho had offered her a lifeline, she had grasped it with both hands.

She would do whatever it took to survive.

Even if that meant betraying a God.

Erika's insides twisted and her gaze was drawn back to

Cara. She winced as their eyes met and she saw the rage flickering in those amber depths. That look promised revenge. Instinctively, Erika found herself flexing her right hand, on which she wore a gauntlet crafted from impossibly fine wires of an unknown metal. It had fused to her very flesh when she'd first put it on and she had been unable to remove it since.

Light blossomed around her knuckles as she clenched the fist. The gauntlet held incredible magic, power enough to strike down the Gods themselves. It was with this that she had captured Cara, taking the Goddess by surprise. A violent, unholy act.

Just a few weeks ago, it would have been unthinkable to Erika. Yet she had done it with hardly a thought. Now she sat sailing through the night, fleeing the kingdom that had supported her for over a decade, intent on delivering the Goddess into the hands of their enemies. Never mind that the Gemaho King had tried to take her life just a few weeks before, or that Cara had rescued her from the Tangata, that she had been Erika's friend.

A shudder racked her and she allowed her hand to relax. The light died and she found herself looking into Cara's eyes again. Now she saw the pain beneath the Goddess's anger. All of Erika's excuses, all her justifications, withered beneath that look.

Finally she looked away, unable to meet the accusation in her former friend's eyes. If the Goddess wanted to live amongst humans, it was time she was taught this lesson. It was one Erika had learnt well as a child. Don't trust, don't allow others to get close. To do so was to invite betrayal. Others were only worth as much as they could benefit you.

And Cara...well, she was the key to a secret world, to powers unknown, ones even greater than the gauntlet. First though, they had to escape the lands of Flumeer.

"Get down," a voice hissed from the back of the boat.

Immediately, Erika slipped from the bench and crouched alongside Cara. Behind, her companion ducked beneath the gunwale. In the darkness, Erika could see little of the woman from Gemaho. Whispers carried through the night and Erika squinted, trying to pierce the mist, seeking the source. An orange light flickered into life and the breath caught in her throat. Another ship was drifting somewhere out on the river.

Fortunately they had kept to the northern shore. The hunters loomed farther out in the currents, though as Erika watched, the light from their ship seemed to grow. She looked back as their boat shifted direction. Her silent companion had her hands on the tiller, directing them towards the shore. There was a *thud* as the bow pressed up onto the mud, barely audible over the whispers of the breeze.

Erika held her breath, eyes on the glow of their pursuers. It continued to grow closer. Silently, she tightened her fist, preparing to summon the power. Then she hesitated, glancing at the gauntlet, wondering. She had come to rely on its magic since finding it in that hidden chamber, come to thrill in its power.

Erika's heart thundered in her ears as she looked on her metallic fist. She had made so many mistakes these past weeks, had hurt so many people. Shouldn't she care? A tremor shook her as she recalled the creatures they had encountered in the caverns beneath the earth, driven mad by the magic they had stolen. Could the same be happening to her?

The gauntlet drew on her own energies—she had discovered as much on the banks of the Illmoor, when its exertion had all but drained away her life force. But she would have known if it was changing her, if it was making her like…those things in the dark. Wouldn't she?

Releasing a breath Erika hadn't realised she'd been holding, she unclenched her fist, allowing the light to die. What was she thinking, anyway? The gauntlet's magic was only useful in close quarters. Her hunters would know that —their archers would pepper her with arrows long before they came close enough for Erika to use the power.

"Make sure the girl is quiet."

Erika frowned as the spy's words drew her back to the present. Her companion never addressed Cara as a God. It seemed blasphemous, though of course, the Gemaho were not known to be a Godly people. Still, with the wings just… hanging there, Erika would have thought they'd be enough to convert the most studious of disbelievers.

Even so, she shifted closer to Cara and made sure her gag was firmly in place. The Goddess squawked in protest, but the cloth muffled the sound and it was easily lost in the lapping of water against the hull. Turning back to the spy, Erika nodded that their…passenger was secure…

…and noticed the light still growing brighter in the mist beyond their white sail. Her heart thudded painfully against her chest and instinctively she clutched a hand to Cara's shoulder, pressing gently. Erika's own strength could never harm the Goddess, but with her gauntleted fist, the threat was clear and Cara ceased to struggle.

At the rear of the boat, her companion cursed softly and reached into a pack. Erika expected the spy to draw out a weapon, but instead her hand emerged with a smooth sphere of glass. Silently, the woman held up the object, a frown wrinkling the plain features of her face.

Erika's gaze was drawn to the sphere as it began to glow. A cry started in her throat—the light would give them away —but immediately the glow faded, becoming muted, the orb itself fuzzy and indistinct. Abruptly, it vanished—and the woman's hand with it, as though they had been drawn into some other dimension. The spy did not react, only raised a finger to her lips as the effect expanded outwards, swallowing her arm, then the woman herself entirely.

Clutching at the Goddess lying alongside her, Erika fought not to scream as the strange magic crept across the boat towards them. Within seconds, half the boat had been consumed, until finally she could take it no longer. Stifling a cry, Erika scrambled up, preparing to throw herself over the side before the magic claimed her as well.

"*Don't move*," a voice hissed from the emptiness where the spy had crouched a moment earlier.

Erika's mouth fell open and she froze. The magic reached her before she could recover from the confusion, and she watched in horrified fascination as it swallowed her leg. Beside her, Cara blinked out, even as the power continued up her waist, her chest, her throat. Silently she sucked in a breath, as though that might save her from being wiped from existence…

Darkness followed as the magic enclosed her, and for a moment Erika thought it was over, that the power had claimed her. Then the black fell away, and she found herself clinging again to the sides of the sailboat. Cara lay alongside her, while the spy sat nearby, finger still to her lips.

Erika's racing heart began to subside. She looked around, seeking their pursuers, and found herself surrounded by a bubble of light. It was as though they had been encased in a snow globe, the plaything of some giant. The outside world could barely be seen through its glow. Surely their pursuers must see it?

But recalling again how the spy and boat had vanished before her eyes, Erika realised that the globe had simply rendered them invisible from without. Her gaze was drawn to the orb still clutched in the hands of her companion. Its crystal surface was aglow, seemingly a reflection of the magic that surrounded them. Somehow, this object concealed them.

They sat in silence, listening for the telltale whispers of their pursuers. Breathing deeply, Erika strained her ears for hint of their approach, for sign they had been spotted. The acrid scent of burning pitch carried to her nose and she caught the occasional whisper, of voices on the breeze, the squeak of boards beneath boots, waves lapping upon a wooden hull, but the hunters came no closer, and slowly even those soft noises faded away.

Silence returned to the night, and finally the Gemaho spy released her grip on the globe. Its light died away and the greater orb vanished, returning them to the world. Erika watched as the woman put the object away. It had to be another artefact from the Gods.

They waited a few minutes more before the spy resumed her station at the tiller and directed them out into the currents.

"Where did you find that?" Erika whispered as the wind filled their sails.

The woman shrugged. "You are not the only one who searches for remnants from before The Fall, Archivist," she replied.

Erika nodded, resuming her seat at the bow. "Why don't you use it all the time?"

The woman frowned as she looked up from the rudder. "Have you not discovered the limitations of your own arte-fact, Archivist?"

"Ah," Erika nodded. "It draws from your own strength?"

The spy obviously didn't deign the question worthy of reply, for her lips remained pursed closed, eyes on the swirling mists. Erika let out a sigh, following her gaze, wondering at the situation she had gotten herself into. She had only this unnamed woman's word that she could trust the king.

"My name is Erika, by the way," she murmured after a time, then: "What should I call you?

Before, Erika had rarely bothered with names. Those worthy of her respect already knew her name, and she knew theirs. Those of lesser rank used the title "Archivist." It was the same with all those who participated in the dance of power amongst the Flumeeren nobility. But after betraying the queen and fleeing her adopted nation, it no longer seemed quite…right.

The spy did not reply immediately, and Erika sighed, returning her gaze to the darkness. It was going to be a long trip to Gemaho—

"You may call me Maisie," her companion finally whispered. "And I suggest you get some sleep. We cannot travel during the daylight. I will need someone to keep watch while I rest, or it will be a long three days to the Fortress Illmoor."

❧ 3 ❧

THE SOLDIER

The Tangatan leader stood in the centre of the clearing, its back turned towards Lukys, gaze lifted to the cliffs hemming the valley. Long white hair hung across its broad shoulders and like most Tangata, its only weapon was a dagger worn on its belt. A plain tunic and cotton leggings would have suggested a simple upbringing amongst humans, but was normal attire for the Tangata. Indeed, with its stiff posture and hands clasped behind its back, there was an almost noble bearing about this individual.

Lukys hesitated at the sight of the lone figure, glancing back at his Tangatan escort, but she said nothing. She had freed him of his bonds and now watched on with an expectant look. Taking his cue, Lukys swallowed and stepped into the clearing. Sunlight washed across his face and he felt his fears dissipate. Lifting his head to the sky, he drew strength from its warmth, the night's chill banished in an instant.

A flicker at the edge of his vision drew Lukys's gaze back to the Tangatan leader. He swallowed as he found the creature now watching him, grey eyes seemingly darker despite the daylight. He'd never paid attention to the differences between individual Tangata, but there was something distinctive about the creature before him, an aura of power, of invincibility, that set his knees shaking.

Human. The voice was louder than those of the guards, than the whispers of the others. Lukys grated his teeth, struggling to hold himself in place, to fight the urge to flee. *It is time we spoke.*

Lukys shuddered, but he was slowly getting used to the voices, and he straightened. "I am a soldier of Perfugia," he said shortly, hoping the creature was unaware of their true reputation, "and you will get nothing from me."

Perfugia? Laughter whispered in Lukys's ears as the creature paced a circle around him. His courage wilted beneath that appraisal and he found himself shrinking, as though to escape his captor's scrutiny. But there was no escaping the words in his mind. *Ah yes, I see the blue beneath the filth. A fitting addition.*

Lukys flinched as the creature came to a stop before him. Its face was just a few inches from his own. A sickly smile twisted its lips as it leaned closer.

Tell me, human, how does it feel to be betrayed by your own kind?

A lump lodged in Lukys's throat and he knew he was exposed, his every secret laid bare beneath this monster's gaze. It knew he was a failure, that the Sovereigns of Perfugia sent the worst of their people to the frontier to die, rather than consume precious resources. His gaze dropped to the forest flaw.

"My name is Lukys." It felt important to speak the words, to remind himself that he was no longer the naïve man who had arrived in Fogmore all those weeks ago. He had made something of himself since those first days, had stood against the Tangata and creatures far worse. Straightening, he looked again at the Tangata. Suddenly his captor no longer seemed quite so intimidating. "What do you want, beast?"

A scowl crossed the creature's face. *Respect, human.* The words rumbled in his mind and he glimpsed the anger in those terrible grey eyes. *I am called Adonis. You would do well to remember the name.*

An icy breeze blew across Lukys's neck as the creature turned away, hands clasped behind its back once more. Lukys opened his mouth, then closed it, struggling to string together a sentence in his mind.

"My apologies," he said, finally managing to approximate something resembling words. "I…didn't realise you used names."

Laughter rasped from the creature's throat as it swung on him, causing Lukys to flinch.

How little you humans think of us, its voice whispered in his mind.

Lukys clenched his fists and met the creature's gaze. He could see the loathing there, the hatred. "Why didn't you kill me?" he asked abruptly.

The Tangatan leader did not reply immediately. It stood watching him with those cold eyes, thin lips pursed, long white hair waving gently in a breeze. Anger touched Lukys as he suffered that piercing gaze, and he found himself stepping forward.

"You killed my friends," he snarled, the fiery heat in his stomach giving him courage. "Slaughtered them, so why spare us? Why go to the trouble of dragging us all this way?"

Still the creature did not reply, only stood staring at him, unblinking. The rage left Lukys as quickly as it had appeared and he found himself retreating a step, a sudden terror sweeping through his veins. The Tangatan leader slowly shook its head.

So…archaic, your kind. Its voice sounded amused. *Screaming your thoughts for all the world to hear.*

It advanced a step and Lukys tried to retreat further. A hand like iron caught him by the arm—he'd forgotten the female still stood nearby. Unable to break her grasp, he stood fixed in place while the leader approached.

Perhaps we are toying with you. Is that not what you humans do, when you take our people captive? It paused, still eyeing him, head bent slightly to the side. *Or is it for some other purpose? Tell me, Lukys of Perfugia, what is the fate of my brothers and sisters you take beyond these lands?*

"I…" Lukys trailed off.

He'd never seen the captives Adonis spoke of—Perfugia did not keep Tangatan captives. But he had read of such practices at the academy. The creatures were extraordinarily difficult to take alive, but human armies had on occasion been known to subdue a Tangata enough to be captured.

Initially, the Flumeeren physicians had hoped to discover the secrets of Tangatan physiology from those captives. But in ten years, they'd made little progress, and eventually the prisoners had been put to other uses…

Images flickered into Lukys's mind, sketches he had glimpsed in his textbooks, of Tangata in cages at the Flumeeren court, of beasts with arms and legs severed, of creatures tormented by their human gaolers. Lukys had thought little of the images at the time—after all, the Tangata were a distant threat to remote Perfugia, an inhuman enemy that occasionally called for them to send soldiers to the frontier…

A soft growl was the only warning Lukys had before Adonis caught him by the throat. He gasped, but the sound was abruptly cut off as the Tangata lifted him into the air. Desperate, Lukys kicked out. His boot connected with the creature's chest, but Adonis took no notice.

And you call us the monsters! Adonis's voice practically screamed into his mind.

The grip around Lukys's throat tightened, fingers digging into his flesh. He would have screamed if he could have drawn in enough breath. Instead, all he could manage was a pitiful squawk. Strength fading, he clasped at Adonis's fingers, trying to pry them loose, but there was no fighting this creature. Darkness circled his vision and the strength began to fade from his limbs. His mouth opened and closed, straining for even a wisp of oxygen.

Adonis! a voice cried in his mind.

Then suddenly Lukys was soaring through the air. He cried out, still aware enough to half curl into a ball before he struck the ground. The impact robbed him of whatever breath remained in his lungs. Dark spots danced across his eyes as he wheezed, gasping, until finally his chest filled.

Rolling onto his side, Lukys sucked in great lungfuls of the chill morning air, hardly able to believe he was alive. When he finally looked around, he was surprised to find the female Tangata standing across from Adonis. No sounds passed between the two, and yet…Lukys heard snatches of their voices. He closed his eyes, trying to concentrate through the pain, to draw meaning from the whispers…

Need…future…assignment…

Groaning, Lukys slumped back against the ground. It was no good. He could understand nothing from the snippets. It seemed he could only make out full sentences if the creatures directed their thoughts at him. He wondered why the female had interfered—Adonis was clearly her superior. It seemed they needed him for something…but what, Lukys couldn't begin to understand.

Bastard, he thought, looking again at Adonis.

Across the clearing, the Tangatan leader's head whipped around, the silver eyes fixing on Lukys. A wicked grin appeared on the creature's face and suddenly it was stalking towards him. Lukys tried to scramble away, but Adonis was faster still, and before Lukys could stand he was clutching him by the front of the shirt and hauling him to his feet.

So you can *Speak!* the creature exclaimed. There was triumph in the creature's words as they sounded in Lukys's mind. *You're the one we've been hearing.*

Lukys struggled to break free of the Tangata's grip, and to his surprise, Adonis released him. He staggered, then slowly backed away. "What are you talking about?" he croaked, throat still in agony.

You're different, Lukys. The Tangata's words chased after him. *We can Hear you. We've been hearing you for weeks.*

What? Lukys whispered in his mind, staring at the creature, unable to believe…

We thought it was the Anahera at first, Adonis continued, though Lukys did not recognise the name. *But no, even young, she would not be so unschooled.*

"What are you talking about?" Lukys said aloud, rejecting that inner dialogue. It felt unnatural, projecting a thought for this creature to hear.

Laughter answered the question. *How little your species understands of our power*, the Tangata said eventually. Then Adonis leaned in close. *Did you not wonder how we discovered your intrusion into our territory, how we found the hidden Birthing Grounds?*

Lukys shook his head, but unbidden, memories flickered into his mind, of the strange dreams he'd experienced ever since arriving in Fogmore. He'd had another of the nightmares that night in the mountains, the night before the Tangata had found them…

"No…" he said. "It's not possible."

It had been him all along. The Archivist had accused Cara of betraying them, before they'd learned her true identity. But Lukys had seen the map, had known where the

Archivist was leading them, the location of the ancient site of the Gods. Unknowingly, Lukys has betrayed them all.

He sank to his knees, thinking again of the bodies they'd found in the abandoned settlement. His fellow Perfugians, betrayed by his careless mind, dead because of him.

I should thank you, Adonis continued, and Lukys could hear the disdain in his words. *We have worked long to keep the secrets of the ancient world from humanity. Had we not arrived first, I shudder to think what new magics might have fallen into human hands. Though it was a shame the Old Ones were…lost.*

Adonis's words ended up abruptly, and Lukys thought he caught a flicker of something in the creature's eyes. Fear? A shiver touched him as he recalled what had waited in those tunnels beneath the earth. The Tangata that had arrived before them had woken something—the "Old Ones" Adonis spoke of. It seemed even the Tangata feared the creatures.

"What are they?" he asked.

A darkness crept across Adonis's face and he quickly looked away. The clearing fell still, and Lukys knelt, waiting, wondering…

The last hope of the Tangata.

The words were so quiet Lukys wasn't sure whether Adonis had meant for him to hear them. He did not respond, and after a moment the Tangata shook himself. Drawing in a breath, he turned to where the female still stood watching.

Put him back with the other one. The order was directed at the female, but it seemed the Tangata were able to make their thoughts heard to more than one listener, should they wish. *The Matriarch will wish to question him further. Perhaps together we can find the source of his ability.*

With that, Adonis clasped his hands behind his back and turned away. Lukys shivered. The action was unnervingly similar to a nobleman dismissing a servant. Shaking his head, he rose as the female approached. Keeping her eyes averted from Adonis, she took his hands and bound them again, thankfully in front of him this time.

She started to lead him away, but Adonis spoke again before they reached the edge of the clearing.

Sophia. Lukys's escort froze at the name, her head slowly turning to look back. The Tangatan leader stood staring after them. *Your insolence has not gone unnoticed.*

The female Tangata swallowed. *Yes, Adonis.*

Then they were retreating, the female leading him back into the trees. Lukys found himself staring at her back, remembering how she had interfered, stopped Adonis from killing him.

"Sophia…" he said suddenly. Ahead, the Tangata froze, spinning to look at him, eyes wide. Lukys spoke into the silence: "That's your name?"

Light filtered through the canopy overhead, revealing the confusion on his captor's face. Seeing such a human emotion made it easier to ignore those terrible grey eyes, and Lukys found himself taking note of her other features. A small scar marked her cheek, accented by copper skin tanned in the southern summers. Twigs and branches tangled in her ash-brown hair and dirt streaked her plain-spun tunic and leggings, though she was probably cleaner than Lukys after his weeks in the wilderness.

Yes, her reply came finally, a frown still creasing her forehead.

"Why did you save me?" Lukys blurted out before he lost his nerve.

The Tangata leaned her head to the side. *You killed my partner*, she replied, her frown deepening. *You are mine.*

✣ 4 ✣

THE FUGITIVE

Exhaustion weighed heavily on Erika's shoulders as the soldier led them through the narrow corridor. Wide windows on the wall opened to the dawn, granting her a view of the shadowed gorge beyond the ramparts of the Illmoor Fortress. After three nights of sailing in darkness, they had chased the rising sun to arrive before the daylight. She could see it even now, its orange glow just appearing on the distant cliffs.

It almost felt strange, to be on her feet as daylight approached. They had spent their days in hiding, the boat pulled in amongst tall reeds that dotted the shallows of the Illmoor. Each day she had lain waiting in that boat for their pursuers to catch them, for the arrows to find her, to strike her down.

Now she was finally safe from the queen's reach. All that remained to be seen was whether the King of Gemaho would keep to his word. She prayed it was so. Walking the corridors of the Illmoor Fortress, she was in his power now.

Guards had met them on the shore outside the fortress, crossbows trained on their little sailboat. Thankfully, they had lowered the weapons when they'd seen Maisie. With the guards help they had been able to lift Cara from the boat with minimal effort. By then they'd covered her wings with a heavy fur coat, thinking it better not to announce her presence to all the world.

Finally they were led into a high-ceilinged room lit by brass chandeliers and furnished with white velvet sofas and tables of glass and steel. The lavish sight brought relief for Erika—she'd half-feared they were being led to the dungeons. The sensation was immediately followed by one of discomfort. Her only bath for the last two weeks had been an unplanned dip in the river water. She had long since ceased to detect her own scent, but with her hair stiff with mud and clothes stained brown, she had no illusions about the current state of her appearance.

She turned to the guards to ask about a private chamber to bathe, but they were already vanishing into the corridor. The door swung closed behind them with a distinct *thunk* that suggested a locking bar had been slid into place on the other side. She looked at Maisie, but the woman seemed unconcerned. Cara, on the other hand, smirked.

"Looks like we're both prisoners now," Cara muttered. Her chains clinked as she wandered across to one of the sofas and slumped into its cushions.

Erika winced as dirt from the Goddess's clothes left streaks of dirt on the velvet. "I don't think our host will appreciate you ruining—"

"Bitch," Cara interrupted. The scowl the Goddess wore suggested she knew exactly what she was doing.

Letting out a sigh, Erika turned away. She'd tried various times during the journey to explain herself, but Cara had remained stubbornly silent, deaf to anything Erika said. The only constant were the looks of hatred the little Goddess sent every time Erika looked her way.

"I wouldn't worry about it," Maisie added, reclining into one of the sofas herself. "Nguyen tends not to care about such things."

"Is he here, you think?" Erika asked. She cast an eye over the sofas, before muttering a curse and falling into the nearest one. She was too exhausted to remain on her feet for a second longer.

"I sent a bird from Fogmore before we left," the spy replied. "I doubt he'll have waited in Solaris for what I promised him."

Erika narrowed her eyes at the woman's words. What *had* Maisie promised the king? Did the spy intend to betray her and claim Erika's offerings as her own? She clenched her fist and felt the pulsing of the gauntlet's magic. If Maisie did betray her, she would find her lifespan measured in minutes rather than years...

Angrily, Erika shook her head, banishing the thought. Despite her chosen discipline, Maisie had been a surprisingly pleasant travelling companion—at least compared to Cara's open animosity. They had developed a system to sleep and keep watch, and the woman had even shown Erika a little about what it took to navigate the swirling currents of the Illmoor. Not enough that she could sail unsupervised, but at least it had taken Erika's mind off the constant threat of the hunters.

Still though, if the king was in the fortress, *where* was he? Surely he'd been summoned as soon as the guards recognised Maisie? A frown wrinkling her forehead, Erika glanced at the door, impatient—

She flinched as her eyes fell upon a man standing in the doorway. Somehow, he'd opened the door and entered without them noticing. No, without *Erika* noticing—there was a knowing grin on Maisie's face as she watched Erika's reaction, and she caught a snort from Cara. Chuckling, the man stepped into the room, allowing the door to close behind him.

"Greetings," he said, spreading his arms. "Maisie, I have had searchers out watching for you. The river is crawling with Flumeer. I was beginning to fear they might exceed even your talent for concealment."

A smile crossed the spy's lips as she rose and gave a short bow. "Gladly, that day has not yet come, Nguyen."

Erika swallowed as she looked from the spy to the newcomer. Nguyen, King of Gemaho. Though he wore no crown or other indication of his position, there was a presence to the man, a power in the sea-green eyes that watched her from across the room. Age had added white streaks to the short-cropped brown hair and his clothes were plain, if expertly tailored. A short sword hung from his belt and he wore leather riding gloves. Had their arrival interrupted other plans the king might have had for the morning?

Her stomach twisted uncomfortably as the king turned his gaze on her, and she stood in silence, suffering his inspection. This man was regarded as a traitor by the Calafe, for he had abandoned the alliance after the disastrous southern campaign. Without Gemaho soldiers to aid them, the lands of Calafe had fallen all the quicker to the Tangata. Erika supposed she should hate him for that— after all, Calafe was her native homeland.

But then, the Calafe had turned their back on Erika's family after the king—her father—had fallen. By birth, she should have been a princess, honoured amongst the Calafe nobility. Instead the council had named her mother the king's paramour, and sent them from New Nihelm in exile.

Why should Erika care whether this man had betrayed the Calafe, when they had done the same to her?

"So this is Queen Amina's famed Archivist," the king said finally.

Erika offered a short bow. "Thank you for inviting me to your kingdom, Your Majesty," she replied.

The king wrinkled his forehead. "It was the least I could do for the daughter of an old friend."

For a moment, Erika didn't understand the man's words. Her heart twisted in her chest and her mouth suddenly felt dry. She swallowed, struggling for words, as the stoic expression she had cultivated amongst the Flumeeren nobility slipped. There was only one man alive who knew the identify of her father, and she had left him in an infirmary bed back in Fogmore. Surely Romaine hadn't told anyone…

"I…what?" she croaked.

The king chuckled. "I came to know King Micah quite well during our campaign in the south," the king replied. "It pained me when he…fell in that last battle. It was some years before I learned what had become of his family. I have followed your progress with interest over the last years."

Erika clenched her fists, struggling to contain her sudden anger. "I suppose that's why your man tried to have me killed," she grated.

The smile slipped from the king's lips. "A regrettable miscommunication," he replied. "I was most relieved to learn you had survived."

"And was it also a 'regrettable miscommunication' when you abandoned my people to the Tangata?" Erika spat, taking a step towards the king. In her anger, her earlier thoughts were thrust aside.

Arms clasped behind his back, the king stood regarding her for a long moment. Then he sighed. "I have made many mistakes over the last decade—first among them leading my soldiers against the Tangata. I argued against the invasion, but in the end, I allowed myself to be convinced." He shook his head. "We were fools to poke the hornet's nest. Thousands of lives were lost in the south, and for what? Our forces were so depleted that we couldn't even defend our own lands."

"You didn't even try to defend Calafe," Erika hissed.

"It pains me, what has befallen Micah's nation," the king replied, "but the sand upon the shore cannot hold back the tides. What we witnessed in the south…" He swallowed, and there was a tightness to his voice as he continued. "The Tangata cannot be stopped, not over open land. Once the Agzor Fortress fell, Calafe was already lost."

Erika opened her mouth, then closed it as she saw the pain lurking in the king's eyes. The anger slipped from her like water through a sieve. He might have only been acting —he was a king after all—but something about the way he spoke about her father, of Calafe, Erika found herself believing him.

"What's done is done," she said finally. "Regardless of the past, it seems you are now the lesser of two evils, Your Majesty." She bowed her head, projecting defeat. It would not hurt for this man to underestimate her. "The Flumeeren Queen is mad—she would do anything to gain the magic I hold."

To her surprise, Nguyen laughed. "The courts of Flumeer have trained you well, Princess." Erika started at the title—only her father had ever called her that—but the man continued before she could reply. "You do not need to flatter me, nor belittle my rivals. I imagine Amina and I are much alike. We both seek to protect our nations, to keep our peoples safe from enemies. Though, I'll admit our approaches tend to differ somewhat."

Erika frowned and glanced at Maisie, struggling to piece together the meaning behind the king's words, but the spy only shrugged. On the other couch, Cara still sat glaring at the two of them. The king had not yet addressed the Goddess, and for herself, Cara had been remarkably quiet for the duration of the conversation. Almost as though—

Click.

A cry burst from Erika's lips as the steel cuffs slid from the Goddess's wrists. With a flicker of movement she was on her feet. The jacket kept her from spreading her wings and chains still bound her legs, but the shimmer in her eyes suggested they would not hinder her.

In panic, Erika lifted her gauntleted hand and the magic ignited in her fingertips. Its power thrummed in her ears and she felt that familiar rush, the feeling of ecstasy that promised she could destroy her enemies…

…a gasp tore from Erika and she staggered, closing her fist, smothering the magic.

What was that?

A growl returned her attention to Cara. A snarl twisted the Goddess's face and before anyone could react, she leapt for the king, fingers outstretched…

…only to slam down into one of the glass tables, all momentum stolen from her spring. A scream tore from Cara's throat as she smashed through the glass, sending shards tumbling across the floor. Then the cry cut off, though her mouth was still stretched wide, the veins of her throat bulging against her skin. Glass cut her flesh as she thrashed amongst the remnants of the table, as though she were in some great agony…

Erika's gaze dropped to her gauntlet, but the light remained dim, its power subdued. It was not she that had struck down the Goddess.

"I see you're getting better with the gauntlet's power," Maisie said as she stepped around the ruin of the table.

Turning, Erika took in the king's outstretched left hand. But he didn't wear a gauntlet, only the leather riding gloves…the breath hissed from Erika's throat as she realised what he'd done. He hadn't been going for a ride—the gloves were to conceal the ancient artefact he wore, a mirror of her own.

Smiling gently, the king finally lowered his hand and Cara slumped amongst the glass, her breath coming in ragged gasps. Despite herself, Erika felt a rush of guilt at the Goddess's treatment. This wasn't right. Cara had been her friend, had saved her life. And this was how she repaid her?

"An interesting weapon, don't you think?" the king said conversationally as he stepped up alongside Erika to regard the crumpled Goddess. "I take it this is the fabled creature that was seen soaring over the waters of the Illmoor?"

Erika swallowed. "Goddess," she rasped, then belatedly added: "Her name is Cara."

"Does it speak?" the king asked.

A muffled snarl came from Cara as she pushed herself to her hands and knees. "Yes," she spat.

The king raised his gauntlet, his smile unchanged. "Well that's an improvement on the Tangata at least."

Breath hissed between Cara's teeth as she looked at the king. "You humans really know nothing about who you fight, do you?"

"Little enough," Nguyen agreed, surprisingly jovial for someone that had just been attacked by a God. "Was there a gap in our knowledge you would like to fill in for us?"

Cara sat back on her haunches. "I'm sure your ignorance could fill the endless miles between the earth and our moon," she muttered. She shifted her shoulders, then winced and glanced at the king. "Am I allowed to stretch, or are you going to smite me again, oh mighty king?"

Nguyen chuckled as he stepped back and gestured for her to stand. Cara climbed to her feet, obviously wary. Slowly, hesitantly, she pulled the jacket from her shoulders.

The king inhaled sharply as wings stretched across the

room. Joints creaked and a moan of relief slipped from Cara's throat. The auburn feathers shone in the light of the chandelier and even Erika found herself retreating a step. Belatedly the king raised his gauntlet, but this time Cara made no move to attack. Instead, she closed her eyes and her face softened, obviously relieved to finally be free of the jacket's confinement.

Erika swallowed, still not quite able to process the sight. A feather had come free with the jacket, and it drifted across the room, coming to rest at her feet. It was almost a foot long and half as broad as her hand. Instinctively she crouched and picked it up, turning it in her fingers. In the days since fleeing Fogmore, her fear had been such that her mind had not lingered on the Goddess, but looking at the feather in her hand, the implications of what she'd done finally began to catch up with her.

Across the room, Cara opened her eyes and saw that they were all staring. Red tinged her cheeks and the wings quickly retracted against her back. Her gaze fell to the floor.

"You really have no idea how uncomfortable that thing is…" she muttered, gesturing at the jacket.

Erika swallowed, unable to summon the words. She figured the sight of Cara's fully unfurled wings tended to have that effect on people. Beside her, though, the king chuckled.

"So this is what you westerners call a God?" he asked. Hands clasped behind his back, he began to circle the room, as though to appraise Cara from every angle.

"What would you call her?" Erika asked, a frown curling her lips. She'd known the Gemaho were not the religious sort, but…surely not even they could maintain their disbelief with the winged Goddess standing before them.

"You know I can hear you, right?" Cara muttered, crossing her arms. A twitch tugged at her cheek.

"My apologies, of course," the king replied politely, as though he hadn't just sent the Goddess crashing through a glass table. He came to a stop before Cara. "It would seem we now have a simple way of answering our greatest theological questions. So…what do you call yourselves?"

Cara hesitated, mouth parted as though to speak. She bit her lips. "We call ourselves the Anahera."

Erika frowned, turning the word over in her mind. Of course the Gods would have their own name for themselves.

"And you are Gods?"

Cara answered the question with a shrug. "What is a God?"

The king nodded, as though her words had actually been an answer, then turned to Erika. "I suppose it is a matter of perspective," he said, gesturing with the hand that wore the gauntlet. "Surely whoever created these artefacts were Gods, and yet, why would they grant the devices power over themselves?"

"The Tangata were born from their magic," Erika said, quoting the legends. "Perhaps the gauntlets were crafted to fight the creatures."

"It could have been so." The king nodded along to Erika's logic. "But, what of this situation we find ourselves in? Cara is now my prisoner. Are your Gods truly so feeble as to be taken hostage by their own creations?"

"Still standing here," Cara muttered.

Looking from Cara to the king, Erika could only shake her head. "There is much I do not understand," she replied.

Her gaze lingered on Cara. The Goddess had relaxed her wings a little, allowing the auburn feathers to stretch out on either side of her. Her eyes were fixed on a point between Erika and the King, but Erika could see the tightness in her jaw, the way she clenched and unclenched her fists. Suddenly the Goddess turned and their eyes met.

Erika shivered as she looked into Cara's amber gaze and found herself transported back to those caverns beneath the earth. Her memory of that time was still hazy—she'd been struck in the head by one of the creatures—but one image stood out in sharp relief.

Cara covered in the blood, the unstoppable creatures dead at her feet, grey eyes piercing the darkness.

Silently Erika swallowed and looked away. Whatever the king said, she sensed that if Cara had really wanted them dead, no chains or weapon on this earth could stop her. Which begged the question: why had she allowed them to come this far?

"Regardless, it seems the good Anahera is to be my guest for a time," the king was saying. "I have had accommodations prepared. I hope you find them suitable. Erika, we shall arrange another meeting once you've rested—I understand there is a map in your possession that has been the source of much interest. For now, though, I must leave you. It seems I will soon have unwelcome guests on my doorstep."

"What's this?" Maisie asked, her head coming up.

Nguyen offered a grim smile. "It seems Cara's arrival and subsequent departure from Fogmore has stirred up quite the firestorm. The queen is on the march."

Erika's heart lurched at his words and she opened her mouth to demand more details, but already the king was striding away, vanishing through the doorway. A thundering sounded in Erika's ears as several servants stepped into the room. She hardly heard what they said. Her gaze fell to the gauntlet she still wore on her hand, and she heard again the last words the queen had spoken to her.

Do not fail me, Archivist. One way or another, I will have that magic.

5

THE FALLEN

Romaine staggered up the steps of the general's quarters, the effort less now than it had been a week ago. That knowledge offered him little comfort. Failure weighed heavily on his shoulders as he reached the door. It opened before he could grasp the handle, a guard within nodding a greeting. A second stood beyond, spear resting casually against his shoulder. These were uncertain times and the general was taking no risks with his safety.

Pain sliced Romaine's chest as he stepped inside and his boot caught on the doorstep. He thrust out his ruined arm to catch himself, and bit back a scream as it struck the door-frame. Belatedly he used his right hand to regain his balance. Teeth clenched, he paused on the threshold, ignoring the stares of the two guards. Stars danced across his vision but he dragged in great lungfuls of air, and eventually they passed.

"Can I…ah, help you with your coat, sir?" the guard who held the door asked awkwardly.

"I'm no damned officer," Romaine snapped, drawing himself up. "And by the Fall, I can take off my own coat."

Just as it had for the past week, it took Romaine a good minute to drag the heavy furs from his shoulders. By the time he hung the coat on a hook, he was panting again, and he cursed this newfound weakness. He had always been a quick healer, but then, he'd never had injuries like these. The loss of his hand was not something one simply *recovered* from. A short sword now hung from his belt, but even that was a façade. He still wasn't strong enough to even practice with the blade.

It dragged at him, to feel so weak. Each day he woke to the whisper of voices, telling him to surrender, to give in to his weakness.

And each day, Cara's face flickered into his mind, and he would force himself to his feet.

He had failed Lukys and the Perfugians, had failed his comrades and his wife, even his own son. He would not fail the Goddess.

Finally recovering his breath, he nodded to the guards and started down the corridor. These visits had become his daily habit, the only thing he felt he could do in his weakened state. Little enough, but it was a start, gave him a reason to leave his house each day.

The general's quarters were in one of Fogmore's original buildings and therefore was better built than the barracks and mess halls, which soldiers had hastily erected to accommodate the standing army now needed to defend the frontier. Panelled walls kept out the worst of the winter drafts and warmth radiated through the corridor from the brazier he knew would be burning in the general's office. Despite his age, General Curtis was renowned as a leader who did not back down from a hard day's work—but neither was he a man to suffer unnecessary discomforts.

Muffled voices carried from adjoining rooms as Romaine strode the length of the hall, the various secretaries and quartermasters of the army already at work. Curtis had not come to be general of the allied armies only for his prowess on the battlefield; it was his administration that kept the mammoth machine of the Flumeeren army running smoothly.

Romaine found the man himself sitting behind his desk, head craned over a stack of papers. Later in the day the general would be amongst the men, overseeing the installation of new defences and checking weapons and armour, or watching battle manoeuvres in the central square. Many questioned why a man so far above the rank and file would bother himself with such trivialities, but those did not understand the nature of soldiers. By working alongside the common soldiers, Curtis had gained a respect few generals could imagine. They would obey his orders without question, trusting he would not send them into danger needlessly.

Unless you were Perfugian, of course.

Anger flared in Romaine's stomach. Despite his respect for the man, there was no denying Curtis had sent Romaine's friends to their deaths. But he kept his anger on a short leash. There was nothing he could do for Lukys and the others now. They slept the endless sleep. But he could still help Cara.

"There has still been no news of the Goddess, Calafe," Curtis said, not looking up from his papers.

The man's dismissive attitude earned another flare of anger from Romaine. He strode to the desk and placed his palm on the papers. His fingers left a streak of dirt on the white.

"Do you not care?" he hissed.

The general looked up with a sigh. "She is a Goddess, Romaine," he said. "If she did not wish to go with the Archivist—"

"She would not have left willingly," Romaine snapped, "not without telling me. You did not see her, after we lost Lukys…"

How could he explain to this man that last look she had given him on the ship? The shared sorrow they had felt, at failing to save their friends. Goddess or no, Cara had been distinctly *human* in that moment, vulnerable, overwhelmed.

"Calm, Romaine," the general murmured, leaning back in his seat. "You were delirious on the river. We cannot pretend to know the mind of a God, the reasons why she came to us, nor why she left."

"She left because the blasted Archivist took her!"

Romaine hammered his fist onto the table to emphasis his point, but the effort only served to steal the breath from him, and instead he was left bent in two, gasping while the general watched on.

"Think rationally," the general said finally, entwining his hands. "We have had scouts out all week. If they had left the city by land or river, we would know of it. Only the Goddess herself could have stolen them away in such secrecy."

Romaine scrunched his eyes closed. The general's calm words made a certain sense, but Romaine knew the truth was different. It was just too convenient that the Archivist would disappear rather than face the consequences of her failure in the south. And Erika had disappeared with the one figure who could answer her questions about the past, about the Gods and their magic. No, something had happened between Cara and Erika. He just needed to—

"The man is right, Curtis," a voice from the corridor interrupted his thoughts. He swung around as a woman entered the office. "It pains me to admit it, but my Archivist has betrayed us. Yesterday, they passed beneath the walls of the Illmoor Fortress."

Romaine stood gaping as the woman crossed the room.

Head held high and arms clasped behind her back, she walked with a cool confidence. She spoke with a Flumeeren accent, and in a kingdom whose women generally did not march to war, she wore chainmail armour stained scarlet. A sword hung from her belt and she carried a full-faced helm under one arm. Golden wires had been fused to the crown of the helmet, marking her as—

"Your Majesty!" the general exclaimed, stumbling to his feet. "What...how...I did not receive word of your coming?"

A smile appeared on Queen Amina's lips as she paused beside the general's desk. "You thought I would remain in Mildeth when the Gods walk the land again?" she asked, one eyebrow arching towards locks of almond hair.

"I..." Curtis trailed off, seemingly lost for words.

Amina *tisked*. "Though, imagine my disappointment when I learned you had *lost* one of the Divine."

Curtis swallowed visibly, but he quickly pulled himself together. "We believed she had left of her own accord, travelling with your Archivist, Your Majesty."

"I did not take you for a fool, Curtis." The queen's words were like acid. "Were your orders not to take the woman into custody the second she returned?"

"I...yes, Your Majesty, but...she said..." He withered beneath the monarch's glare.

"She said what?" the queen asked. "That you should ignore your queen's orders? You disappoint me, General." The queen paced to the rear of the office, where several medals hung on display. "After so many years of service, I had thought you knew me better. I ordered you to seize the Archivist for one simple reason: she has betrayed us to a foreign king."

Romaine's heart lurched at Amina's words and for a

moment he thought she spoke of his own king, the man Erika had claimed as her father. But no, if she had passed into the Illmoor Fortress, Erika was heading east. The queen was speaking of Nguyen, king of the Gemaho.

"I suspected something was amiss when she claimed to have survived an attack by one of Nguyen's spies," the queen went on, once more facing Curtis. "That man is many things, but careless is not one of them. It seemed unlikely one of his agents could fail to best a simple Archivist. But I deemed it an acceptable risk, sending her south to retrieve artefacts of the Gods, knowing you would be here to detain her when she returned." There was a stringent pause as the queen eyed Curtis. "It seems in that regard, I was wrong."

The general bowed his head. "I have failed you, my queen."

"Yes." The queen's eyes shifted, focusing on Romaine. "It would seem this Calafe has more sense than my own general."

Romaine inclined his head as a show of respect, though he did not bow. She was not his queen.

Amusement danced in the woman's eyes at the gesture.

"Regardless, it seems the time has finally come to confront our eastern neighbours."

Hope flared in Romaine's stomach at the queen's words, while behind the desk, the general started.

"What?" he blurted out, then seeming to remember his manners, added: "Your Majesty, the frontier cannot afford the troops for a second campaign…"

"Of course not, General," the queen replied, "though I trust you will continue defending our lands against the scourge of the Tangata while I am otherwise occupied."

The general hesitated. "Your Majesty?"

The queen gave a throaty chuckle. "Thankfully, the Gods have blessed me with great foresight," she replied. Turning, she gestured in the direction of the town. "I did not leave Mildeth alone. The Queen's Guard marched with me, five thousand of our finest soldiers. By their might, I will finally claim retribution against the Gemaho for turning their back on our alliance."

A long silence followed the queen's proclamation. Romaine could see the indecision in the eyes of the general, the doubt. It was clear Curtis did not think it prudent to start a war against Gemaho while the Tangata still threatened the frontier. Despite Cara's abduction, Romaine was inclined to agree. Yet if this was the only way of getting her back...

"Your Majesty," Curtis said, clearing his throat, "I must advise against—"

"Your concern is noted, General," Queen Amina replied, her voice cold, "but you would do well to trust more in your queen. Just as I trust that you will defend these shores to the last man."

The general hesitated for another long moment, but finally he nodded. "I will, Your Majesty. You have my oath."

"Very good, General," the queen said. She turned her eyes on Romaine. "And what of you, Calafe?" she murmured. "What path will you take?"

"Your Majesty?" he asked, eyebrows drawing into a frown. He clenched his one good hand, though it only served to remind him of the missing one. Surely she couldn't be asking...

"The Gemaho have assaulted the personage of our Gods," Queen Amina mused. "It is my understanding you are familiar with her Divinity. I would have your aid on this journey, Calafe, if you wish it."

Romaine swallowed. "I would march through the fires of hell itself for Cara, Your Majesty."

The queen nodded. "As would I, Calafe," she replied. Then she smiled, and Romaine saw in her emerald eyes an anger, a rage that could only come from betrayal. "Besides," she added, "the good Archivist has something of mine I would like back."

❧ 6 ❧

THE SOLDIER

New Nihelm.

Standing on a hilltop, Lukys looked across the valley to where two great rivers came together on their long journey from mountains to ocean. At the point where they converged, an island had formed amidst the swirling waters. It was there the Calafe had built their only city.

Lukys had never seen anything like it. New Nihelm's rustic beauty equalled even that of Ashura, the ancient capital of his own kingdom. Yet unlike its rival capitals, this city had no walls, no spiralling guard towers or fortifications. New Nihelm had only been founded a hundred years before, long after the warring tribes of humanity had settled into kingdoms. Its creation had been constrained only by its architect's imagination.

Instead of walls, walkways led around much of the island's circumference, set atop the breakwaters that protected the inner reaches of the city from the river's wrath. Beyond, great domes of platinum and silver dotted the city, rising above the slate rooftops of the common buildings. And higher even than the domes, spires sliced the skyline, their gold and marble materials shining in the morning sun, forming a jagged pattern that seemed to mirror the mountains rising to the east.

The daylight slowly illuminated the shadowy streets, revealing a broad, tree-lined avenue that ran from one side of the city to the other, connecting with the northern and southern bridges that were the island's only physical connection to the mainland.

Lukys could only shake his head. He had not expected to find such a wonder amidst the vast wilderness of Calafe. They had been a nomadic people even before the Tangata came, only settling in stone cottages during the worst of the winter months. All except the inhabitants of New Nihelm, it seemed.

Movement on the hillside drew Lukys's attention back to the present. Dale came alongside him and they shared a glance. A week had passed as they marched south, always in darkness, so long that Lukys had begun to feel he were a creature of the night himself. At least the journey had allowed time for their bruises to heal, and some life to return to his friend's face.

"You think this is where they've been leading us?" the larger man asked, his hazel eyes drifting to the city.

Lukys shrugged, rolling his aching shoulders. The Tangata had granted them more freedom since that first night, only binding them when it came time to sleep. That did not mean they went unguarded. A flicker in the corner of his eye revealed Sophia hovering nearby. He shuddered, haunted by her words from a week before.

He had killed her mate. He should have realised it earlier—the creatures usually came in pairs. Now it was only a matter of time before she took her revenge.

Swallowing, he forced his thoughts back to Dale and the city below.

"Romaine said the city was destroyed," he said as they started down the hillside, shepherded along by their Tangatan captors. "Why would they have spared it?"

Neither had an answer, and silence resumed between them. Lukys could feel the exhaustion dragging at him, a creeping fatigue that called for him to sleep, but he fought it off. He had no desire to draw their captors' wrath—at least, not any more than he already had.

He hadn't told Dale of his conversation with the Tangatan leader. That would have required revealing the truth about his newfound ability. Guilt still hung about Lukys's shoulders at the role he had inadvertently played in bringing the Tangata down upon them.

About the role he had played in their comrades' deaths.

Adonis had not called him again to speak, and for that Lukys was grateful. Though the Tangatan leader held a certain...civility about himself, he had proven no less vicious than the others Lukys had encountered in battle. It was as though a beast lurked in every one of the species, chained in some, set loose in others, but always there, waiting for its opportunity to strike.

It was only a short journey from the hills to the flood-plains of the Selman basin, though the bridge to New Nihelm was another mile downstream. They had left the denser northern forests behind a day ago and the land before them now was of verdant grass, the open fields dotted with wandering herds of sheep and goats.

Several of the creatures grazing near the riverbanks raised curious heads at the group's approach, but soon returned to their meal. They wore thick coats of wool, untouched for a season by the shearers of men, and Lukys felt a touch of pity for them come the summer. If left unshorn for much longer, their coats would become so heavy as to make them slow runners, easy prey for predators.

Or did the Tangata already know this? He glanced at Sophia and her companions, recalling then that most of the species wore clothing spun from wool. How had humanity come to be so ignorant of their enemy, that they had not even questioned where the creatures found their clothing?

The Tangata leading their group reached the riverbanks and turned towards the west, where the bridge beckoned. Looking into the waters swirling below, Lukys was shocked to see they were crystal clear. After spending so long around the Illmoor, he had come to assume all mainland rivers must be murky and polluted. But then, the Illmoor ran for hundreds of miles through Gemaho before reaching Flumeer. Turning his gaze to the mountains rising to the east, Lukys could see no break in their endless peaks; the waterways of Calafe must run directly off those snow-capped summits.

Looking ahead, Lukys was surprised to see a slow trickle of people moving across the bridge. The sight brought a frown to his face, but it wasn't until they got closer that he began to recognise the smooth, balanced movements of the Tangata. He shared another glance with Dale, but neither said a word. So it was true: the Tangata had taken up residence in the husk of Calafe society. New Nihelm was their destination.

What are they doing here? he wondered, watching as the creatures left the bridge and started into the surrounding pastures.

You think us such savages, human. Lukys started as a voice whispered into his mind. Jerking around, he found their ever-present guard watching him from nearby. Sophia. *Why should we not desire a place of safety for our people to shelter?*

Lukys swallowed, unnerved that Sophia had heard his

thoughts. He quickly turned his eyes ahead again before Dale noticed. What else could she hear—and how could he prevent the creatures from listening? He knew it was possible; otherwise he would hear more than just muffled rumblings from the other Tangata. Unfortunately, he doubted any of the creatures would be willing to instruct him.

I'm sorry. He tried to broadcast the words to where Sophia walked. *I am...ignorant of your kind.*

A rumble that might have been laughter—or a growl—whispered in his mind, but Sophia did not reply. He swallowed, her words from that first morning returning to him again. Just now though, she did not seem angry or vengeful, and Lukys decided to press his luck.

But...why here? he tried again, pushing the words from him in the direction of the Tangata.

To his surprise, Sophia leapt as though someone had just grabbed her by the shoulder. Landing in a close approximation of the fighting stance Romaine had taught him just a few months past, she swung around, eyes wide, teeth bared.

Lukys froze midstride, while Dale leapt backwards away from their guard and raised his fists.

"What the—" He bit back the words as the other creatures turned towards them.

Thankfully, Sophia had been walking a few paces ahead; otherwise Lukys feared she might have struck him. With the strength each of the Tangata possessed, such a blow could easily have proven fatal.

There was a moment's tension before Sophia lowered her hands. Dale quickly did the same, his eyes on the surrounding creatures. Slowly the others relaxed, and finally one of the other Tangata gave a grunt, indicating they were to move on.

Letting out a long breath, Lukys obeyed, though as he fell into step alongside Dale, he flicked a glance at Sophia. She was still watching him, and for a moment their eyes met.

You do not need to shout, her words whispered gently in his mind.

Despite the danger of his situation, Lukys felt his cheeks grow warm. He quickly dropped his eyes to the river, focusing on the rocks that shimmered beneath the surface rather than his mortification. Shout? He barely knew how to speak this way!

It is strange for us too, hearing a human Speak, Sophia's words chased after him. There was a pause before she continued. *There is a beauty in this place, even for our people. The Matriarch saw no reason not to make use of it.*

Her words inspired a dozen more questions in Lukys's mind, but before he could formulate a sentence, Dale shifted closer to him.

"What was that about, you think?" the other recruit hissed, looking in Sophia's direction.

Lukys shook his head, struggling to shift back to a verbal conversation. "Something startled her," he offered finally. "We're lucky she didn't tear our throats out."

That seemed enough for Dale and he let the topic drop.

I would not have harmed you, human. There was a touch of humour to Sophia's words now.

Frowning, Lukys glanced in her direction. He was about to mention to her something of their words in the forest, but at the last moment thought better of it. There seemed to be little point in reminding the creature of her loss. Instead, he offered an observation.

My name is Lukys, he tried, reaching out more gently with his mind now.

57

Yes, it is. Her voice turned cold again, and Lukys swallowed as silence fell across his mind.

It was a strange sensation, having a conversation all in his mind—almost like he were talking to himself. He wondered how the Tangata did it, how they distinguished their own thoughts from those of their fellow Tangata. Sophia's voice had a distinct tone to it, but often the whispers he heard coming from the others were indistinguishable from his own inner musings.

Finally they reached the bridge spanning the Shelman River. It stretched some six hundred feet to the distant island, built from great blocks of granite that plunged down into the swirling waters. Bricks had been laid to protect the structure from the endless traffic, but these had been worn smooth over the decades, and twin ruts in the centre revealed the gradual erosion left by the wagons.

There were no wagons now, though. The few Tangata leaving the city were on foot, many carrying great packs upon their backs. Lukys expected them to stop and stare at the human prisoners Adonis had brought to the city, but instead the passersby paid them little attention.

Halfway across the bridge, the polished stone turned abruptly to wood. Lukys paused, eyeing the ragged section of planks spanning a gap between the granite blocks. He guessed the allied forces of humanity must have blown this section of the bridge to protect their retreat to the north. The Tangata had evidently lacked either the skill or the patience to repair the damage with stone.

Sophia and the other Tangata continued across the patched section without hesitation, leaving Lukys with no choice but to follow. The boards groaned as they took his weight, but thankfully held, and a moment later he returned to the bricked path.

They continued, reaching the shores of the island and

passing onto the broad avenue that split the city in two. Lukys was surprised to find the street awash with colour. Trees lined the avenue, pink blossoms sprouting from their wiry branches, their petals swirling at every breeze and filling the air with the sweet scent of flowers.

More than that, though, the buildings themselves were each a display of individuality. Just like in the border city of Fogmore, the Calafe had built their city of wood. But the similarities ended there. Where Fogmore appeared to have been thrown together overnight, New Nihelm had been built with care, the wooden beams and panels of every building fitted together with precision.

Each house had also been painted in different colours from its neighbours. Façades of red and yellow and blue and green led away down the street, creating a vibrant, picturesque image of a city united by its differences.

Sadness touched Lukys at the thought, as he remembered that the families who had so lovingly crafted the image were gone, forced from their homes by the threat of the Tangata.

The sun was lifting higher into the sky, bringing with it more of New Nihelm's new Tangatan occupants. They moved about the paved streets much the same as the citizens of his own city back in Perfugia, though they were not half so numerous. It would have been easy to forget the creatures around him weren't human.

Easy, but for the fact they lived in a city stolen from its rightful owners. It had not been the Tangata who had thought to build their city upon this island. It had not been their skill that had crafted such beautiful homes, nor their hardship that had maintained it for a century. No, the only thing built by the Tangata on this entire island were the wooden boards they had used to span the broken bridge.

Everything else they had stolen from the Calafe.

Eventually, their captors led them off the main avenue into the smaller streets that crisscrossed the island. There they began to see further signs of life—vendors standing behind stalls, groups of Tangata on street corners, and still others carrying great packs of goods on their backs. Only… Lukys could not help feeling there was a strangeness to it all, an unnaturalness that hung about the city.

It was a while before he could put a finger on the abnormality.

It was the silence.

In every city, every town he had ever visited, there was a constant buzz, a distant rumbling of wagons and beating of hammers, of voices, of life. With the Tangata in New Nihelm, there was none of that.

They crossed a number of bridges spanning smaller watercourses, though these were broad, arcing things that lifted several yards higher than the surrounding streets. Crossing them, Lukys began to realise New Nihelm was not one island at all, but many, divided by canals that criss-crossed the city. At the edge of each channel, stone foundations were revealed, plunged deep into the mud and hidden by the structures that had been built atop them.

Anger touched Lukys as he was again reminded of the effort the Calafe had put into the construction of their city, only to have it stolen away. He found himself glaring at the creatures they passed in the streets, wishing there was something he could do, some magical way of restoring to Romaine's people what was rightfully theirs—

Lukys froze as he caught a glimpse of a figure amongst the Tangata gathered around a nearby fruit stall. Frowning, he came to a stop, watching them, aware there was something different about this group. Sophia and the other guards did not immediately realise his absence, and silently he stepped towards the stand. Two males and a female stood perusing the vegetables on display. In another time, he might have wondered at the oddity of the monsters from his nightmares out shopping, but something about the female's movement had caught his attention.

Struck by a sudden suspicion, Lukys darted forward and reached out to grasp the woman by the shoulder. A belated cry came from behind him as Sophia finally realised his absence, but she was too late. Crying out, the female he'd accosted spun, hands raised in fright, eyes wide.

Eyes of a brilliant sea green.

The woman was human.

THE FALLEN

The Illmoor Fortress was five days ride from Fogmore, though the queen lingered a day in the riverside town to prepare supplies before pushing on. Her Guard rode large destriers bred for war, their iron-shod hooves capable of caving in the skulls of even the most ferocious of the foes. Behind them came the supply wagons, though many would be left in the smaller forts that lined the shores of the Illmoor, restocking them for the coming months of conflict against the Tangata.

Romaine himself rode a smaller mare, for which he was thankful. The destriers might make great warhorses, but their thumping gait would have been agony for his injuries. Even with the smoother strides of the mare, Romaine was aching by the time the sun set on the first day. It was a relief when he finally topped a rise and found the vanguard setting camp on the floodplains below.

Tugging on his reins, he drew the mare to a stop and watched the preparations. Still far from Gemaho, there was little chance of an attack by Nguyen's soldiers. Indeed, if they were lucky the man might not yet know of their advance.

As for the Tangata…an attack seemed unlikely, but with the Illmoor River less than a mile from their position, nothing could be guaranteed. The soldiers below were certainly taking no chances. There were no trees available for a stockade wall, but a defensive ditch and embankment were already nearing completion.

The thumping of hooves came from below and a moment later a rider topped the rise and approached Romaine.

"Have to admit, those Royal Guards sure are an efficient sort."

Lorene wore a broad grin on his youthful face as he pulled his mount to a stop alongside Romaine's. He'd volunteered for the expedition when the queen had asked for scouts to help navigate the journey east. There were no roads or passageways in these parts, and so close to the river it would have been easy for the queen's forces to become bogged in the marshland. The seemingly solid ground in the open pastures had a habit of sinking beneath the weight of horses, so it paid to have scouts along who knew the territory.

Romaine only grunted and swung from his saddle. He would walk the rest of the way down the hill—his body could use the stretch. Grinning at some unspoken joke, Lorene did the same, and together they started down the hill.

Romaine did his best to keep the pain of his injuries from his face, but it was difficult to ignore the searing that touched his chest with each step. How much longer until he healed? Days, weeks, months? Despair swelled in his throat and he struggled to push it back down. What good was he to anyone, let alone a Goddess, if he couldn't even walk without pain?

"You think she's really going to attack the Gemaho?" Lorene asked as they threaded their way down the hillside. There was a path that wound around in a gentler manner, passable for the wagons, but they had opted for the more direct route.

Romaine flicked a glance at the man but said nothing for the moment, keeping his attention focused on the ground beneath his feet. The grassy slope fell steeply to the campsite and they were doing their best to zigzag the horses down. The mare snorted and tugged at her reins but otherwise followed Romaine without question. No doubt she was relieved at the break from his weight upon her back.

"You know, you didn't need to join us," Romaine said, skirting the man's question, then muffled a curse as a patch of earth slid beneath his boot.

These hills had once been covered in forest, much the same as his own homeland across the distant waters, but for the last decade the banks this side of the Illmoor had been progressively burned away. The Flumeeren soldiers had feared the Tangata would use the forests as cover to pass their defensive lines and attack settlements further inland. Now though, the land lay exposed, and many hillsides were slowly crumbling beneath the forces of erosion.

"I know," Lorene replied with a shrug. "It's just…it didn't feel right, staying behind last time. I should have gone with you lot when you went south."

"If you had, there'd be one more corpse lying in the forests of my homeland."

"Maybe," Lorene said, a self-deprecating grin appearing on his lips, "or might be I could have helped. Can't know now, can we?" His eyes turned ahead, to the distant mountains. A sharp V between the soaring peaks marked the valley through which the Illmoor passed. Beyond, the plateaus of Gemaho waited. "But at least I can still help the lass."

Romaine chuckled at that. "Can hardly call her a lass now, you know."

Lorene grinned. "Nah, maybe that's the real reason I'm coming. Didn't get a chance to see her before her untimely departure. Wouldn't mind a glimpse though. Something to tell the grandkids about, you know?"

"The Gemaho might have something to say about that."

"Ain't that the truth."

They fell silent at that, each pointedly turning his eyes from the distant mountains. Before anyone could reach the plateaus of Gemaho, they first had to pass the granite walls of the Illmoor Fortress. And the defenders wouldn't let the queen's army pass without a fight.

Reaching the bottom of the hill, Lorene nodded a farewell and mounted up again to set off around the perimeter of the camp. Romaine watched him go, then led his horse on through a gap that had been left in the fortifications for the arriving army.

With no tasks of his own to occupy him, Romaine wandered through the camp. The vanguard had staked out areas for the army's tents, which would soon arrive in the wagons. Watching the men work, Romaine found himself thinking of the coming conflict. Again, doubt touched him. The Tangata were massing beyond the Illmoor. With an attack imminent, was now really time for the queen to start a war between the kingdoms of man, the first in more than a generation?

Yet…neither could Romaine bring himself to disagree with the queen's decision. After all, it was his only chance of rescuing Cara. And perhaps the dispute could be ended without bloodshed. After all, surely the King of Gemaho did not intend to hold one of the *Gods* against her will. The eastern peoples were not known for their devotion, but not even they could deny Cara's divinity.

Though Romaine had to admit, he still hadn't entirely come around to that truth. It seemed impossible the innocent young woman that had spent so many weeks at his side was one of the Divine. What had a God been doing here anyway, sparring with the Perfugians, eating with the other soldiers in the mess hall, even befriending Romaine? But then, that was the way of the Gods, was it not, that mere mortals could not understand their motives?

Shaking his head, Romaine returned his attention to his surroundings. The queen had been riding with the vanguard and now he saw her ahead, supervising the last touches on the camp fortifications. Romaine's horse gave a soft whinny, announcing his approach. A smile lit the woman's face and she waved a greeting.

"Romaine, come, join me," she called. "I trust the ride was comfortable?"

Romaine nodded. Thankfully, Amina did not call him out on the lie, though he feared the truth was written on his face.

"What do you think?" she asked, gesturing to the men at work.

Romaine cast a professional eye over the fortifications. The ditch was a good four feet deep, the mound rising behind it almost the same. Enough to stop the most determined of cavalry charges, but against the Tangata...the creatures could easily leap the width of the trench, and a mound of dirt was not likely to slow them.

Turning to the queen, he shrugged. "Good work."

A smile tugged at the queen's lips and there was a hint of laughter in her eyes as she drew him away from the working men. "You may speak truthfully with me, Calafe," she said. "You think such measures inadequate against the threat of the Tangata?"

Romaine glanced over his shoulder at the soldiers. They were out of earshot now, but several had broken away to follow the queen. Her personal guard. Shaking his head, he regarded the woman.

"You are no fool, Your Majesty," Romaine replied. "And the fortifications will at least provide a line for your men to hold, should the Tangata strike. But...if the creatures were to attack in any force, there is little a mound of dirt will do to stop them."

The queen nodded and they continued away from the boundaries of the camp, heading towards the centre. The supply wagons had arrived now and many were hard at work setting the tents for the night. One of the queen's grooms approached as they walked, eyes on Romaine's horse. He handed over the reins with reluctance—a man should always care for his own horse.

"You are right, of course," the queen said as the groom led his mare away, "but a leader must think not only of the day at hand, but those to come. Would you believe I had my soldiers perform this ritual every night we spent camped between Mildeth and Fogmore?"

Romaine frowned. There would have been little risk of attack by man or Tangata in those lands. "No wonder you travelled so slowly."

The queen gave a throaty chuckle. "Of course, without such precautions, we might have reached the city a day sooner." She gestured to the soldiers moving past. "However, in a matter of days, we will be faced not by Tangata, but men. My soldiers must be ready to repel any attack. I thought it prudent that they have some practice at setting a war camp before we marched into enemy territory."

"You truly think it will come to that?"

"This is war, Romaine. I discount no possibility when it comes to my enemies. Especially one so wily as King Nguyen."

She came to a stop at that, and Romaine realised they were now standing in front of a canvas tent at least five times the size of the others that were being set up around the campsite. Two of the queen's personal guard already stood outside, spears held upright, eyes fixed on Romaine.

Romaine shook his head. "What does that man want with Cara?" he murmured, more to himself than the queen.

"There are several possibilities that come to mind," the queen mused. "However, I had hoped you might shine some light on the subject. You knew the Goddess best. Would you join me for a drink, Calafe?"

For a moment, Romaine was tempted to turn the woman down. His chest was aching something fierce and he wanted little more than to lie down and sleep a dozen hours. But...one did not simply turn down a request from the Queen of Flumeer. Muffling a sigh, he nodded, and the queen led the way inside. Ignoring the hostility of her guards, Romaine followed.

Within, the tent was more luxurious than he had expected for a woman who wore a full suit of armour. But then, he supposed even a warrior queen needed a few indulgences. The floor of the tent had been lined with stone tiles and Romaine quickly did his best to wipe the mud from his boots in the doorway. Warmth greeted him as he stepped inside, drawing his attention to a brazier set in the corner. Several plain wooden chairs had been set there, while beyond a feathered mattress lay on a slate bed.

Surprised they had managed to fit so much into the supply wagons, Romaine returned his gaze to the queen.

"Take a seat, Calafe," she said, gesturing to the chairs

beside the brazier. "Perhaps the warmth will ease your injuries."

The warmth was only adding to Romaine's weariness, but he did as he was bid while the queen moved to a cabinet set beside the bed. She joined him shortly though, proffering a glass of amber liquid. Accepting the drink, Romaine sniffed gingerly before raising an eyebrow.

"Calafe gold?" he murmured. It had been almost a decade since he'd last drunk the wine. One of the first attacks by the Tangata had burned the grapes on their southern vines.

"Of course," the queen replied, lifting a glass of her own in salute. She leaned forward then, the glow of a lantern setting her emerald eyes alight. "So, tell me of her, Romaine. What was it like to sup with the Divine?"

Romaine found himself unable to hold the queen's gaze. Instead, he took a sip of the wine, and instantly found himself carried away to another time, one lit with sunshine and love and hope, to days spent with his wife and son, before the Tangata had stolen everything away. He sighed as the images faded, to be replaced by one of Cara, sitting in the plaza of Fogmore, lit by the winter sun.

"In many ways, she was just like us," he murmured. "A little strange, innocent, but I doubt we would have ever realised her true identity if not for the creatures we found in the caverns."

He clenched imaginary fingers at the mention of the beasts, a shudder running down his spine. His memory of the time beneath the earth was foggy—he'd lost a lot of blood—but he could still recall the faces of those ancient creatures with terrifying clarity.

"I have read your report," the queen murmured, pursing her lips. "The Goddess fought them off?"

Romaine nodded. "Her eyes turned grey, just like the

Tangata—and those…other things. We believed it meant she was one of them. The creatures had slain several of the Tangata and we thought the sight had enraged her." The words were bitter in his mouth, for that had been the first of many mistakes he'd made in the south. "It wasn't until…the river that I realised who she truly was."

"A shame," the queen murmured, "though understandable, given the eyes. They were amber normally, no?"

"Yes," Romaine replied. It seemed the queen had done her research well. "Those creatures, Your Majesty, I've never seen the like. If there are more of them…" He swallowed, lifting his left arm instinctively, and the queen's eyes were drawn to the bandaged stump. Despite her calm demeanour, she shivered and rubbed her own wrist. Ignoring the gesture, Romaine went on: "Let's just say, we could not have defeated them without Cara's help. She fought like nothing I have ever seen, killed them with hardly a thought."

As he spoke the words, Romaine was drawn back to the battle on the banks of the Illmoor. The way Cara had fought against the Tangata had been utterly different to the conflict in the tunnels of the Gods. In the darkness, her eyes had been mad, her blows wild, sickeningly strong. Beside the river though, she had fought with a cool precision and skill, and the Tangata she had downed had not been slain.

"Such a wonder, that the Gods allowed their magic to fall into the hands of humanity. No wonder it drove those sorry souls you discovered in the depths mad."

"Mankind is not meant to wield such power," Romaine murmured in agreement.

The queen only smiled. "It does lead me to wonder how Erika has wielded her magic gauntlet for so long. Tell me, did you notice a change in her, during your time south of the Illmoor?"

Romaine hesitated, recalling for an instant the way Erika had tortured Cara with the magic, when she'd thought the woman responsible for her ill fortune. That had been before they'd discovered Cara's true identity, when they'd thought her a Tangatan spy, but even so, her actions had been vicious, vindictive…

…but then again, after discovering the Perfugian recruits butchered, Romaine had not acted much differently. Finally, he shook his head.

"No, not that I noticed."

"A pity," Amina mused, "though I suppose when we recover the artefact, her experimentation will serve me well." She chuckled. "I admit, that was one of the reasons I permitted her mad expedition. The magic needed testing before I claimed it for my own."

"That 'mad expedition' claimed the lives of my friends," Romaine replied, struggling to keep the anger from his voice.

The queen looked up at that, her eyes widening with surprise. "The Perfugians, of course," she said after a moment. "Their loss was…regrettable."

Romaine ground his teeth, but said nothing. It was not his place to criticise the Flumeeren monarch, however much her decisions angered him. Instead, he found himself staring at the open grate of the brazier. The occasional *pop* came from the burning coals.

"You think me cold," the queen said after a time. "I cannot deny it. The skill is one I have perfected much over the years, that ability to weigh my decisions without thought to personal sentiment. But then, that is the burden of a monarch."

"Not to care for the people you rule?" Romaine asked, unable to keep the words to himself any longer.

"To focus on what creates the greatest good for my people, that which will protect the greatest number of lives."

Silence fell at her words and Romaine couldn't help but feel a touch of guilt. He said nothing, though. The queen might be forced to justify the death of dozens, or even hundreds, in protection of her nation, but he could not. Would not.

"I suppose she told you of the map?" the queen asked finally. "A shame I listened to her paranoia." She snorted. "No doubt my rival king will be delighted to know the Archivist escaped with the only copy."

"I saw the map." Romaine hesitated. "I do not recall much of its details."

"Nor I, sadly," the queen replied. "Though there was one site…"

"The home of the Gods?" Romaine nodded, recalling the scarlet star that had marked the secret location, deep in the mountains east of Calafe. "Something a man isn't likely to forget."

"Yes, it would be quite the discovery," the queen said, turning her head in the direction of those distant peaks. "I fear that is the reason Nguyen chooses now to act against me."

"You cannot think he would be so bold as to break the prohibition?" No human had set foot in the Mountains of the Gods for centuries—or at least, none that had lived to tell the story.

The queen's eyes remained distant, even as she spoke. "It is one of several eventualities I am considering," she mused. Then she blinked, returning her gaze to Romaine. "Assuming your Goddess is her prisoner, where do you think the Archivist would go, should she be given the choice?"

Romaine hesitated, remembering the fervent glint that had come over Erika's gaze when she spoke of the Gods and their power. A shiver ran down his spine as he realised the truth.

"If she were desperate enough…" He swallowed. "If the king allowed it, you're right, she would make for the home of the Gods. There are no other sites left to explore, other than a handful deep in the southern territories of the Tangata."

Amina sighed. "Yes, that is as I thought." She shook her head. "No matter. With luck, we will have both the Goddess and my Archivist returned before the king can make his move."

Romaine's stomach twisted, though he wasn't sure it was for the hope of Cara's return, or the prospect of an approaching war between the kingdoms. Before he could find the words to reply, movement came from the entrance to the tent, and a man appeared between the flaps.

"Amina," the newcomer said informally, then hesitated at the sight of the two of them by the brazier. "Didn't realise you had company."

A frown touched Romaine's forehead as the man stepped closer to the light. His clothes were mud-stained and there was a weariness about his face that spoke of a long journey. He wore a rough-spun cotton tunic rather than the red uniform of a Flumeeren soldier. The guards outside must have recognised him though, for they had admitted him without commotion, despite the longsword he wore at his waist. The handle of a crossbow also hung over his right shoulder. A broad grin split the man's face as he looked from the queen to Romaine, though he did not speak whatever unseemly thoughts might have generated it.

"Yasin," the queen said in greeting, rising from her chair. "I hadn't thought you would arrive until morning."

"We rode for three days straight after I got your

message, my lady," Yasin replied, falling into a half-bow that seemed more mocking than respectful.

Romaine's frown deepened and he found himself reaching for the hilt of his own sword. The newcomer did not miss the movement. He straightened, feet slipping into a defensive stance, though his hands did not stray near his blade. Romaine froze, shifting his gaze to the man's face. He still wore the mocking grin, but there was a hardness to the sky-green eyes now. Whatever the man's outward appearance, this Yasin was a warrior.

Silence hung over the tent as the two regarded each other, until the queen stepped between them.

"Enough of that," she snorted, waving a hand. "Romaine, this is Yasin, captain of my…private security. Yasin, this is Romaine, soldier of Calafe."

The two warriors eyed each other for a moment longer, before Romaine finally nodded and took his hand from the sword hilt. A trickle of despair touched him as he realised how little good the weapon would have done him anyway. The weapon was unfamiliar in his hand. Even his greater size and reach would not have meant much against an expert swordsman—and Romaine had no doubt the queen only employed the best. Silently, he resolved to start practicing from that night onward.

"Thank you for the drink, Your Majesty," Romaine said finally, "it was a rare treat. But I will bid you goodnight. My injuries still bother me, and I must rest if I am to be any use to you in the coming days."

The queen smiled. "Of course, Calafe, rest well."

Nodding his thanks, Romaine strode past the two and out into the night—though not before he caught a soft snort of laughter from Yasin. Anger flared in Romaine's stomach but he ignored the man. He was in no position to fight the man, or any other. No, he needed to regain his strength, and his skill.

Clenching his fist, he breathed in the night air. Then he strode into the night, seeking Lorene. If the man truly wanted to redeem himself for not travelling south, he could volunteer as Romaine's sparring partner.

❧ 8 ❧

THE SOLDIER

Fear shone in the woman's eyes as she tore herself free of Lukys and retreated. Before he had a chance to question her, a hand of iron grasped him by the arm and dragged him away. He stumbled, almost falling, before straightening to find himself face-to-face with Sophia.

What are you doing? her voice hissed into his mind.

Seeing her anger, Lukys tried to shrink away. She held him fast, looking for all the world like she was about to take the revenge he had been anticipating these last days.

"She's…human!" he gasped, panic forcing the words from his mouth before he could stop them.

Sophia hesitated, a frown furrowing her brow. Behind her, Dale was struggling with one of the other Tangatan guards, but he froze at Lukys's words.

"What?" he gasped, twisting to try and see past Lukys and Sophia.

But the woman and the Tangata that had been with her had already fled. Lukys's heart pounded in his ears as he locked eyes with Sophia.

"What was she doing here?" he hissed, yanking at the

arm that held him. To his surprise, she released him. He paused, drawing in a breath. "What are *we* doing here?"

Dale looked confused by the outburst, but Lukys paid him no attention. Glancing beyond his fellow recruit, he scanned the other Tangata moving about the streets, squeezing their way past the roadblock their group had formed across half the avenue. With the sun now streaming down between the rooftops, it was easy to see their eyes, to recognise the eerie greyness—

There!

A man walked by, hazel eyes focused on the path ahead. Then another, this one a woman with brown eyes. Humans. There were humans in New Nihelm, in a city of Tangata. And suddenly he thought he knew why he and Dale were there.

"They're slaves," he croaked.

"Wha—" Dale broke off as the other guards gripped him by the arms and started dragging him down the street.

Lukys turned his gaze on Sophia, waiting for her to do the same with him. But she made no move to grab him again, only gestured in the direction the others had taken Dale.

Come, Lukys, she said. *You will not find your answers here.*

Swallowing, Lukys considered trying to run. But even if he could evade Sophia's lightning reactions, where would he go? The Tangata were everywhere; they would catch him before he made it a block. Finally he let out a long breath and nodded. Sophia took hold of his arm again and led him along the street.

They soon caught up with Dale and the other guards. His friend had given up his struggles, though a look of relief appeared in his eyes when he saw Lukys. Released from their guards, they fell into step together, though now Sophia and the others hardly gave them a foot of breathing space.

They must have covered another half a mile after that. Lukys paid more attention to the faces of those they passed this time, and soon spotted more of the strange, human citizens of the city. He didn't try to contact any of these others, and for their part, the humans kept their eyes downcast, averted from the fresh prisoners being marched past.

Finally they found themselves at the edge of the island again, though this time in the western reaches. There they passed beyond a low flood wall, out into a broad plaza of ash-stained tiles. The river bordered the opened space to north and south, while directly across the plaza from where they had entered stood a single building in the shape of a pyramid.

Lukys's heart throbbed as he recognised it as a Basilica to The Fall. Stretching from the swirling waters to either side, the sloped granite walls loomed over the plaza, seeming to have a presence of their own. Most older cities had at least one of the structures, built in the early days of civilisation as appeasement to the Gods that had brought the darkness down upon them. Today few believed the temples had placated anything, and so it was surprising to find one in a city as young as New Nihelm. He supposed that living in the shadow of the Mountains of the Gods, the Calafe might have erred on the side of caution when it came to inciting Divine Wrath.

Regardless, the Tangata seemed to have found a use for the structure, for a large group waited outside the polished gold and brass doors. The rest of their party was already halfway across the plaza, Adonis in the lead, and at a push from Sophia, Dale and Lukys started after them.

As they neared the basilica, Lukys saw that the group standing outside the doors was similarly streaked in mud and filth. He frowned, wondering whether another group of

Tangata had also returned from the wilderness. The gentle buzz of conversation carried to them on the breeze…

Lukys's heart lurched as he realised the group was speaking out loud. They were humans, others captured by the Tangata and brought to the city as prisoners. But where would the Tangata have found so many humans this side of the river…

…he glimpsed a face in the group. His mouth fell open —then he was rushing forward, leaping past Sophia, Dale only a step behind. He recognised that face, these people, those filthy blue uniforms.

"Travis!" he bellowed.

Travis's eyes widened in shock, before a grin split his face. Stepping away from the rest of the Perfugians, he opened his arms and dragged Lukys into a hug. Lukys gasped as the bigger man crushed the air from his lungs, but there was laughter on his lips as they broke apart.

"What are you doing here?" he gasped, still gaping at the sight of his friend alive.

The rest of the Perfugian recruits gathered nearby, though they were not so bold as to approach Lukys as Travis had. Their numbers had been reduced to just fifteen including Lukys and Dale, just a fraction of the fifty men and women that had arrived on the frontier just a few short months ago. But still a far cry more than he'd feared.

"Where else would I be?" Travis replied with a grin.

His beard had grown out in the two weeks that had passed since they'd seen each other. Between his dishevelled uniform and the grime covering his face, he had seen better days. Footsteps came from behind them and Travis offered Dale a nod as his fellow noble born approached.

Beyond, Sophia and the rest of their escort didn't seem overly concerned by their reunion, though they did not take their eyes off the group of humans. Adonis had already reached the Tangata that had been guarding the Perfugian recruits and now seemed to be waiting for something.

"We…found the village," Lukys said finally, recalling the moment he'd stumbled into the cluster of abandoned buildings and seen the bodies of his comrades.

Travis's face darkened and a scowl twisted his lips as he glanced at the nearby Tangata. "We were so close." He shook his head, looking away. The village had been less than a day's march from the safety of the Illmoor. Drawing in a breath, Travis went on: "There were too many to fight, but we stood our ground anyway. Only…after the first clash, with a dozen of us dead on the ground, the bastards just stood there, watching. Eventually one of us threw down their spear. Rest of us followed. Guess we figured it was worth trying to surrender." He shrugged. "So here we are."

Tears touched Lukys's eyes, and without speaking he dragged his friend into another hug.

"I'm glad you're here," he said as they broke apart.

A grim smile appeared on Travis's face as his gaze swept the plaza. "And the others?" he asked softly.

"We lost Groner," Lukys said, feeling guilty that he'd hardly thought of the man since that terrible time in the tunnels beneath the earth. "Romaine lost his hand, but the others are fine. They got away." He hesitated, thinking about Cara. Travis didn't know what she was. "We, ah, have a lot to catch up on."

Beside them, Dale snorted. "That's an understatement."

Travis exhaled hard, relief momentarily showing on his face, though there was still confusion in his eyes.

Lukys shook his head. "Later," he said, looking past Travis and the other Perfugians to where Adonis and most of the Tangata had gathered before the polished doors. "What's happening here?"

"Your guess is as good as mine," Travis replied with a shrug. "We arrived in the night. They put us in some building until the morning, then brought us here." He shivered, and Lukys glimpsed the fear his friend was hiding behind the calm façade. "Isn't it creepy?" His eyes were fixed on Adonis's group. "They never make a sound, yet they're communicating."

"It's that damned magic they stole from the Gods," Dale answered, his face hardening. "I wonder if that's why Cara came, to take it back?"

"What?" Travis said, his eyebrows knitting together in a frown.

"Ah…" Dale trailed off, turning to Lukys for help.

Lukys swallowed. "Err…you know how Cara was always wearing her furs, even inside?"

Travis nodded, though his eyes showed he didn't know where Lukys was going with the subject.

"Well…you see…it turns out she was hiding something…"

"She's got bloody wings!" Dale exclaimed.

Lukys suppressed a groan. "It's true," he said to Travis's confusion. "She's one of them, one of the Gods."

Before Lukys's eyes, the colour drained from his friend's face. "Wh…what?" Travis's mouth opened and closed, but no further words came out.

"Easy, man," Dale said gently, patting Travis on the back.

Lukys nodded and was about to speak further when he felt another presence brush against his mind.

Lukys.

A shiver ran down his spine and he turned to find Adonis approaching, Sophia at his side. Behind him, his friends froze, and even the murmurs of the other recruits faded to silence. Lukys swallowed as he looked into the eyes of the senior Tangata, remembering his rage back in the clearing. He'd hoped Adonis was done with him.

Come with us, Lukys. Sophia's voice was softer than the senior Tangata's, but it was clear the instructions were not optional.

He swallowed as the two came to a halt before him. He hesitated, waiting several moments before turning to his friends.

"I…I think they want me to go with them," he rasped, still unsure about how to tell them of his ability.

Sophia caught him by the arm before the others could respond, and Lukys was dragged away. Travis and Dale watched after him, lips downcast, eyes haunted. They looked for all the world like they had just attended his funeral.

Swallowing, Lukys forced his eyes ahead. *What are you going to do with us?* he asked, trying to direct the question at Adonis.

That is for the Matriarch to decide.

He offered no further explanation. Lukys allowed himself to be shepherded past the other recruits towards the polished doors of the basilica. They swung open as two of the Tangatan guards entered first, revealing darkness beyond. Swallowing, Lukys took one last glance at the sunlit sky before the black swallowed him up.

Bright spots danced across his vision as the doors closed again behind them, and he blinked, struggling to pierce the gloom. Movement flickered somewhere within, betrayed by the gentle whisper of clothing, of leather boots upon stone.

A gentle push from behind urged Lukys forward. He staggered, and glancing around, he managed to pick Sophia's face from the shadows. Swallowing, he obeyed her silent command, taking tentative steps on the smooth floor, afraid the ground might drop out from under him at any movement.

Slowly his eyes adjusted, and he began to make out shadows around the room. Light from above led his gaze to tiny windows set at the point of the pyramid high overhead. Returning his eyes to the ground, the room began to take shape from the dark.

The basilica had only one enormous chamber, its inward sloping walls leading up to that single point above. Amidst the shadows, he could see no other entrances or inner rooms, not unless they were hidden behind the altar of the Gods.

Set upon a dais raised some four feet above floor level, a giant slab of marble dominated the room. Otherwise the place was unadorned, though as Lukys took another step, he caught a shimmer from the base of the dais. He frowned, moving closer, and realised the dais was situated in the centre of a great pool of water. It seemed to be flowing slowly around the stone, though a glance at the walls did not reveal a source.

Movement drew Lukys's eyes back to the altar, and a figure stepped forward. Rustling came from around the room as all the Tangata knelt and pressed foreheads to stone. Before he could ask what was going on, Sophia gripped him by the shoulder and pressed him down. He cried out, legs weakened from the endless march south giving way beneath her strength, forcing him to his knees.

Quiet! Sophia hissed in his mind.

There was a sense of urgency in her voice, and Lukys bit back his cry, heart suddenly racing. Turning to face the altar, he stared at the figure that had appeared there, trying to make out her features through the gloom. Swathed in long robes, she could only be the Matriarch that Adonis had spoken of. She stepped closer, and the light from above fell across her face.

The breath hissed from Lukys's lips as he looked on the aged face. He had never seen an older Tangata before—those they fought were always young, their appearance that of humans in their twenties. This creature though, her face was more wrinkles than skin, and her hair was a pale grey, drained of its colour by the countless passage of years. Her hands were speckled with age spots, and her eyes…Lukys swallowed. They were pure white. Without the grey of the Tangata, he might have thought her human…yet there was something about her manner, about the way she stood, that left Lukys in no doubt as to what she was. And those eyes were looking directly at him.

Adonis, what have you brought me?

✿ 9 ✿

THE FUGITIVE

Sitting on the pillowed bed, Erika stared down at the intricate lattice of metal fibres that covered her hand. It clung to her flesh, so close she could run her hand from gauntlet to her arm and hardly feel the difference. The strange metal was even warm to the touch, as though it had become a part of her, feeding off her energies.

Without thinking, she clenched her fist and felt the familiar thrum of its magic. The soft glow bathed her face, radiating a new heat now, one that promised power, promised glory. She shivered and released it once more, and the sensation faded. Disgust replaced it, clogging her throat, and she thought of all the terrible things she had done with this gauntlet.

Ibran, her assistant turned traitor, deafened, blind, abandoned in the darkness.

The Tangatan prisoner in Amina's court, screaming its agony.

Cara, writhing beneath the gauntlet's power, begging for her mercy.

Standing suddenly, Erika strode to the window and looked out over the rooftops of the fortress proper. It had been five days since their arrival, and she had only seen the king one other time, a brief visit in which she'd handed over the map showing the hidden locations of ruins that had once been occupied by the Gods. Little good it had proven —there was but one site inside the bounds of Gemaho, and it had apparently been discovered years ago.

The remaining stars were beyond their reach, mostly hidden deep in the south, in lands that had been claimed by the Tangata generations ago. All but for the one marked high in the Mountains of the Gods. But not even Nguyen seemed interested in that venture. The Gemaho might not be religious, but even they avoided those forbidden peaks.

Letting out a sigh, Erika turned from the window and began to pace. The inactivity was starting to grate on her, and the knowledge that Queen Amina was approaching had not helped at all. The woman was vicious, her resolve hard as iron. She would stop at nothing to get what she wanted.

And she wanted the magic that had fused with Erika's arm—even if it meant cutting it from her corpse.

The room the king had placed her in was large and well-adorned, with furniture crafted of pinewood and lit by chandeliers of silver and brass. She had been forced to share the accommodations with Maisie, but thankfully the spy was rarely there—her bed had not even been slept in last night. Cara had been taken to separate quarters; Erika had not seen the Goddess since.

Slumping back to her bed, she found herself staring at the gauntlet once more, wondering again at its power. The king's words about how it worked on Cara had stayed with her. It had proven an effective weapon against the Tangata, but it still seemed strange that the Gods—or the Anahera, as Cara had called them—would create a weapon that could be used so easily against them.

Did that mean it had been created by somebody else?

A cold breeze blew across Erika's neck. She had used the magic so recklessly these last weeks, with hardly a thought to the consequences. The Tangata had been changed by the magic they had stolen, and she wondered now if the same could happen to her. But…it *hadn't* harmed her, hadn't changed her.

Had it?

No, surely not, or the king would not use its power so freely. Unless he too did not understand the power he wielded. How had he come by another of the artefacts anyway?

Erika shook her head and scrunched her eyes closed. Questions upon questions. In her mind she recalled the way the king had struck Cara down. He had acted quickly, without hesitation, without even knowing Cara's identity. A vicious act, without mercy.

A *click* drew Erika's attention to the entrance as Maisie entered. Rings circled the woman's eyes and there was mud on her leggings, as though she had spent the night wading through the marshland beyond the walls of the fortress. Erika raised an eyebrow as the spy crossed the room and dropped onto the other bed.

"I take it these nightly disappearances aren't to see some secret lover?" she asked, trying to be friendly.

The Gemaho woman grunted. "Afraid not." Letting out a groan, she sat up and eyed Erika from across the room. "Your queen is drawing close."

A vice closed around Erika's throat at the woman's words and it was a moment before she managed to reply. "She's heading here?"

"With an army," Maisie confirmed.

Fear drove Erika to her feet. She paced the room again, fists clenched, warmth radiating through her body…

She froze, her eyes falling to the gauntlet. Light shone from the metallic fibres and she realised she'd summoned its magic again without thinking. Letting out a slow breath, she relaxed her hand and the magic died.

"How long do we have?" she asked quietly.

"Less than a day."

"*A day!*" Erika cried.

She swung around, panic gripping her…but there was no escaping the Queen of Flumeer. A moan built in her throat and she clutched her hands to her hair. What had she been thinking? Better that she had thrown herself upon Amina's mercy than betray such a woman. She would get no clemency now.

"Oh, calm down," Maisie snorted, lying back on the bed. "You're safe here, or had you forgotten? A *fortress* lies between us and the woman. Her army could hurl itself upon the walls of the Illmoor Fortress for a decade and never come a step closer to taking you."

"You don't know her like I do," Erika argued, though she ceased her pacing. Drawing in a breath, she sought calm. "The woman is devious."

"And you think Gemaho has survived all these years because Nguyen is not? Believe me, he has been three steps ahead of Amina for years."

The breath hissed from Erika's nose as she exhaled sharply, but she did not argue further. There was little point. She slumped back to her bed.

"Sorry," she murmured. "It's just…I've never felt so lost. None of this makes sense. Even this magic…I think it's doing something to me."

"Oh?" Maisie asked, leaning forward on the bed. "Why would you think that?"

Erika shook her head. "I don't know." She made a gesture, as though to dismiss her concerns. "Though… maybe you can help. The orb you have, the king's gauntlet…how long have you had them?"

Maisie eyed her for a long moment, as if weighing up whether that was information they could trust Erika with. In the end though, she must have proven herself worthy, for the woman let out a sigh.

"Two years," she replied. "We found them in our only ancient site, far to the east. There was a sealed room, much like the one you discovered in Flumeer, I hear. It held several artefacts, though only Nguyen's gauntlet and my orb retain any power."

Erika nodded. "And the king…he hasn't changed, having the gauntlet for so long?"

"Not to my knowledge," the spy replied with a smile.

Despite herself, Erika let out a sigh, relieved. If the king hadn't changed after using the gauntlet after two years, then…she frowned, glancing again at Maisie. She too wielded one of the artefacts of the Gods; could that have altered her perception of the king?

Angrily Erika shook her head. She was being paranoid, wasn't she? Surely Cara would have said something about the gauntlet earlier, if it could corrupt them. But then, the Goddess had rarely offered information freely…

"I need to see Cara," Erika said suddenly, coming to her feet. "It's time I asked her some more questions."

"Ah…" The woman hesitated. "I don't think she's taking visitors right now."

Erika narrowed her eyes, suddenly suspicious. She should have checked on Cara days ago, but she'd been preoccupied with the queen and her own magical dilemmas.

Now something about the spy's behaviour set her suspicions aflame.

"Where is she?" Erika demanded.

Maisie sighed. "She's safe…and secure."

"You put her in a cell, didn't you?"

"Well, we could hardly leave her in those chains after she got the first pair off, could we?" Maisie argued.

"I want to see her."

Air hissed between the spy's teeth as she exhaled, but after a moment she nodded. "Come on."

Maisie led her through the long corridors of the fortress until they came to a narrow stairwell of cold granite, leading down into the depths beneath the keep. Erika hesitated as the spy took a torch from its bracket, memories of other underground tunnels flickering into her mind.

"You ready?" the spy asked, raising an eyebrow.

Erika nodded quickly and they started down into the darkness. Maisie's torch lit a bubble of light around them, but watching the flames flicker, Erika couldn't help but think how easily they might be extinguished. Then the darkness would claim them. A shiver ran down her spine and she clenched her fist, reaching for the magic, before stopping herself.

The stairwell ended in a narrow corridor lined with the iron bars of several cells. It stretched only a few yards— apparently Fort Illmoor hadn't had a great need for jail cells until now. Maisie led her past several empty cells before coming to a stop at the last one. She held up the torch and glanced at Erika.

"Well…ask your questions."

The breath caught in Erika's throat as the flames illuminated the room beyond the bars. It held no furniture but for a steel-framed cot bolted to the stones and a bucket placed in the corner. There were no windows or other exits, though movement came from the corner as a rat squawked at the light, disappearing into a hole between the bricks.

Erika's gaze was drawn to the bed, where a figure sat, knees pulled up to her chest. Dirt-stained wings hung limp across the bed, though Erika was surprised to see the cuts the Goddess had suffered from the king's attack already appeared to have healed. Slowly, Cara lifted her head, her amber eyes glinting in the lantern light.

"So you finally decided to come," she said as their eyes met.

A lump lodged in Erika's throat and she quickly dropped her gaze, unable to face that accusation, that anger. How far had she fallen, that it had come to this? She had seen her friend, the Goddess that had saved her life, imprisoned, locked away, all to save herself.

"I was meant to go home, you know," Cara's voice whispered through the bars. "That night in the mountains, before I led you to your precious hidden site. I was meant to go *home*."

"I'm sorry," Erika rasped, and her vision blurred. She turned to Maisie. "You can't leave her like this. It's not right. She's a *God!*"

"One of your Gods, not mine," Maisie said, but her face flickered as she spoke the words, as though she found herself doubting them. Her fingers played with the hilt of her sword as she glanced into the cell. "Besides, it's not my call."

"That's right—it's mine, Princess."

Erika swung around as the king's voice carried down the corridor. He appeared a moment later on the granite stairwell, his way lit by the unnatural glow of his gauntlet. Apparently, he had decided not to wear the riding gloves today.

"She doesn't deserve to be treated this way," Erika

argued, taking a step towards him. "Whatever you think she is, Cara has done nothing wrong."

"She did try to attack me," Nguyen replied as he strode up. "I'd say imprisonment is a fairly light punishment for assaulting a monarch, wouldn't you?"

A growl came from inside the cell and Erika only shook her head. "You cannot be serious—"

The king waved a hand, cutting her off. "Calm yourself, Princess," he said, still using the moniker, much to Erika's annoyance. He moved to stand before the bars of the cell. "The good Anahera has proven…difficult, but these are only temporary accommodations, while I have been making…other arrangements."

"Other arrangements?" Erika asked as Cara's words echoed her question from inside the cell.

Nguyen chuckled. "All in good time," he replied, then offered a bow to the Goddess. "For now, I am afraid I must steal your visitors, Cara. There is something pressing we must attend to."

"Oh?" Maisie asked as the king turned away from the cell. Within, Cara had sat up and was watching them closely.

"Yes, I am afraid things are coming to a head rather faster than I had forecast," he said, looking from the spy to Erika. "The queen has arrived. There is to be a meet. With luck, I can forestall an attack long enough for my preparations to be completed."

"You're going to *talk* with her?" Erika hissed.

She clenched her fist, realising suddenly how precarious her situation was. The king already had a gauntlet of his own. With Cara and the map, there was little reason for him to protect her—not when the choice was between peace and a terrible war. Being the daughter of a dead king certainly wasn't going to save her.

The king's eyes glinted in the light of his magic. "You're afraid I will betray you?" he asked, as though he had read Erika's thoughts.

Erika swallowed. "Are you?"

Nguyen grinned. "On the contrary, princess. I was hoping you might help me."

❧ 10 ❧

THE SOLDIER

*A*donis, *what have you brought me?*

Adonis had dropped to his knees with the other Tangata, but now he stood.

An anomaly, Matriarch, he replied, apparently making no efforts to shield his words from Lukys. *This human possesses the ability to Speak, and to Hear.*

Is that so, human? Milky eyes turned on Lukys. *You can Hear us?*

Lukys flinched—this time the Matriarch's voice was far louder in his mind, as though all her will had suddenly focused upon him. The creature lifted its eyebrows at his reaction.

So it's true. Her attention returned to Adonis. *An anomaly indeed. How did you make such a discovery?*

Chance, Matriarch, came Adonis's response. *He was broadcasting when we pursued the Anahera into human territory.* He hesitated. *She may have a connection with this human. She revealed herself trying to free him.*

Pieces fell into place in Lukys's mind at Adonis's words.

The Anahera were the Tangata's name for the Gods. His blood ran cold as he realised the truth. His first day on the frontier, the Tangata had attacked, slaying dozens and suffering heavy losses themselves. But that had also been the night Romaine had arrived with the injured Cara. He frowned, staring at Adonis. Did the Tangata really hate the Gods so much that they had pursued Cara across the river, even thrown away so many of their own lives for a chance to slay her?

So the Anahera are finally returning to the world, the Matriarch mused. *Perhaps there is hope yet.* Her eyes shifted back to Lukys, and again the strength of her voice redoubled. *Tell me, human, what interest do the Anahera have in humanity?*

Lukys's skin crawled at the power of her words, though this time he thought he managed to keep the reaction from his face. Suppressing a shudder, he made to climb to his feet. A hand from Sophia stopped him until the Matriarch nodded her permission.

"The Goddess is a friend to my people," he said out loud, the words echoing in the silent chamber, "and she will come for us."

Laughter rasped around the room as the Matriarch shuffled to the edge of the dais. *Goddess?* A smile curled her lips. *Yes, of course, humans are such superstitious creatures.*

There was a flicker of movement, and suddenly the Matriarch was leaping forward, clearing the pool of water in a single bound and landing beside Lukys. He cried out and tried to retreat, but a wrinkled hand caught him by the shirt and dragged him back.

Tell me, human, are you truly a friend to the Anahera?

"I…" Lukys swallowed, suddenly finding himself trapped in that awful gaze, in those bleached white eyes.

Words abandoned him, but images flickered through his mind, memories of Fogmore, of time spent with Cara and

Travis and Romaine. Good times, gone now, swept away by the madness of the Archivist's expedition.

So you speak the truth, the Matriarch murmured, and Lukys shuddered as he realised she had seen the memories. Then she sighed, and released him. *Still, it must be a faint hope that she would come to this place of her enemies.*

Lukys swallowed as she swung away from him, his entire body trembling. Had she simply read his mind, or had he been broadcasting those memories? Swallowing, he forced the fears away. He had to be strong.

"What do you want with us?" he asked, taking a step towards her.

A hand caught him before he could take another. He muffled a curse as Sophia dragged him back to where the other Tangata stood, though the Matriarch paid him no attention now.

I understand there are other humans without, Adonis? she asked, moving to stand before him.

Yes, Matriarch, he replied. *We brought fifteen for assignment.*

So many, the Matriarch mused. *And have you chosen one of your own?*

Adonis hesitated, but finally he shook his head. Lukys frowned at the exchange, but the Matriarch continued.

You are of the third generation, Adonis, she reproached him. *The last of my true progeny. You cannot delay forever, however distasteful you consider the chore.* Then she sighed and waved a hand. *But let that be a matter for another day. Tell me, how did so many come into your possession?*

Adonis's eyes flickered to where Lukys stood before returning to the Matriarch. *The humans led an expedition into our territory*, he said, his mental voice dropping to a murmur.

An expedition? To what ends?

Adonis swallowed visibly. *They had discovered another of our*

WRATH OF THE FORGOTTEN

Birthing Grounds. Thankfully, the human's broadcasts forewarned us. We arrived first.

Good. Perhaps now the humans will respect our territory, she paused. *And what did you discover there?*

The Old Ones, Matriarch, he whispered.

His words were met with a stunned silence. Watching the Matriarch's face, Lukys thought he glimpsed something there…of wonder, or hope? The thought sent a tremor down his spine as he remembered the creatures Adonis spoke of, the so-called "Old Ones." He could still recall the madness in their eyes, the bloodlust. They had slain even the Tangata that had woken them.

Suddenly he realised that words were no longer flowing through his mind, and looking up he saw the eyes of Adonis and the Matriarch on him. Adonis licked his lips, glancing uncertainly at his leader.

The human is right, he said finally. *The centuries had destroyed their minds. We fled before the creatures killed us all.*

Is that so? The Matriarch took a step towards Lukys, her eyes boring into him once more. *And how did the humans know where to look for this Birthing Ground?*

We do not know, Matriarch, Adonis replied.

The milky eyes did not leave Lukys. *Well, human?*

Lukys shivered, an image of the Archivist's map rising unbidden in his mind. Desperately he tried to press it back down, to hide it away. Laughter rasped from the aged creature as she stepped closer.

He resists me. Her whispers reverberated through Lukys's mind. *Let us see your strength then, human.*

A sudden, searing pain blinded Lukys at her words. In that instant, he felt as though his very being were being washed away, and in the distance he heard a voice crying out, agony ringing in his ears. The strength went from his legs and he sank to the ground. For a second the cold stones offered relief—but then another wave broke upon his soul, and the map he had glimpsed just once sprang to life in his mind.

Coloured lines and stars and circles appeared before his inner eyes, each depicting some real-life feature of the world in which they lived—mountains and forests and rivers and so much more. Inevitably his eyes were drawn to a scattering of scarlet stars spread throughout the kingdoms. The ancient sites of the Gods, what the Tangata had called their Birthing Grounds.

Lukys's pain vanished as quickly as it had appeared. Letting out a cry of relief, he slumped against the ground, sobbing softly into the granite floor. He knew, in that moment he had betrayed his people. The secrets of that map were important in a way none of them had ever realised, not until they'd stepped foot in those dark tunnels and discovered the Old Ones waiting.

Ahhh, so there is a map! Despite his misery, Lukys could not keep out the words of the Matriarch. *It shows all of our Birthing Grounds, even those long forgotten.*

There are others? Adonis asked, his mental voice betraying his excitement.

Several… Lukys looked up as the Matriarch hesitated, and saw a frown creasing her face. *Even…could it be…the home of the Anahera?*

Truly? Adonis hissed. *Then there is a chance—*

No, the Matriarch interrupted. *I have seen your memories; our people are not prepared for a confrontation with the Anahera, not yet.*

Then let us forge an accord! Adonis cried. *Surely they must understand our plight—*

Guard your thoughts, Adonis, the Matriarch interrupted, flicking a glance at Lukys. Adonis swallowed visibly at the creature's admonishment, and Lukys wondered what he had been about to reveal. After a moment, the Matriarch went on: *No, the risk is too great. The Anahera are as likely to slaughter us as treat with us. But…there is another Birthing Ground yet to uncover. Perhaps…*

Matriarch…is that wise?

An icy feeling spread through Lukys's gut—fear. But not his own. Images flickered through his mind as he stared at Adonis, of bloodshed and death and vicious creatures screaming in the darkness. Adonis too feared the Old Ones.

We must take the risk, she said, dismissing his objections. *Go, Adonis. If you will not take an assignment, then this is your task. Take five of our finest warrior pairs and find this final Birthing Ground. If the Old Ones slumber there, wake them, and do your best to bring them back to us.*

The map welled in Lukys's mind again, but this time it came not from him, but the Matriarch—she was projecting it to Adonis. He found his focus drawn to one of the scarlet stars he'd paid little attention to. There, far in the south, deep in the ancestral lands of the Tangata, on an island not far off the coast.

"No," he whispered, finally struggling to rise. His heart hammered in his chest and he held out a hand. "No, you can't, those creatures, they're insane!"

But it was already too late, as Adonis bowed his head and left the chamber. Alone before the Matriarch, he swallowed as her eyes fixed back on him.

We do as we must, human, she spoke into his mind.

You can't control them, Lukys replied, so desperate now that he cast the thought at her, and all the memories of bloodshed and death he had taken from that dark place beneath the earth. *They'll kill us all.*

The Matriarch remained unbending. *So be it*, came her reply. *Better the world burn than have my children go whimpering into extinction.*

Lukys shook his head, wishing he could somehow

convince this strange creature, but already she seemed to have dismissed him. Then movement came from alongside him. He looked around in time to see Sophia approaching. He'd almost forgotten she was there.

Matriarch? she murmured, her head bowing slightly in deferment.

The Matriarch started at her words, seemingly surprised at her interference. *Yes, my child?*

I wish to claim my assignment.

The Matriarch's frown deepened and the pale eyes looked Sophia up and down. *You are of the fifth generation?* She paused, only going on when Sophia nodded. *You are still young, child. There may be time for you yet.*

My partner was slain, Sophia replied. Suddenly her grey eyes fixed on Lukys. His blood ran cold as she continued: *Slain by this human.*

Blood pulsed in his ears and he longed to flee. But there was nowhere for him to run, nowhere he could escape Sophia's gaze. So instead he stood fixed in place, knees trembling, and waited for his fate to be decided.

Ahhh, the Matriarch murmured, joining Sophia now. *Are you sure, my child?*

Yes, Sophia replied, turning again to Lukys. *The human slew many of my generation. He will be a good assignment.*

There was a long pause before the Matriarch spoke again, and all the while her eyes watched Lukys. He could feel them drilling into his soul, the touch of her mind upon his, and finally he was forced to look away.

Very well, my child, the Matriarch said finally. *He is yours—though beware, the Anahera may yet come for him.*

Then we will deal with her, Sophia replied, bowing her head deferentially. *Thank you, Matriarch.*

Lukys swallowed as footsteps approached. Fear and anger warred within him as Sophia moved forward. He would not be made a slave, would not surrender to these creatures, his will crushed so he only served them. Silently he steeled himself.

Then his eyes met Sophia's, and he felt something brush against his mind. His emotions faded as she stepped up before him, grey eyes piercing him just as the Matriarch's had. The resolve he'd felt just moments before drained away like a plug had been pulled in his core. And her voice whispered in his mind.

Now you truly are mine, Lukys.

❧ 11 ❧

THE FALLEN

Standing atop the river terrace, Romaine let out a long breath as he looked across at the Illmoor Fortress. Curtain walls of stark granite swept out from the cliffs, the blocks seeming more an extension of the mountains themselves than a manmade structure. Watch towers marked the ramparts at intervals, their twisted rooftops flying the yellow of Gemaho.

Their approach would have been noted days ago and now hundreds of soldiers stood atop those walls, armour shining in the noon sun. Looking on the men and women who opposed them, Romaine was reminded again of the madness of it all, that humanity should war upon itself while the Tangata still threatened their very existence. Not that he would be involved in much of the fighting. He had been training in the sword with Lorene and his injuries were healing well, but he would be little use in a pitched battle.

Pushing the thought aside, Romaine continued his appraisal of the enemy fortress. Away to the right, the waters of the Illmoor River had narrowed until they were just half a mile wide. The currents rushed between the twisted peaks of the Mountains of the Gods—and beneath the broad walls of the fortress. An incredible feat of engineering had erected a bridge of stone above the rushing waters as an extension of the curtain walls. Iron grates between the support pillars prevented the passage of ship or swimmers, and could be raised during storms or to allow debris to be removed. Only in the centre of the river were ships allowed to pass through a giant portcullis—at least during peacetimes.

The walls continued on the southern banks of the river, ensuring none could pass unnoticed into the lands of Gemaho. Other than the water portcullis, the only way through was the land gate—massive doors of heavy oak bolted by steel. Without ships for an aquatic assault, it was there that the queen would launch her attack.

Silently, Romaine turned his gaze to the floodplains before the fortress, where the queen's army had formed up, shields and spear tips glinting in the noonday sun. Behind the formation, others were hard at work preparing the camp fortifications. Romaine was again impressed by the speed at which they were securing the position. Unlike some of the irregulars he'd fought alongside on the frontier, the Queen's Guard were professional soldiers, and each knew his role.

Dozens had already paced out a perimeter for the camp and were now directing men with shovels where to prepare the defensive ditch. Others were preparing latrines downwind from the main camp, while still more went about setting the tents and organising the now-empty supply wagons into a second defensive perimeter. All the while, a squadron of archers stood in reserve.

Within an hour the camp would be set. Shaking his head, Romaine spurred his horse down the hill in search of the queen.

He found her amongst the soldiers standing in formation, her banner fluttering overhead, as though daring the Gemaho forces to attack. Sitting on her great destrier, garbed in the scarlet armour of the Flumeeren royalty, Romaine could imagine for a moment how it must have looked when she had led the charge against the Tangata in the disastrous southern campaign.

A smile lit her face as she turned and saw his approach. "Calafe, we've been waiting for you. Are you ready?"

Romaine frowned as he drew his horse to a stop alongside the queen. On her other side, Yasin grinned, though the gesture was mocking. Ignoring the silent taunt, Romaine rested his hand on the pommel of his saddle.

"Ready for what?"

"There is to be a truce for discussion. I plan to demand the Goddess's return. Given your affiliation with her Divinity, I thought you might wish to attend the meet."

Romaine hesitated, flicking a glance at the towering walls, but there didn't seem to be any activity atop the ramparts to indicate an attack was eminent. So instead he nodded, and the queen kicked her horse forward. Romaine followed. The ranks of scarlet soldiers split ahead of them, while a squadron of guards formed up behind the queen's delegation. Leaving behind the shelter of her army, they rode some hundred yards towards the fortress before pulling their horses to a stop. There they waited.

It wasn't long before the gates to the fortress creaked open to emit a column of riders. The queen's soldiers tensed, but Romaine was thankful to see their opposites numbered the same as their own party. They approached at a slow trot, finally drawing up a dozen yards from the queen and Romaine.

"King Nguyen," the queen said as one of the riders heeled his horse forward a step. "I had not expected you to welcome me personally to your kingdom."

A grin appeared on the rider's face and still in the saddle, he offered a mocking bow. "Of course, my lady," Nguyen replied. "When I learned of your movements I made for the Illmoor with all haste. I would be a poor king indeed if I did not offer greeting to a neighbour who comes to visit."

"Ay, poor indeed," the queen said, her voice as frigid as the snow-capped peaks towering above. "Though no more poorly than sending thieves behind a neighbour's back."

"Thieves, my lady?" the king said, feigning horror. "What has become of the world that such suspicions enter between friends?"

"The Gemaho have not been friends to Flumeer for a decade," the queen snapped.

She edged her horse forward and the soldiers behind the king reached for their swords. One, though, flinched at the queen's advance. Romaine frowned as he looked past the king to the soldier…

…only the rider wasn't a soldier at all. It was Erika, the queen's former Archivist. The one who had taken Cara.

"*You!*" he hissed, pointing a finger at the woman. He kicked his horse forward, but several of the king's soldiers drew between him and the opposing party. Teeth bared, Romaine bellowed a challenge. "What have you done with Cara?"

Blood hammered in his ears as he looked past the soldiers at Erika. The Archivist's face had grown pale at his challenge, but now her features smoothed as she quickly masked her emotions. Nearby, the king smiled.

"Ah, so I see you have met my new Archivist," he said with a laugh.

Watching at Erika sitting amongst the Gemaho, Romaine felt himself a fool. She had convinced him to trust her, to believe she was the long-lost princess of Calafe, but it had all been a ploy, a way to escape the clutches of the queen.

"So you admit to the crime," the queen snarled.

Behind the king, Erika tensed, but Nguyen laughed and gestured her forward. The woman hesitated, but one of the soldiers prodded the backside of her horse, and with a nicker it trotted forward until she sat alongside the king. His face hardened as he turned and regarded the queen once more.

"I am here because a foreign monarch has camped an army on my doorstep," he said, and now his voice had lost all humour. "Gemaho does not take kindly to threats against our sovereignty. I would ask you to remove this army from my border, lest blood is once again spilt between the kingdoms of man."

The queen sneered at his words. "So now the cowardly king concerns himself with the kingdoms of man," she spat. Clutching her reins, she stared across the field at the enemy king. "Surrender the thief, and the Goddess Cara, and perhaps I will consider leaving your pitiful walls standing."

Nguyen stared back at them, his expression kept carefully masked. Beside him, however, Erika was a picture of terror, her carefully crafted persona shattered by the queen's threats. Romaine couldn't help but feel a touch of satisfaction as he watched her squirm. He cast his eyes over the other soldiers, but there was no sign of Cara. He clenched a fist and swallowed another outburst.

"I am afraid the Calafe princess has requested my asylum," the king said finally. "In respect for my fallen brother king, that is a pact I will not break."

Romaine's heart lurched at the king's words—not least because this was the man who had abandoned his nation to its doom. Teeth clenched, he looked from Nguyen to Erika.

Did the man truly believe her claim, or was he using it as a political tool, a weapon he could wield against the queen?

"What nonsense is this?" the queen hissed, her eyes flicking from the king to Erika. "The bitch is no princess."

Mock surprise showed on the king's face. "You did not know?" he gasped, then *tisked*. "Amina, I am disappointed. I thought your spies were better than that."

The queen narrowed her eyes and a strained silence followed. Romaine guessed that Amina was weighing the king's words, trying to decipher whether he spoke the truth. Erika's potential royalty might mean little, or her appearance could stir up unrest amongst the hundreds of Calafe refugees camped outside her capital.

"You may keep the Archivist," Amina said finally, though her voice was strained. "It is the artefact she uncovered which concerns me. Her expeditions were funded by Flumeeren coin—the gauntlet belongs to me."

"The gauntlet?" the king murmured. Then his eyebrows lifted as though he had suddenly remembered something, and he pulled off one of his riding gloves. A gauntlet of silver steel was revealed beneath. "You mean this?"

For just a second, the queen's mask cracked, and Romaine saw the terrible rage simmering beneath the surface. Around him, her guards recoiled, hands tightening on spears and swords, but the king only held up the gauntleted hand. His eyes glinted in the sunlight.

"I'll admit, it is an interesting trinket."

"The Archivist had no right to gift it to you. It belongs to me," the queen hissed through clenched teeth.

"Is that so?" the king mused.

He chuckled, and with his free hand he grasped the gauntlet around his wrist. There was a muffled *hiss*, as of steam from a kettle, and even in the bright daylight the metal began to glow. Then something went *click* and he slid the gauntlet from his hand.

"Take it," he said, tossing it across the open ground. It struck the ground before the queen with a heavy thud. "Its power did not...sit right with me anyway," he added with a smile.

The queen stared at him for a long moment before turning her eyes to the gauntlet. Romaine swallowed as he glimpsed the greed there. He had seen what that gauntlet was capable of, the power it held. In the span of a second it could reduce grown men to agony, could knock even the Tangata from their feet.

The queen indicated for Yasin to collect the artefact. Eyes never leaving the enemy, the man dismounted and claimed the weapon, then handed it to Amina. She took it reverently, though not without another glance at the king.

Still sitting on his horse, Nguyen spread his hands. "So, we have peace then?"

The queen's eyes narrowed. "What of the Goddess?" she asked. "She was taken against her will. Flumeer will not stand idle while you assault the personage of the Divine."

The king chuckled. "I would have thought your Gods better able to protect themselves," he replied. He waved a hand, as though to dismiss Amina's concerns. "I will speak with the Goddess, though I believe she has already made arrangements for her future."

"Liar," Romaine snapped, the king's words finally pushing him beyond the bounds of reason. "You took Cara against her will."

"You must be Romaine." The king smiled as their eyes met. "Good to finally make your acquaintance. I have heard much of the last soldier of Calafe. Cara was most concerned for your health."

Romaine was forced to bite back a rude retort as the

queen raised her hand. "My army will not be leaving while Her Divine Personage remains your prisoner, Nguyen."

The king let out a sigh. "Then it seems we are at an impasse."

Amina's eyes were hard as stone as she stared him down. "I know the Divine was brought here in chains by the woman who stands beside you, Nguyen," she grated. A growl rumbled from Romaine's chest at her words, but the queen went on: "I will not stand for it. Grant the Goddess her freedom by the morrow, or the bloodshed that follows will be on your hands."

With that, the queen turned her horse and started back towards the camp. For a moment, Romaine sat on his own horse, staring at Erika. The Archivist shrank beneath his gaze, before she finally broke and tugged on her reins, turning away. Shaking his head at her cowardice, Romaine went after the queen.

"—really his daughter?" He caught the queen's words as he approached.

Riding alongside her, Yasin shrugged. "Was a long time ago, but it could be true. Hair is the right colour."

"Romaine," the queen said as he came alongside her, "what do you think?"

"She claimed the same to me on the banks of the Illmoor," he grunted.

Amina cursed. "Nguyen is no fool. If he says it's true, more than likely he's right."

"Does it change things?" Yasin asked.

The queen did not reply immediately. Her eyes had fallen to the gauntlet she held across her saddle pommel. "What game is he playing, giving it up so easily?" she murmured. Then she shook her head and looked at Yasin, as though finally hearing his question. "No," she replied. "I don't believe so."

"Then I'll have my men ready by nightfall," Yasin replied.

"What's this about?" Romaine asked softly.

"Nguyen has been a step ahead of me since all of this began," the queen replied, "but no more. This time, I know what he's planning to do next."

"How?" Romaine breathed.

"Because it's what I would do." A grin spread across the queen's face. "Are you ready for a rescue mission, Calafe?"

Romaine swallowed, clenching the reins in his fist. "Anything for Cara."

The queen nodded. Then her eyes returned to the gauntlet, and she held it up to the light. A twitch tugged at her cheek, but then she seemed to steel herself, and in one fluid movement, she slid her hand into the ancient artefact. Light burst from the shimmering links as she clenched her fist.

"Good," she breathed, "because it's time we took back the initiative."

❧ 12 ❧

THE SOLDIER

Lukys woke to darkness. For a moment he felt panic, that the nightmares of his sleep had somehow followed him to the real world. His heart hammered in his chest and he cried out, fumbling desperately at the black, and was rewarded by slamming his hands into something solid. Pain lanced through his fingers and he cursed, rolling away—

Thump.

The breath hissed from Lukys's lungs as he toppled off the ledge on which he'd been lying and slammed into the ground. He lay there groaning for a moment, memories slowly returning to him.

After his encounter with the Matriarch, Sophia had led him to the back of the basilica. There an opening hidden behind the dais had revealed a staircase leading down into the earth. Below, they'd discovered a seemingly endless corridor leading away into the depths of the earth, lined by iron doors.

A prison.

Sophia had not spoken as she locked him in his cell,

leaving him alone in this awful darkness. Lukys had spent the hours since pondering his fate. Why had Sophia locked him in this place, if he was to be her slave? What was a prison even doing hidden beneath the Calafe's Basilica to the Fall?

Eventually Lukys had fallen asleep on the low bench that lined the walls, though there was no way of telling for how long. Time did not seem to move in this dark place. He found himself wondering what had happened to Dale and Travis and all the others. Had they too been locked in this awful place? He'd tried yelling through the heavy iron door, but from the way his voice echoed in the tiny space, he guessed little noise escaped.

A shiver ran down his spine as he began to wonder how long he would be kept here. How much time would it take before he went mad in the absolute black, robbed of all sense of time, of hope? He had found a crevasse of water in his first moments within the cell, but his stomach was already starting to rumble. Would they feed him, or was starvation part of his punishment?

Lukys…

Lukys yelped and almost fell off the bench as Sophia's voice whispered in his mind. He swung around, half expecting to find that the Tangata had snuck into his cell. But that was impossible—the first thing he'd done was run his hands around the walls in hope of finding another way out, and there'd been nothing. Slowly he turned towards the door. She was outside.

"What do you want?" he snapped, then cursed as his words echoed within the cell.

She must have heard him though, for laughter whispered into his thoughts. *Careful, you'll wake the dead with such noise.* She paused, before adding: *This would seem a good opportunity to practice Speaking...Lukys.*

The hairs on the back of his neck lifted at her words. *The dead?*

That's better. There was amusement in Sophia's inner voice. *It's said that many of our ancestors perished in places such as this, in the time before The Fall. Perhaps their spirits do haunt these corridors.*

The Tangata believe in spirits? Lukys frowned; even after a week with the creatures, he hadn't contemplated the thought they might have a concept of an afterlife. A dozen questions rose unbidden in his mind, but he brushed them off. Now was not the time for scholarship. *What is this place, then?*

Another of our Birthing Grounds. The Calafe tried to cover it up, but my people are good at sniffing out secrets.

Lukys nodded to himself, recalling how the Tangata had managed to locate the entrance to the other ancient site, despite it lying buried in an empty plateau.

Why did you bring me here?

There was a pause before Sophia replied. *We have been assigned,* she said finally, as though that explained everything.

Frustration touched Lukys and he crossed to the door, placing his head against the cold metal. "But what does that *mean?*" he hissed out loud, trying to cast the thought through the iron at the same time.

I told you—it means you are mine, Lukys. There was a pause.

Lukys's skin crawled at her words. *So that's it, then,* he murmured, turning away from the door, his heart suddenly racing. *You're going to lock me here in the dark forever, taunt me and torture me, all because I killed your partner?*

His words were followed by a long silence and he closed his eyes, thinking she'd left him again. Panic touched him and he realised he didn't want to be alone down here, trapped, starving, lost. Better he had someone's company, even if it *was* only to punish him.

A sudden *clang* came from the door as Sophia drew back the locking mechanism. Lukys leapt as a soft light spilled into his cell, first just a fine crack where the door opened, then growing larger to reveal a lantern. He swallowed as Sophia entered the cell, retreating the rest of the way to the rear of his little prison. But she made no move towards him, only watched him for a moment with those terrifying eyes, then sat herself on the bench. She placed the lantern down beside her.

I do not seek to hurt you, Lukys.

For a moment, Lukys did not understand the words she'd spoken into his mind. He blinked, hesitating. *What?*

I fought alongside Zachariah for many years, Sophia murmured. *But such bonds are…complicated for our people.*

Lukys frowned, the pounding of blood in his ears fading slightly at the calmness of Sophia's words. He hesitated, glancing at his hands, recalling the conversation that had passed between Sophia and the Matriarch. In his fear, he hadn't really taken in the words, but now he found himself wondering…

"The Matriarch told Adonis to take his best warrior pairs," he said finally.

Sophia nodded. *When we come of age, my people are partnered with another of our generation. We are required to serve five years as warriors, to ensure the safety of our people from…humanity.*

"Then…he wasn't your mate?" Lukys asked.

Mate? Still you think of us as animals, Lukys!

"No!" he gasped, raising his palms in a gesture of peace.

He hesitated when he saw the grin on her lips, and a peal of laughter rang through the cell. His racing heart slowed as he watched the Tangata. What was this creature playing at? Slowly he lowered himself down onto the bench opposite her.

We were many things, Sophia said finally. She leaned

forward, her eyes fixing on him once more. *But…our time together was coming to an end.*

Lukys swallowed. "You…don't seem…overly bothered by his death."

To his surprise, Sophia looked away at that. He thought he might have glimpsed a touch of red to her cheeks, but in the flickering lantern light he could not be sure.

Zachariah was…passionate. She glanced at him. *He loathed your kind, and joyed in his…role as a warrior. Alas, I never felt that same passion.*

"Oh…" Lukys hesitated. "Well, I for one am thankful that you haven't torn me limb from limb."

The hint of a smile appeared on Sophia's lips, surprisingly feminine. *It was lucky you sparked Adonis's curiosity,* she replied. *He is another who…dislikes your kind's role in our society.*

Her words gave Lukys pause and he found himself looking away, eyes caught in the lantern light. He savoured the orange glow, even as its brightness caused stars to dance across his vision. Despite everything Sophia had told him, there was still one thing he did not understand.

What am I doing here, Sophia? he murmured, reaching out with his mind.

A sigh slipped from the Tangata's lips but she did not answer. Lukys forced himself to look at her again and was surprised to find her watching him. He swallowed. The sight of those grey eyes still terrified him, caused something primal in him to cry out.

"Am I to be your slave?" he asked at last, unable to keep the despair from his voice.

No. Sophia rose abruptly. She walked to where the iron door still stood open and for a moment he thought she would depart. But she swung back, fists clenched, lips pursed tight together. She shook her head. *This isn't how it is meant to go.*

"And how is it *meant* to go?" Lukys snapped, anger rising in the face of Sophia's disappointment. He found himself on his feet. "Was I meant to just bow down to you, submit to my new overlord? Is that what humanity is to become, if you conquer our world? Your playthings?"

We do not want your world, Sophia replied.

You took this one! Lukys hurled the words at her. *This city belonged to my friend's people once. You stole it from the Calafe, slaughtered their families, drove them from their lands. Now you make slaves of those who were left behind.*

They are not slaves! Sophia snarled into his mind.

She stepped towards him, teeth bared, her whole body trembling. Lukys was suddenly reminded of what he faced. For a moment he'd managed to convince himself he spoke to another human, to forget what she was. Now that realisation came rushing back and he retreated from her fury.

Sophia's eyes widened at his movement and the anger drained from her face. Silently she took a step back from him, and he thought he saw something in her eyes…terror, revulsion? Then she shook her head.

They are not slaves, Lukys, she repeated. *All chose their fate, chose to live amongst us.*

Lukys clenched his fists. "Then I am free to leave?"

Air hissed between Sophia's teeth and she looked away. *You cannot,* she replied finally. *You have seen too much.*

"Then I am your prisoner," Lukys stated.

A sigh slipped from the Tangata's lips. *I cannot force you to accept our assignment, Lukys.* Her voice came as a murmur, as though she barely dared to speak. *But neither can I release you, not until you swear yourself to me. The Matriarch would not stand for it.*

So you're to be my jailor? he spat back.

Sophia's eyes narrowed. *If that is how you wish to view it.* She turned and strode to the door. *I will return tomorrow, and every day after.* She pushed open the iron door and picked up the lantern from the bench.

Panic touched Lukys at the sight of the light being taken. "Wait!" he gasped.

Grey eyes turned on him. *What?*

Lukys hesitated, unsure of what to say. The thought of lingering in the darkness for another day, for all his remaining days, made his entire body shake. Yet he could not surrender his freedom so easily. He thought again of Travis and Dale and the other recruits.

What of my friends? he asked finally. *What has become of them?*

Silence lingered in his mind, then: *A few have already sworn themselves to their assignments,* Sophia admitted finally. *Most... still resist, as you do.*

Reassured that at least his friends had not been butchered, Lukys nodded. Sophia might have been lying, but somehow he didn't think so. Speaking mind to mind, he sensed it must be difficult to tell a falsehood.

"Thank you," he murmured.

Sophia only turned away, preparing to leave, and Lukys's stomach twisted again with fear.

Wait! He hesitated. *Can...you leave the light?*

Looking over her shoulder, Sophia regarded him for a moment. Then in silence she set the lantern on the bench beside the door and slipped out. The door clanged shut. And he was alone in the silence.

❧ 13 ❧

THE FUGITIVE

Panic ate at Erika as she lay awake in her bed, staring up at the hidden ceiling. Darkness clung to the room and the only sound to break the silence was her own breathing. Maisie was gone again, off completing some task or another for the king, no doubt. But despite the tranquillity of the night, Erika found sleep would not come.

She could not stop picturing the queen, could not stop seeing the hatred in her eyes, the promise for vengeance. Princess of Calafe or not, the woman wanted her dead. And what Amina wanted had a habit of coming true. Would she send Romaine to take his revenge?

No, it would be a true killer, someone well prepared to strike another down in cold blood. Immediately the face of the other man who had ridden alongside the queen leapt to Erika's mind. There had been a darkness in that man's eyes, and something else…a familiarity, as though Erika knew him from somewhere. But Erika could not quite put her finger on it.

Grinding her teeth, she sat up suddenly and threw off her covers. Rising, she crossed to the window and looked out at the silent vista. Stars shone in a cloudless sky, but the moon was hidden behind the mountains that bounded the fortress. Somewhere in the distance, though, between the stark cliffs of the canyon, she glimpsed the faintest of glows.

Dawn was already approaching. She shook her head, returning to her bed, though she did not bother to close her eyes. Instead, Erika turned her mind to the king and his actions. Why had he given up the gauntlet to his enemy? Had he truly thought to buy peace with the queen—or was there something more nefarious in his actions?

Erika's eyes were drawn to her own gauntlet. In the darkness, the faintest shimmer of light could be seen amongst the metallic fibres, though she had not unleashed its power in days. Was there some danger to that glow, some effect of the magic she did not understand? Regardless, she needed it now. It was her only protection should the queen's killers come for her.

Her heart twisted as she turned her thoughts to Cara. How badly she had repaid her friend's kindness, to allow her to be imprisoned, locked away like a common criminal. Teeth clenched, she lurched from the bed and threw on a tunic and coat, then boots. It was time she began making up for her mistakes.

Erika was just starting for the door when it swung open. A lantern carved the darkness and she raised a hand and squinted against its brilliance.

"Oh good, you're up," came Maisie's voice from the doorway. "Grab your things, the king wants us away before dawn."

"What are you talking about?" Erika gasped.

"We're leaving," Maisie replied, as though it made perfect sense. She turned away as Erika's vision began to adjust to the light.

"What?" Erika repeated. Her heart hammered in her

chest as she looked around the room, but her only possession was a small day pack. Scooping it up, she followed the spy out into the corridor. There, though, she hesitated. "What about Cara?" she said softly. "I'm not going anywhere until I know the Goddess is no longer locked in that cell."

Maisie paused at that, one eyebrow arcing towards her fringe. "Oh, so now you've developed a conscience, have you?" She chuckled and swung away. "Don't worry about it, Cara is coming with us."

Erika opened her mouth, then closed it. She'd already made herself look ignorant enough. Recovering her composure, she strode after the Gemaho woman. A cocoon of light spread out from the lantern Maisie held, shielding them from the night's darkness, though Erika caught glimpses of the approaching dawn through the windows they passed.

"So where are we going?" she asked finally.

"Here," Maisie replied, pressing a steel tube into her hands without breaking stride. "We're going to the home of your Gods."

Distracted by the object she'd been handed, Erika didn't immediately understand the significance of the spy's words. Removing the top of the tube, she drew out an aged piece of paper, before quickly replacing it in the protective cylinder. She didn't need to unfurl it to know what it was—the map she had recovered, the one she'd given to the king…

"Wait, what did you say—"

Erika's words were cut off as her foot caught on a wrinkle in the carpet. Crying out, she lurched forward, arms windmilling, until a hand from Maisie settled her upright once more. Cursing, she looked at the woman.

"You can't be serious?" she gasped, abandoning all attempts at keeping her cool.

The spy laughed and continued down the corridor. Erika hurried to catch up. It wasn't like she hadn't considered the idea. Ever since she'd seen that distant star marked in the Mountains of the Gods, she had wondered. But it was forbidden to enter those mountains. Now that they knew the Gods truly dwelled there, what they were capable of, surely such an expedition was suicide.

"Can't say I'm too thrilled with the plan," Maisie said matter-of-factly as they turned down a set of stairs that led towards the river, "but *Nguyen* is serious, and therefore, so am I."

The stairwell opened out onto a series of berths nestled in the space behind the bridge wall. Several ships of varying sizes were currently docked, though at this hour the only movement came from a large galley further down the jetty. Beyond, Erika glimpsed an arcing dike of boulders that stretched out into the river, sheltering the port from the currents.

"Maisie, Erika, I'm glad you made it," Nguyen greeted as they approached the vessel.

Erika came to a stop alongside the king. Taking a moment to gather her thoughts, she glanced at the ship the man had prepared for them. It looked much the same as the galley that had once taken her across the Illmoor to Calafe, though the mast currently bore no sail. With the wind blowing down the canyon from Gemaho, the sailors would have to use the oars until they passed beyond the sheer cliffs.

From there she could imagine the path they would take from the map she held in her hand—sail south through the plateaus until they reached the valley that would lead them up into the icy peaks, up to the ancient site marked by a scarlet star. It was madness, though…Erika couldn't help but feel a thrill of exhilaration. What fresh wonders must await in the home of the Gods themselves?

"Excited, Princess?" the king asked, though his eyes were on the preparations.

Erika swallowed. "I'm…not sure we'll be greeted warmly," she replied.

"No, I imagine not. These Anahera have distanced themselves from human civilisation for centuries. They are unlikely to welcome uninvited guests."

"Then why…" Erika trailed off as she glimpsed a new figure approaching along the jetty.

Cara still wore iron manacles on her wrists and ankles, but it looked like she'd at least been allowed to bathe and change her clothes. A heavy cloak of wolf fur hung around her shoulders, concealing her wings, and her copper hair had been tied back in a ponytail. She also still wore her familiar scowl, and a troop of some twenty soldiers followed behind, swords and spears held at the ready. Apparently they had been told to treat this prisoner with extreme caution.

"Welcome, Your Divinity," the king said, adopting a cheerful smile. "I trust the facilities were to your liking?"

Cara's scowl deepened as she stopped before them. "Where were all the 'Your Divinities' when you had me thrown in your dungeon?"

"Ancient history," the king replied, dismissing the complaint.

"It was happening up until an hour ago."

"Yes, well," the king continued, apparently unperturbed. "I do hope that we might put the past behind us."

The Goddess folded her arms—or as best as she could with the heavy manacles. "How about I knock you out first and stuff you into a cargo hold for a week. Then maybe we can talk."

"A rather unproductive proposal, I would say." Nguyen

smiled. "I would much rather learn more about the Anahera."

Cara narrowed her eyes. "I will talk no more of my people."

"Yes, yes, you've made that quite clear," Nguyen replied. "Only, if you must know, I am growing quite desperate. The threat of the Tangata grows ever closer, and now the Flumeeren queen brings an army against me. I have a need for allies."

"The Flumeer are here?" Cara's head perked up. "Is Romaine with them? Is he okay?"

Erika snorted. "Seemed fine to me when he was threatening my life."

Cara flashed her a glare but the king interrupted before the Goddess could say anything else.

"Yes, yes, the Calafe is quite fine, though I fear that Amina has her claws in him now. We were discussing how you might aid me, Your Divinity."

Cara snorted again and lifted her hands, giving the chains a rattle. "Why don't you take these off, and I'll think about smiting these enemies of yours."

The king sighed. "It is not your powers I require," he replied. "Though your cooperation would no doubt be of great aid. I seek to contact your people, the Anahera, to ask for *their* aid."

The Goddess stilled at his words, her eyes taking on a look of surprise. "You can't."

"I must," Nguyen said, then gestured to the ship. "The sailors will take you as far as the river allows, the soldiers the rest of the way into the mountains."

"*You can't*," Cara repeated, taking a step towards the king.

Swords rattled against shields as the soldiers behind her

advanced, but Nguyen raised a hand to stop them. The Goddess's amber eyes never left him.

"They'll…stop you," she croaked.

"Ahh, but my dear Cara, we have *you*," the king replied, eyes shining. "I am sure the Anahera will welcome the return of one of their own."

Cara's shoulders slumped at that and she looked away. "You don't understand," the Goddess grated between clenched teeth.

Erika swallowed. There was no missing the anger in Cara's voice. How much longer would she endure such treatment? The king wore his riding gloves, no doubt to hide that he had given away his power, and the gauntlet still hung heavy on her own arm, but…it would be a long journey. Erika didn't savour the thought of being alone with an angry Goddess high in those icy mountains.

But the king was right: humanity needed allies, and Gods or no, the Gods alone had the power to defeat the Tangata. Their strength and magic would be a substantial advantage to whichever kingdom won them as allies.

"Well, I suppose it's time the three of you set off," the king announced, bringing his hands together in a clap that made them all jump.

"You're not coming?" Erika asked, surprised.

The king chuckled. "Much as I would enjoy the adventure, I have a kingdom to run." He gestured towards the wall. "Not to mention your old mentor to handle—"

As though summoned by his words, a horn sounded in the distance. A frown touched the king's forehead and together all eyes on the dock turned towards the walls. Another blast of the horn sounded, closer this time, followed by a faint roar, as of a thousand voices crying out as one.

Crack!

The stone shook beneath Erika's feet and she swung around, as though expecting some giant to come charging towards them. The king only shook his head.

"It seems Amina is early," he said, turning to Erika with a grim smile. "Time for you to get moving then, Princess. Fate of the world and all. Best of luck."

With a final wave, he turned and strode away. Erika stood for a moment staring at the towering walls, until Maisie grasped her by the arm and dragged her aboard the ship. Cara followed, trailed by the soldiers, and moments later they were adrift in the currents of the Illmoor, each stroke of the oars sending them ever closer to the legendary home of the Gods.

And the screams of the dying chased after them.

❧ 14 ❧

THE FALLEN

W *hooorl.*
Romaine came to a halt as the sound of horns carried up the slope. His gaze was drawn past the plunging drop just a few feet from where he stood, down to where the walls of the fortress stretched across the valley. They looked smaller from his vantage point, the soldiers upon its ramparts like beetles in their shining armour.

Beyond the walls, a second swarm of beetles raced across the open ground, covering the green grass in black. The horn sounded again and moments later the cry of a thousand voices raised in unison reached them on the mountainside.

"I take it back," Lorene murmured, standing just behind him. "Going south might have been safer."

Romaine did not reply, as the first screams began from below. He forced himself to look away. It felt wrong, to see humans fighting against humans, while the threat of the Tangata loomed so close, less than an hours boat ride away. From their vantage point he could see the wild lands of

WRATH OF THE FORGOTTEN

Calafe, stretching almost to the walls of the fortress. It might be the last glimpse he ever got of his homeland.

"Come on, you two," Yasin's voice came from ahead. "Amina's guards can only distract them so much. We're exposed out here."

Below, the clash of weapons began as the first of the Flumeeren soldiers scaled their ladders and reached the ramparts. Shaking himself free of his misgivings, Romaine shared a final glance with Lorene before continuing. Seemingly determined to finally set eyes upon Cara and her wings, the man had volunteered to join them on this mad journey, though neither he nor Romaine knew where it would take them.

Along with Romaine and Lorene, Yasin had brought another thirty men, though none were of the calibre that Romaine had come to expect of the Queen's Guard. Rugged and unkempt, if not for their polished weapons and armour, Romaine might have guessed them to be brigands or mercenaries. As it was, from the scars most sported, it was clear they were veterans of some sort.

Yasin took the lead once more, leading them along a goat track high above the Fortress Illmoor. From below, Romaine would not have thought it possible to traverse these rugged cliffs. Indeed, the trail was not without risk. Not only were they exposed should any of the defenders decide to look up, but a single misstep would see them plummet hundreds of feet to the rocks below.

No wonder they hadn't started this section of the trail until the sun had begun to rise. Thankfully the queen had timed her distraction well, and with their weapons and armour covered by cloth to prevent them reflecting the sun, Romaine prayed their passage would go unnoticed. If not... well, then no doubt Nguyen would have a welcoming party waiting for them.

Romaine tightened his fist at the thought. He was still practising the sword with Lorene and the queen had gifted him a shield which could be strapped to his left arm rather than held. But the chest injury still hindered him and his progress had been slow. He needed more time to regain his former skill—time he did not have.

At least he was healed enough not to slow their progress. Yasin did not seem overly happy to have them along, but Amina had insisted. They needed someone Cara knew if they were to rescue her out from under the Archivist's nose, though Romaine still hadn't been filled in on the details of that plan.

Their journey continued, winding along the tops of cliffs and across treacherous slopes. All the while, the battle raged on. When the queen had first mentioned this trail, Romaine had wondered why she didn't send a larger force to attack the fortress from behind. Afterall, the Illmoor Fortress had only been designed to defend against a foreign aggressor. Now he understood. It would be a miracle if they passed unnoticed and without incident—a greater force would be spotted in minutes.

Entering the centre of the pass, Romaine wondered at the queen's boldness. Nguyen's soldiers were well-armed and taking a terrible toll on those attempting to reach the ramparts. The bloodshed was terrible to behold. It seemed a terrible price to pay for a distraction. And all for what? To save one woman.

Or to save a God?

The distinction was still muddled in Romaine's mind, his memories of Cara seemingly split into two people. There was the Goddess he had seen on the shores of the Illmoor, wings spread, eyes burning with untold power. But there was also the sweet, innocent young woman he had known in Fogmore. That woman felt far more real to

Romaine, his memories of the days they'd spent training together, the sharp smiles and her flitting romance with the recruit Travis crystal clear. Despite the importance of the Goddess, it was that Cara he searched for, that Cara he sought to rescue.

An hour passed quickly in their desperate race across the mountainside, up spires of rock and down into twisted gulleys, their passage all the time punctuated by the distant shrieks of weapons clashing, the howls of the dying. Romaine kept his eyes on the trail, thankful that Yasin seemed to know his way. It made him wonder how many times the man had crossed this way, what other undertakings he might have performed in the lands of the Gemaho.

Though whatever disreputable actions the queen might have taken against the kingdom, Romaine couldn't help but think it was justice. The king's cowardice in abandoning the alliance had left Calafe exposed, their armies too weak to withstand the Tangatan assault. As their kingdom inexorably fell to the creatures, Romaine and his comrades had often cursed the man's name.

What sort of king hid behind his walls while the rest of the world burned, while his former allies fought and died in the name of freedom?

Such cravenness could only bring fate down upon such a man—and his kingdom, too. Romaine prayed to the Gods above that he would live to see the day.

Finally they moved beyond the sheer cliffs into deeper grooves in the mountainside. Pillars of stone rose around them, shielding the company from view of those below. The path also widened, allowing Lorene and Romaine to walk abreast. The normally cheerful scout wore a grim expression as they started the climb down towards the lands of Gemaho.

"You okay, lad?" Romaine grunted.

The scout flashed Romaine a glance. "That battle seemed far too bloody for a distraction," he said after a while. "What is Queen Amina thinking, committing so many of our soldiers to an assault on Gemaho?" He gestured towards the south. "Has she forgotten the Tangata are still out there?"

Romaine said nothing for a while, though the scout was voicing the same concerns that had plagued him these last days. Finally he shook his head.

"Best not to question the scheming of monarchs," he murmured, though he could see his words did not mean much to the soldier. After all, it was Lorene's countrymen who were dying below.

"You really think we can find her?" the scout said after a time. "I doubt the king would be so foolish as to keep her in the fortress."

Romaine grimaced, recalling Nguyen's words from their meeting. "No," he replied, eyeing the men who went ahead of them. "But I have a feeling the queen is relying on that."

A frown touched Lorene's forehead as he followed Romaine's gaze. "Who are they?" he said softly, so the words would not carry to Yasin or the others. "Seems strange to send a bunch of mercenaries on a mission of such importance."

"They're not mercenaries," Romaine replied. "Yasin is far too comfortable with the queen. And despite their appearance, they're just a little too professional about all this business."

Lorene nodded. "You're probably right." Then he smiled. "Ah well, least we're not marching with a bunch of sellswords who'd turn on us the second old Nguyen offered a bigger pile of gold."

Romaine grunted his agreement, but did not voice his own concerns. Yasin's men might not be mercenaries, but the ease with which they'd taken to this assignment suggested they were far from regular soldiers. He suspected Yasin and the others were the people she sent when she needed something carried out in secret.

As they continued down the mountainside, Yasin slowed, allowing others to take the lead and falling into step alongside Romaine. While his sword and armour had been covered by cloth for the crossing, the crossbow was mostly wood and so hung from its usual strap across his back.

"How's the hand, Calafe?" he asked with a grin.

Romaine gritted his teeth but ignored the not-so-subtle gibe. "As well as it's going to get," he replied, doing his best to keep the dislike from his voice, then quickly changing the subject. "What is your plan for infiltrating the fortress, once we leave the mountains?"

"The fortress?" the soldier said, a look of surprise crossing his face. Then he snorted. "We won't find your Goddess lass inside those granite walls. Old Nguyen started making preparations to move her soon as he learned Amina was coming."

Romaine nodded at the confirmation of his earlier suspicions. "Then what are we doing?"

Yasin chuckled. "All in good time, Calafe," he replied. "Amina is more than a match for the old Gemaho bastard. We already know where they're taking her, we just have to catch up!"

"And how will we do that?" Lorene cut in, his voice light. "Seems to me the Nguyen wouldn't be so foolish as to send the Goddess by foot, when he's got such a nice river on hand."

All trace of mirth left Yasin's face as he turned his gaze on the scout. "Do you think your queen an idiot, soldier?"

"I..." Lorene trailed off beneath Yasin's glare, perhaps sensing what Romaine had that first night he'd met the strange warrior. The knowledge that he was staring into the eyes of a killer. Swallowing, the scout tried again. "Do you have a ship tucked away in some magic pocket we don't know about?"

The joke fell flat in the emptiness of Yasin's stare. Lorene clamped his mouth shut, glancing at Romaine.

"The man's got a point," Romaine commented.

He did not flinch as the warrior turned on him, and after a moment a smile cracked Yasin's face.

"By the Gods, your training buddy is jumpy, Calafe!" he laughed. Beside them, Lorene frowned, but Yasin only chuckled and gestured to the way ahead. "You'll see when we reach the ground." With that he set off ahead once more, leaving them to trail behind the group.

Lorene watched the man go, his jaw clenched, forehead still marked by frown lines. "I'm not sure I like that man," he remarked finally.

Romaine sighed. "I'm not sure we're meant to, lad," he replied. "Doesn't matter though, so long as they help us get Cara back."

The scout nodded, though the expression on his face suggested he wasn't convinced. They continued after the others, winding their slow way down towards ground level.

While the most dangerous part of the crossing needed to be completed in daylight, they had climbed much of the mountainside in the night and so it was only several hours more before they neared the bottom of the gorge.

Only once was their journey interrupted, as movement in a nearby gully sent them all scattering for cover. The action sent loose rocks tumbling down the mountainside, disturbing the group of Guanaco that had been hidden in the shadows. The long-necked creatures leapt nimbly across the trail, disappearing into a nearby ravine, knocking hardly a stone out of place.

Yasin and the other soldiers cursed the creatures, but in the tradition of the Calafe, Romaine took them as a sign of good luck. Covered in heavy wool with long ears and beady eyes, the Guanaco were considered the flock of the Gods. Their presence before a long journey was meant to herald good fortune, though that had not entirely been true the last time he'd crossed paths with the creatures. That had been just hours before they'd unearthed the monsters beneath the earth, to which he'd lost his hand—and almost his life.

After that, Yasin called a stop and they waited there for the sun to finally set behind the distant peaks. With the twisting ravines falling into deep shadow, they continued for another hour until they finally reached the floor of the canyon.

There, Yasin led the way confidently across the narrow floodplains, following the gentle whispering of the Illmoor River. By then the darkness was complete, with only the faint glimmer of the emerging stars to light the way. Romaine almost tripped several times as they made their way downriver, and his irritation with Yasin grew with each passing hour.

Finally, the sound of the river changed, and he heard the tell-tale squeak of wooden boards shifting on water from ahead. His heart picked up and he strained to pierce the night, seeking out the ship he was sure must be waiting for them. By then he hardly cared how the queen might have gotten word to her informants, nor even that she apparently had enough connections in Gemaho to procure them a ride.

The ship emerged slowly from the gloom, its features mostly obscured by the darkness, though he could see the movement of sailors upon its upper deck. Lorene inhaled sharply alongside him and he flashed the scout a grin.

"Looks like they had a ship in their pocket after all."

The scout only shook his head, and together they picked

up the pace, eager to catch Yasin and his men before they decided to leave the pair of them behind. Broad sails stretched high above them, and dozens of oars poked from the gunwales, lifting Romaine's heart. For the first time in weeks, he felt a touch of hope. His gaze was drawn to the east, to that distant, unknown land of Gemaho. Somewhere out there, Cara was waiting for him.

I'm coming, he whispered to the universe.

⚜ 15 ⚜

THE SOLDIER

L ukys passed a week in his cell—or at least a week by his best approximation. Without any hints from the outside, Sophia's daily visits were his only measure of time. He said nothing during those occasions, though Sophia spoke sometimes, talking of the goings on in the city above. Lukys could do nothing to prevent the whispers from entering his mind, and so he would sit in silence, staring into the distance, determined not to acknowledge her presence.

But even Lukys's anger could not last forever—particularly when the Tangata was his only source of light and food and water. The food was mostly fish, trout and salmon caught in the crystal waters of the surrounding rivers, along with tubers and the occasional helping of red meat. In fact, he had to admit the food was far better than anything the Flumeerens had ever fed him.

That thought ate at him during those long hours beneath the earth. What reason did he have to be loyal to humanity? Had his own kind not failed him at every turn? The Flumeerens had refused to train him, to prepare him in any way for the battles to come, had even sent him on the suicide mission that had ended in his capture. Even the Sovereigns that claimed to rule Perfugia for the good of all had betrayed him, ordering him to the frontier to die.

Yet despite Sophia's apparent kindness, he could not submit himself to the Tangata. After all, they too were guilty of terrible deeds, of driving the Calafe from their lands. Even before the war began, they had raided the Calafe southlands. No, to give in to the Tangata would be to betray everything and everyone he had ever known. And yet…

…gave us a long chase. It might have escaped had it made the river, but its heart gave out.

Lukys blinked, pulling himself back to the present. Sophia sat across from him, lips pursed, eyes on the wall as she recounted the story of a stag the Tangata had brought down that night. Apparently she had been assigned to a hunting pack. Lukys's attention was drawn to the wooden plate she had brought for him, where half the venison lay uneaten.

"Has Adonis returned?" he asked suddenly.

His sudden communication shocked the Tangata so much that she half leapt off the bench. Gasping, Sophia sat upright for a moment, hand on her heart. It was the first time he'd said anything since that first day in the cell.

What? came her voice to his mind.

Adonis, Lukys repeated, looking her in the eye. *The Matriarch sent him to seek the Old Ones. Was he…successful?*

Sophia stared at him, as though suspicious he had come up with some secret plan to escape. Finally, though, she shook her head.

No, he has not returned. The Birthing Ground is many days' journey from here, even for a Tangata.

Lukys nodded. "Good," he murmured, turning away for

a moment. "Were you...with him, when they woke the others?"

Images flickered into his mind by way of response, memories that were not his own. He found himself looking at two giant cylinders filled with liquid, lit from below by magical lights of purest white. Within each of the cylinders, two seemingly human figures stood suspended, eyes closed, their bodies somehow sustained for centuries by the magic of the Gods.

Shuddering, Lukys tore his mind from the horror. "A simple 'yes' would have been sufficient," he said softly.

Sophia nodded and rose. She began to pace the cell, moving with the graceful, balanced posture he had only ever seen amongst the Tangata. Well, the Tangata...and Cara. Jealousy touched him as he watched Sophia's movements. He had spent weeks with Romaine training to improve his balance, to give himself a fighting chance when the Tangata came. He'd improved slightly, but Sophia moved with a natural fluidity he could only ever dream of.

I know you can't understand it, but what Adonis does is necessary, Sophia said at last, though Lukys could still sense the fear radiating from her.

He only nodded by way of answer—it was clear that the Tangata would divulge the true reason they were seeking the Old Ones. After a moment, Sophia sat once more beside him.

So, you're speaking again?

Lukys sighed. Sophia sat with one leg propped up on the bench, elbow leaning against her bent knee, chin in her hand. She arced an eyebrow, obviously expecting a reply.

Lukys rolled his eyes. Carefully he picked a piece of venison from his plate and began to chew. It was cold as always, but the rumbling in his stomach hardly cared. *Was* he speaking again? There seemed little point in his silence now. He wasn't going anywhere regardless.

"I guess so," he muttered finally, flashing her a glare, "but it changes nothing."

Very well. Despite his hard words, a smile tugged at the Tangata's lips. *Though you should know, the last of your friends have now sworn to their assignments.*

A chill touched Lukys and for the first time, he felt truly alone in that cell. He was the last one, the only Perfugian that still refused to accept his new place in the world. How could the others have given in so quickly? Unless Sophia was lying, trying to convince him to do the same. But there was a ring of truth to the Tangata's words, and he shivered, unconsciously hugging his arms to his chest.

Are you okay, Lukys? Sophia whispered, concern showing on her face.

He shook his head. *I'm glad you did not kill them.* The words slid from his mind. *It…is more than my people would have offered your kind.*

A visible shudder shook Sophia and he caught a wave of revulsion from her. *Yes, I saw what you showed Adonis.*

Showed him? It was a moment before Lukys realized what she meant. Of course Adonis had seen images of the Tangatan captives in his mind—Lukys had known nothing of his strange skill that day in the clearing. He swallowed. *I am sorry you had to see that. We…do not all support such atrocities. My own kingdom does not take Tangatan prisoners.*

Perfugia… The word slipped from Sophia like a sigh. *The kingdom beyond the great sea. It amazes me, the distant lands humanity has reached in the short years since The Fall.*

Lukys looked down at that. *They say we were founded by those who sought to flee the wars that humans once fought amongst themselves.*

Sophia's eyebrows lifted in surprise. *Your kind wage war amongst yourselves?*

The Tangata do not? Lukys asked. When Sophia only shook her head, he sighed. *They say the first century after The Fall was terrible. What little knowledge we had of the days before was lost to the darkness. I guess I can't blame my ancestors, for fleeing that.*

A smile touched Sophia's lips. *What are they like, your people? We know little of distant Perfugia.*

We are a…practical people, he replied without thinking. *Our children are taken from their families at eight, to be raised in an academy.*

Shock registered on Sophia's face as she reeled back. *Why would they do such a thing?*

Lukys shrugged, though he was surprised at the strength of her reaction. *To ensure all are given an equal opportunity in life…though it doesn't entirely work that way in practice. The noble born are still favoured by the professors, receive better accommodations. Only a handful were so unlucky as to be chosen in our cohort of recruits.*

Is it not an honour to fight for your people? Sophia asked, her head tilted to the side.

Lukys snorted. *That is what we thought, until we reached the frontier,* he replied. He looked at her and let out a heavy breath. *Myself and the others here with me were chosen because our leaders judged us failures. We served no purpose in their perfect society, so we were sent here, untrained, to fulfil their quota of soldiers on the frontline.*

That is…terrible. Sophia seemed at a loss for words.

As I said, we are a practical people.

Sophia looked away. *The Tangata are also practical. There was a time when we too sent away our weakest, to preserve the strength of our species. It did not work.*

Lukys swallowed. *Maybe my people could learn from the Tangata.*

He was surprised by the smile that lit up Sophia's face. *Perhaps one day*, was all she said, then: *You are getting better at Speaking.*

What? Lukys started as he suddenly realised they'd conducted the entire conversation in their minds. His cheeks warmed. *I guess I am.*

Silence fell for a while then, and Lukys found his mind turning to his friends once more. Had they truly abandoned their loyalty to humanity so easily? Or had they simply realised their loyalty had been misplaced? He wished he could speak with them. Maybe then he would understand.

Sophia, he said after a time. *Is…possessing a slave truly so important to your people?*

Sophia winced. *I…wish you would not use that term. As I said, we do not force your people into assignments. Neither do we treat them poorly. Your friends are happy with their new lives.*

I wish I could believe you, Lukys sighed.

He flinched as Sophia stood suddenly, lifting an arm to defend himself, but the Tangata only stood there, eyes shining in the light of the lantern.

Maybe I can show you.

Lukys frowned. *I thought you said I could not leave…*

I will tell the Matriarch you have sworn yourself to me.

You would…lie to your leader? Lukys asked, regarding Sophia with a frown.

*Yes…*Sophia hesitated. *But…this would require you to trust me.*

Lukys might have laughed. Trust one of the Tangata? And yet…the prospect of leaving his cage, of seeing daylight again, was tempting. Could he so easily dismiss a lifetime of mistrust for her kind?

His eyes were drawn again to his plate. He had almost finished the venison now, and the tubers had vanished as their conversation went on. There was a warm, satisfied feeling in his stomach. He had only felt such contentment once in Fogmore, when Romaine had insisted they eat with him in the main soldier's mess hall. Every other night, the gruel they'd been given might as well have been river water for all the nutrition it had held.

"I trust you." He spoke the words before he could change his mind.

And Sophia smiled.

16

THE FUGITIVE

"I don't understand why you're doing this," Cara hissed as Erika settled down alongside her.

The Archivist let out a sigh. The sun was just beginning to lift above the endless plateau to the east and the sailors were preparing the ship to sail. They had anchored for the night in a broader section of river where the currents were sluggish, but everyone was eager to depart, the memory of screaming soldiers and clashing of weapons still fresh in their minds.

Not that the queen could have taken the Illmoor Fortress so easily. Not once in centuries had its walls been breached. It was just…better to be prudent when Amina was involved. The warrior queen had a reputation for achieving the impossible.

Shivering, Erika focused her attention on the Goddess. She still wore her manacles, though this pair had apparently been permanently welded shut to ensure she did not pick the lock again.

"Humanity is desperate, Cara," Erika said after a moment. "Surely you've seen that?"

They were sitting on the benches on either side of the raised bow, Erika's customary position when setting sail. She enjoyed the feeling of journey it brought, of heading off to explore unknown lands, to discover fresh secrets of the ancient world. It was the elation of discovery that had led her to become an Archivist in the first place.

"And you think my people will help when you show up on their doorstep with their daughter in chains?" Cara asked pointedly.

Erika sighed. "What have we got left to lose?" she replied. "You won't help us, won't show us the way. So we have to use you as a bargaining chip."

"You don't *have* to do anything, Erika," Cara said, turning away. "You chose to attack me, to kidnap me, to give me to the king. All of this is by your own choice."

"The queen wanted me dead," Erika rasped, though the words seemed inadequate now, and she found her gaze drawn again to the gauntlet encasing her hand.

"Maybe you deserve it," Cara snapped.

Erika found herself nodding. "Maybe," she replied.

Silence answered her reply. When she finally looked up, Erika found the Goddess staring at her, lips turned down in a frown.

"I'm sorry," Erika croaked finally. "None of this makes sense to me, Cara. Ever since I uncovered this gauntlet, since I discovered that map, it feels as though I've been cast adrift. I'm barely keeping my head above the water—and now the tide is coming in."

Cara said nothing, only stared back at her, amber eyes unreadable. Erika let out a sigh and rested her head back against the bulwark. Above, the sky was an endless blue, barely marked by a single cloud.

"Why are you here, Cara?" she whispered finally.

"Good question," the Goddess replied archly. "I think I mentioned something about a kidnapping…"

"I meant, why has a God returned to the lands of humanity?"

The Goddess did not reply immediately, and when she did speak, the words were whispered: "It was…an accident." Erika looked sharply at Cara and was surprised to see her cheeks had coloured. "I'm not meant to be here," she added, her voice becoming hoarse.

"What?" Erika asked. "How is that possible?"

Cara shrugged. "I'm, err…somewhat of a rebel." The Goddess offered a sheepish smile. "We aren't allowed to leave the mountains, according to the Elders, but…" She trailed off, a tinge of anger appearing in her eyes. "I mean, how would you feel, being able to soar through the clouds, go wherever you want…but not having the freedom to do it?"

"I…ah, the Elders?"

Cara scowled. "My family, you might say…" She hesitated. "It's not like I haven't done it before," she mumbled. "Only this time…"

"You were attacked by the Tangata," Erika surmised, remembering Romaine's story. "He said…you had a broken arm?" She frowned. "But…you fought off dozens of the Tangata on the Illmoor. How could two have done anything to hurt you, even with your injury?"

"It wasn't just my arm that was broken," Cara replied, her face losing some of its colour. "I…fell." A shudder ran through the diminutive figure. "That's never happened before."

"You fell?" Erika asked softly.

"There was a snowstorm," Cara answered shortly, then paused before going on: "I was caught in it on the way home, it drove me out of the sky. Before I knew how low I was…the tree came out of nowhere! My wing…" Her voice grew taut, as though she were remembering some terrible pain. "I almost passed out from the pain. And then those Tangata caught my scent."

Erika shook her head. "That doesn't make any sense; why would the Tangata follow you? Why stay in Fogmore? Why come with us to Calafe?"

"I stayed because they were kind," Cara whispered. "Because I wanted to help Romaine and Lukys and all the others. Because I wanted to help *you*."

The intensity in Cara's voice forced Erika to look away. Her gaze fell upon the sailors moving below, on the soldiers as they lounged about the deck, the packs of supplies and weapons. The sight reminded her briefly of her other expedition under Flumeeren rule, the miserly supplies and poorly trained recruits that had been sent to protect her. There could be no comparison to the preparations Nguyen had made for her, to the bearded veterans that would march with them.

But…could she trust them? Lukys and the Perfugians might not have been the most skilled of warriors, but they had been earnest, without a bone of treachery in their bodies. And Romaine, Cara—they had volunteered to come, despite the danger. These men and women, how far would their loyalty to the king stretch, when faced with the dangers in the Mountains of the Gods?

"I think they're desperate as well," Cara said suddenly.

Frowning, Erika looked across at the Goddess, but her gaze was on the open plateaus. "Who's desperate?"

"The Tangata," Cara replied, meeting Erika's eyes now.

"The Tangata?" Erika shook her head. "Desperate? I doubt that. They've enjoyed a decade of victories against our forces, taken an entire kingdom from the hands of humanity. What do they have to be desperate about?"

"I don't know," the Goddess said, "but I could sense it in their voices when they chased me, when they tried to capture me on the banks of the Illmoor."

Erika blinked. There was a lot to unpack in the Goddess's statement. "Their voices?" she started, before adding: "They were trying to capture you?"

Cara smiled. "You know, for an intellectual, you're not the most observant." She hesitated, before continuing. "They're afraid of something, the Tangata."

"Fear?" Erika snorted at that. "You think that was fear?"

The Goddess stared back at her, those amber eyes seemingly aglow in the morning light. Finally Erika swallowed and changed the subject. "Why would they want to capture you?"

The way the Tangata had launched themselves at Cara, it had not seemed like the creatures were interested in taking the Goddess prisoner. And yet…there *had* been a moment when Cara had been knocked to the ground, pinned beneath a horde of the creatures. Surely then one of the creatures could have managed a fatal blow…

"I don't know," Cara replied with a shrug. "There is much about their people I do not understand."

"Maybe they wanted to capture your magic?" Erika suggested. After all, that was how the Tangata had first been born.

"My magic?" Cara looked at her blankly. "Whatever… power I have, they could not take it. I don't think."

Erika let out a long breath, turning her memories of the battle over again in her mind, trying to piece together the clues. But recalling the fight, another thought occurred to her.

"Why didn't you kill them?" she asked, running her hand over the metallic links of her gauntlet. "I didn't think much of it at the time…but the Tangata you struck all got back up."

Cara bit her lip, suddenly looking nervous. Rubbing her shoulder, she looked away, and Erika didn't think she was going to answer.

"My people…do not kill," Cara croaked finally.

"What?" Erika frowned. "But you killed those…things in the caverns."

A visible shudder shook Cara and she hugged her knees to her chest. "Please…don't remind me."

Erika was about to press the matter when she noticed Cara's face had lost all colour. Whatever had happened in the caverns of the Gods, it had shaken Cara just as much as Erika and the others. At least Cara's claim helped Erika make sense of why she hadn't tried to kill them at the earliest opportunity.

Letting out a sigh, she let the subject drop. Silence fell between them, and finally Erika rose. "You'll stay here?"

The hardness returned to Cara's eyes as she looked up. "Not like I have any choice."

Erika's stomach twisted, but there was no correcting the situation now. Without anything else to offer, she left Cara where she sat. The ship rocked beneath Erika's feet as she crossed the deck, searching for Maisie, finding her at the tiller with the captain. Sails cracked overhead as she wandered towards them, the ship surprisingly steady beneath her feet. But then, the river was smooth today, with hardly a ripple to impede their passage.

Maisie waved as she saw Erika approaching and stepped away from the captain, nodding her thanks, then beckoned Erika across to the railings. Joining her, Erika leaned against the bulwark and looked out across the empty plains. The lands of Gemaho were said to be as large as the other three kingdoms combined. Without the threat of the Tangata, it was difficult to imagine how such a kingdom had united beneath a single ruler—and had remained that way down through the centuries.

"Why are we doing this?" Erika said suddenly. Regardless of her assertions to Cara, she still found herself doubting their path, not sure whether what they did was best for humanity, or if it was for her own personal gain.

The spy flashed her a glance. "The world is changing, Erika," she murmured, her words so soft as to be barely audible over the cursing of the sailors. "Magic has fallen again into the hands of mankind and ancient creatures walk the earth. A new age is approaching for humanity."

"Assuming we survive," Erika snorted.

"We're a resilient species," Maisie replied. "Here in Gemaho, we have watched the war from afar, read the reports. You think you're losing, but each battle costs the Tangata more in blood. Ten years ago, when the war first began, we lost five soldiers for every Tangata we slew. Nowadays the number is down to three."

Erika frowned; she hadn't heard that piece of information. What would cause such a change? She supposed it made sense; over ten years, humanity had come to learn the enemy's tactics. But even so, Maisie's numbers still meant they were significantly outmatched. "That doesn't mean we can defeat them," she argued.

"Perhaps not yet," the spy mused. "Regardless, it is the magic of the Gods that will determine our future. Imagine a hundred soldiers equipped with gauntlets like yours, or an army wielding orbs like mine, able to march under a blanket of invisibility."

Erika looked self-consciously at her gauntlet. "It would be an edge," she admitted. "That was why I went looking for their magic in the first place. But do you think the Gods will just *give* us such weapons?"

Maisie shrugged. "I do not know." She looked at Erika then, and her face was grim. "But I *do* know that whoever is first to gain their power will do more than just defeat the Tangata. Whoever controls that magic, controls the world."

A shiver ran down Erika's spine. "Then why would Nguyen give away his gauntlet?"

A smile tugged at Maisie's lips. "Nguyen is cunning; he knows how it will play with the queen's mind. And besides, one device will not change either kingdom's fate."

Erika eyed the woman, wondering how much truth there was to her words. "And what of Nguyen? Do you believe the king is worthy of the power you would place in his hands?"

All sense of mirth slipped from the spy's face as she looked at Erika. "Would you prefer the power fell into the hands of your queen?"

"Of course not," Erika said, pursing her lips.

Maisie nodded, turning her eyes to the water passing below. "He's a practical man, Nguyen. He does what he must, but he is never cruel or vindictive." She sighed. "And there is a kindness in him that few ever see."

Erika snorted.

"You don't believe me?" Maisie murmured. "I don't blame you—he hides it well." She hesitated, the breeze whistling through the rigging overhead. "I was a street rat once," Maisie said, her voice so soft Erika almost missed her words. "Years ago, before the war began. Belonged to one of the gangs in the capital. I was just a child. Nguyen found me, saved me. Even trusted me with his magic."

The spy looked at Erika then, and she glimpsed something in her eyes, something beyond the respect or even loyalty she professed. Love, perhaps? Maisie looked away again quickly, as though realising she had revealed something secret. Her hands tightened on the bulwark, her knuckles turning pale.

"Eventually, you'll have to make a choice, Erika," she said softly.

"I thought I already had."

The spy laughed. "You chose Nguyen out of self-interest. One day, though, you'll have to choose someone to put your faith in, without regard for what they can give you. Regardless of what it might cost."

With that, the spy pushed away from the railings. Offering Erika a nod, she wandered away. Alone now with her thoughts, Erika stared down at the swirling currents, and wondered when her life had become so complicated.

⚜ 17 ⚜

THE TANGATA

Adonis sucked in a lungful of air as the wave swept towards him. A second later the white waters washed over his head, plunging him into the swirling depths. With a powerful kick he fought the currents, struggling to rise to the surface. Sound came rushing back as he burst again into open air and dragged in another breath.

The water lifted him as the next wave rushed past and he scanned the way ahead, desperate for a glimpse of the island. Surely it couldn't be far now. Through the surging harbour he thought he caught a flash of rock, but it was difficult to make out, still so far, so far…

Forward!

He kicked out again, sending silent encouragement to his brothers and sisters. They would make it—they were Tangata after all, not some weak humans to fail against the raging of mother earth. The storm might hurl its strength against them, but the Tangata would endure, just as they had for centuries.

Roaring against the swirling clouds above, Adonis fought on, and was finally rewarded with a view of the island. Sheer cliffs rose from the seas ahead, stretching high above, a small ledge of shore beckoning them on.

Still so far, though. They probably should have waited out the storm, Adonis knew. The Matriarch's need was urgent, but while he and his warrior pairs could survive the crossing, they needed their strength for what lay ahead. Adonis had not forgotten what had transpired in the last Birthing Ground they had uncovered. The unbridled rage of the Old Ones had been terrifying to behold. Whatever the Matriarch said, he could not dismiss his reservations about her plan.

The Old Ones were not Tangata, not as they had been since The Fall. They were something else, something that might save his species—or perhaps might doom them all.

Exhaustion weighed heavily on Adonis by the time he finally pulled himself ashore, the pain of endless hours spent on the move. He had pushed his brethren hard to reach this remote outpost, travelling day and night at a pace that would have broken lesser creatures. But Adonis was of the third generation, and those warrior pairs he had chosen were of the fourth. They relished the challenge.

It pained him to learn this Birthing Ground had been here all along, hidden in the Tangata's own territory. Their plight would have ended long ago had they uncovered the Old Ones sooner.

But he was getting ahead of himself. Despite the Matriarch's hopes and his own fears, it was unlikely anything remained of this place. The Birthing Ground might have gone undiscovered all these years, but that did not mean the Old Ones slumbered here too. The ones they had woken in northern Calafe could have been the last…

Despite his orders, Adonis felt himself hoping that was true.

One by one, his warrior pairs emerged from the waters.

Adonis had lost his own partner years ago, but had resisted swearing himself to an assignment. The thought of spending so much time amongst humans made his skin crawl. The creatures were loud and undisciplined, and the images he'd glimpsed in the mind of Lukys only added to his distaste. Unfortunately, the Matriarch would not tolerate his disobedience much longer, despite his parentage.

Not unless he found another way.

In silence, he and his followers left the sandy shores. Each of his five pairs carried a great hammer between them —they would need the tools should they find the entrance sealed. Behind them, the ocean continued to rage, the crack of thunder echoing from the nearby cliffs. Sand gave way to gravel beneath their feet and ahead, Adonis's sharpened vision spotted a goat track leading up between the escarpments.

Adonis picked up his pace, making for the track. He did not know where on the island they would find the entrance to the Birthing Ground, but the view from up high would give them somewhere to start.

The others followed, their inner voices silenced. This was holy ground, one of the hidden sites from which their ancestors were said to have first emerged. He could sense their doubts. Some had been with him when they'd freed the Old Ones before. They had witnessed the madness in the eyes of those creatures, had experienced the same feeling of powerlessness as their fellows were slaughtered. Against the Old Ones, his people might as well have been humans, for all their powers aided them.

Adonis slowed as they reached the top of the track, taking a moment to recover his breath as he scanned the area atop the cliffs. Before him the ground flattened out into a plateau of unnaturally smooth stone—a sure sign that one of the ancient sites had once occupied this island. The hairs on the back of Adonis's neck tingled at the sight. There could be no doubt now.

Spread out, he ordered as the others joined him. *Seek the entrance.*

They moved quickly, fanning out across the plateau, scanning the stone for some clue of an entrance into hidden tunnels. It didn't take them long.

Here.

Adonis joined the pair that had called the discovery. Dirt and moss had built up through the years, but the harsh winds blowing across the island had kept them from completely covering the unnatural rock. At first glance the spot where the two stood looked no different from the rest of the plateau, but a closer inspection revealed there was a slight mound here, circular in shape.

Crouching, Adonis scraped aside the moss for a better look at the rock beneath. It was rougher than the rest of the plateau, and the rain and wind had carved rivulets across the surface. He looked at the Tangata who held the hammers.

Break it.

They set to the task, the harsh crash of steel against stone ringing across the plateau. Adonis left them to their work and wandered back to the clifftops. No evidence remained of what had been here before The Fall and his people had not visited this place before. The Tangata might be capable of defeating the waters, but they did not needlessly hurl themselves into the murky depths either.

Beyond the shores of the island, the storm was finally breaking. It had come upon them quickly and now seemed intent on departing with the same speed. The winds would linger—they rarely ceased on this part of the coast. It made him wonder why the humans had once built a city here, of all places.

Standing atop the high cliffs, Adonis looked across the waters to where the ruins of the original Nihelm stood. Jagged spires of iron lay rusting on the distant shores and blackened stones formed great mounds. He suspected the fallen city's existence had been lost from the records of humanity—certainly those humans assigned in New Nihelm never spoke of it. Even the Tangata knew little of that broken place. The time of their awakening was recalled only in the mind of the Matriarch now, passed down from her forebearers. But one thing was known: the Tangatan homeland had once belonged to humanity.

Some claimed those early days had been peaceful, that the Tangata and humanity had lived together in harmony. Adonis doubted such claims. The humans feared that which was different from themselves—especially when those others threatened their supposed superiority amongst the species of the earth. Tangata were faster, stronger, *better*. How could humanity *not* loathe them?

Besides, humanity had shown time and again they could not be trusted. Their invasion of the Tangatan homeland ten years ago had slaughtered thousands of innocents. Only the Matriarch's harsh retaliation had prevented further losses and driven back the enemy forces.

That victory had seemed to herald the fall of humanity as a danger to his people. Even the Matriarch spoke now of maintaining the peace, of leaving the humans to live beyond the great river.

But Adonis feared the war had only just begun. Humanity had proven surprisingly resilient. Despite their inferiority, they fought with a frightening ferocity. And after ten years of war, their numbers seemed untouched, as though the more soldiers they lost, the more their pairs produced.

Meanwhile, the Tangata dwindled, their strength shrinking with each passing year.

No, the Matriarch was wrong in that regard. There could never be peace with such creatures. Their fear, their anger, their *greed* had proven such aspirations mere delusions. He had no doubt what the creatures would do if they ever realised the Tangata's weakness. His people would be hunted down, slaughtered like animals.

Or worse, put in cages to be tortured, as the human had shown him.

I will burn their civilisation to the ground before I allow them to destroy us.

But for that they needed to renew their power, fresh blood to restore the Tangata to their former greatness. The Matriarch was right, the Anahera would not aid them. That left only the Old Ones.

Adonis, a voice sounded in his mind. *The entrance is open.*

Despite his resolution, Adonis felt a thrill of fear. Angrily he brushed it aside. Whether the Old Ones slumbered below or not, he would face them with courage. Humans allowed terror to control them; he was Tangata.

Smiling, he crossed back to where the others waited. Their strength had made short work of the mound of stone, and a hole now lay open to the howling wind. Darkness beckoned beyond.

Adonis leapt without hesitation.

❧ 18 ❧

THE FUGITIVE

Three days passed before Erika and the others finally disembarked from the ship. By then Erika was more than a little fatigued by the endless hours of inactivity, of sitting in the bow and staring into the distance.

Unlike the ever-varying landscapes of Flumeer and Calafe, Gemaho never seemed to change. Beyond the Mountains of the Gods, endless plains stretched onwards to the horizon, their pastures stained brown by the warm spring sun, and not even the golden crops offered much in the realm of contrast. There were no forests to speak of, hardly any trees at all. While grasslands and rainforests flourished beneath the heavy rains of the west coast, here the very air seemed dry, a strange phenomenon, considering how far they had travelled on the broad waters of the Illmoor.

Now standing on the banks of the river and looking up at the towering peaks, Erika wasn't surprised to see they offered little more in the way of variety. Here the farmlands of Gemaho ended, to be replaced with a low, almost grey scrub, the rocky soils lying exposed beneath. A stream trickled down from the valley in which they stood and a few taller bushes grew along its path, though even these barely came to her breast, and their leaves were short and stunted, their branches dotted with thorns.

Shouldering her pack, Erika glanced at Cara. The Goddess's mood hadn't improved much during the three-day journey, probably something to do with the shackles she still wore. At least she had shown no outward signs of resistance, other than her reticence to speak of their final destination. Beyond the Goddess, the last of their soldiers had disembarked from the gangplank, allowing the vessel to pull away. The sailors were to continue upriver to Vanror, where they would collect supplies for the war effort then return to the Illmoor Fortress, hopefully picking them up on the way past.

If we're still alive by then.

"Ready?" Erika asked, forcing a smile as she looked again at Cara.

The Goddess held up her manacles and glared at her. Letting out a sigh, Erika gestured for the Goddess to go ahead. The chains on her legs were not so tight as to hinder her ability to walk. Several of the king's soldiers had already started up the valley, scouting the way ahead, while those remaining spread out around Cara and Erika, their eyes alert for trouble. Only one man lingered near the shore, but upon seeing their departure, he brought up the rear behind Erika.

As they started off, Erika found herself wondering at the men and women the king had sent with them. From her conversations over the past few days, she had come to realize they knew little of Cara's true identity—only that she was dangerous. They hadn't asked any question, though from their whispers Erika surmised they thought Cara to be some new kind of Tangata, just as she and Romaine had believed all that time ago.

More surprisingly, the soldiers didn't seem concerned about their expedition into the Mountains of the Gods. Erika wasn't sure what to think of such loyalty—did it speak of a king who earned his followers' faith, or a man that did not suffer disobedience?

Shaking her head, she set her mind back to the trail. Reaching the home of the Gods was her most pressing concern. The going was easy for those first few hours, the trail sloping gently upwards. But soon they reached the first of the foothills, hills of scarlet rock rising around them, and the way became steeper. Sparse vegetation marked the slopes and the gentle bubbling of the stream grew louder as the waters picked up pace, racing over ever larger rocks.

A chill wind blew down the valley, but as the sun approached its zenith, Erika found herself beginning to sweat. For a time, undoing the buttons of her jacket relieved the heat, but the next time they stopped to rest, the cold quickly found its way back. The warmth drained from her body at a frightening speed and while Erika refastened the buttons, even when they started off again, she never regained the lost heat.

Cara herself seemed little bothered by the trek, despite the hinderance of her shackles. Where Erika slipped and stumbled on the loose rocks scattered across the slopes, the Goddess nimbly picked her way up the path. Again Erika found herself wondering at the Goddess, why she came along with them. Even if her people were forbidden to kill, surely Cara was powerful enough that she could have escaped by now. Could it be she *wanted* to be here?

Night found them camped on the shores of a small

mountain lake, its waters no more than a few hundred yards wide. The stream had led them there, up between the ever-narrowing slopes of the winding valley, and now stark cliffs hemmed them in on either side. They had been forced to clamber over boulders for the last hour, the remains of a landslide that in ages past had filled the valley.

Though spring was already underway, the days were still short and darkness came quickly to the mountains in Gemaho, the sun stolen away by the walls of stone rising around them. With the dark, the cold came in earnest, and Erika huddled close to their fire, glad for the ring of boulders surrounding them that provided shelter from the wind. There hadn't been enough room for the entire party, and half the soldiers had set a second camp close by. The whisper of laughter came from the other camp.

Listening to that distant mirth, feeling the warmth of the flames on her face, Erika thought again how different this journey was from her last. In Calafe they had been moving through enemy territory, never knowing when the Tangata might stumble upon them, whether their lives would be measured in days or even hours. Now though, despite the significance of this expedition, despite what might await them, Erika could almost convince herself to relax.

Almost—but not quite. Her gaze was drawn to where Cara crouched nearby and her heart twanged. Seeing the sadness in the Goddess's eyes, she quickly looked away. The fire was beginning to burn low. She rose, then crossed to the pile of wood the soldiers had gathered from beneath the scraggly trees that grew alongside the lake. Adding a stick to the flames, she watched as tongues of fire licked their way up the offering.

The soldiers nearby paid her no attention and Maisie

had vanished a little while ago, probably to scout their surroundings or check on the other camp. Letting out a long breath, Erika moved to where Cara sat and lowered herself down.

"How was your food?" she asked quietly. The soldiers had cooked a stew using dried meat and grains they'd taken from their packs. It didn't compare to the meals she'd been provided in the fortress, but then, she wasn't sure what the Goddess had been fed in her cell.

To her surprise, an audible rumble came from Cara's stomach, though the Goddess only shrugged. Back to one of the boulders and her knees drawn up to her chest, she kept her gaze on the flames.

Erika frowned, studying Cara's face. She'd eaten as much as any of them, but perhaps that wasn't enough for one of the Anahera. Rising, she found the pot the soldiers had set aside. There was still enough for another serving inside. Taking the handle and a spare spoon, she returned to Cara's side and held out the pot.

Cara eyed Erika for a moment before taking her offering. She settled herself back down as the Goddess ate, though after leaning against the stone for a few minutes, Erika began to feel the cold seeping through her heavy furs. Apparently Cara's wings gave her a little more insulation— or perhaps she was simply unaffected by the cold. These mountains were her home, after all.

Pulling herself off the boulder, Erika hugged her knees to stay upright and looked again at the Goddess. The stew was disappearing rapidly, giving her the distinct impression she'd been right about Cara's metabolism.

After a moment, the Goddess flashed her a glance. "You know, for a species who claims it's rude to stare, humans sure do it a lot."

Erika's cheek warned at the remonstration. "Sorry," she said, "we're not exactly used to having one of our own Gods amongst us."

Cara's amber eyes were aglow in the firelight. "Sorry?" She grimaced. "Another word that has no meaning for your kind." Her brow furrowed. "They really mean nothing to you, do they? Your words. You say whatever you like and it doesn't matter to you, the falsehoods. There is no honour, no fairness amongst your kind."

"I…" Erika hesitated, caught off-guard by the directness of the Goddess's attack.

A dozen excuses rose in her mind, that she hadn't lied, that she regretted the things she'd done, but…there Cara sat, dragged halfway across the world against her will, hands and ankles still bound in chains. Erika could apologise all she liked, but Cara was right: what did it matter if she continued doing the very thing she was apologising for?

"You're right," Erika whispered finally, choking on the words. Her vision blurred as tears formed in her eyes. "It wasn't fair of me to treat you like this." She blinked then, forcing herself to harden. "But our world, it isn't fair, Cara. I don't expect a God to understand, but humanity is only what our environment has forced us to be. When I was young, my future was stolen from me. I have spent every day since fighting to win it back. For years I worked to earn a place in the queen's court, but in a matter of days that too was stolen away. I'm not sorry for doing what I needed to save my life."

The last words left her mouth in a rush, giving way to silence. Cara still watched her, though to Erika's eyes it seemed her expression had softened somewhat, as if the outburst had helped her finally understand something. Letting out a long breath, Erika swallowed the last of her emotion.

"As I said," she added finally, "I wouldn't expect you to understand. You're a God."

Cara shrugged. "So you say," she started, looking uncertain. "But you're wrong. I do understand. At least a little." She raised her eyes to the sky, and in that moment, she looked more like a young woman than she'd ever looked a Goddess. "You say you lost everything, but at least you once had freedom. That's something I've never tasted before. At least, not until Romaine found me in that forest." A tear streaked her cheek. "I'm not even sure…not sure how my people will receive my return. It is a terrible crime for us to leave the mountains, let alone reveal ourselves to humanity. But after so many decades—"

"*Decades?*" Erika interrupted, eyes widening.

The hint of a smile tugged at Cara's cheeks. "How old do you think I am, Archivist?"

Erika opened her mouth, then closed it again, unwilling to take a guess, though she would have said a human of Cara's looks couldn't be older than twenty.

Cara chuckled. "I would be close to fifty in your years, though amongst the Anahera I am still but a child."

Erika shivered. She shouldn't have been surprised that Cara was older than she looked. She was a Goddess after all, with the strength to hurl a man across a room as though he weighed no more than a few pounds. And wings. Yet it was still disconcerting, to look on the face of a teenager and know the soul within had seen fifty years of life.

"My night flights, they were my little show of rebellion." Cara's eyes danced as she spoke. "Is it still called the rebellious teen years? It seemed so harmless, flying from the mountains in the night. That is, until that storm. God, I was so *stupid*."

"We all make mistakes, Cara," Erika said, feeling more than a little strange to be comforting a being twice her age.

How did new Gods even come into existence? Yet another question she would like to ask, though perhaps another time would be more appropriate.

Cara sighed but said nothing, and Erika settled back against the boulder. There had been few clouds during the day and now the night sky was an open tapestry of light, an orchestra of stars stretching overhead into infinity.

"I won't run." Erika's head jerked up as Cara spoke again and she found the Goddess watching her. She frowned, not understanding, and the Goddess elaborated: "If you freed me, I wouldn't fly away."

"You know I can't trust you," Erika whispered.

"I know," Cara said, nodding sadly. "You're too accustomed to falsehoods. But my people, the Anahera, we do not lie. I don't expect a human to understand that." She smiled wryly. "But it's the truth."

Erika swallowed, and in her mind, she saw again a vision of Cara in flight, swooping down to pluck her from the clutches of the Tangata. How poorly she had repaid that deed. Her words now about the unfairness of the world seemed hollow, and to her surprise she found herself rising. Light lit her gauntlet as she reached for the shackles that bound the Goddess, but at the last moment she hesitated, a thought occurring to her.

"But you lied to Romaine, when you said you were Calafe."

Red tinged Cara's cheeks. "I...never actually *said* I was Calafe," she mumbled. "I just...never corrected anyone when they assumed..."

Laughter burst from Erika at the Goddess's words and she shook her head. "Now who is accustomed to falsehoods?"

Even so, she reached again for the shackles. She'd never used the gauntlet in such a way, but it felt right, to use it for at least one good deed. Not quite knowing what she was doing, she took the shackles between her fingers and squeezed. Magic lit the metallic fibres and she focused on directing it into the steel chains.

There was a flash as the gauntlet brightened, followed a sharp *crack*. Steel rang against rock as the locking mechanisms failed in both shackles and they fell from Cara's wrists. Erika blinked, surprised it had worked so well, then glanced at the Goddess. When Cara made no move to attack, she turned her attention to the ankle chains.

Those too fell away and Erika backed away, waiting to see how Cara would react. The Goddess rose slowly, pulling the jacket from her shoulders. Freed of their confines, her wings spread wide with a sharp *crack* of feathers. Gasps came from the soldiers on the other side of the fire, but Erika kept her eyes on the Goddess, wondering if she had been wrong.

"I trust you, Cara," Erika whispered finally. "I'm sorry I didn't earlier."

Before Cara could react, movement came from the shadows nearby and Maisie appeared between the boulders. The spy paused when she saw them both on their feet, then her eyes were drawn to the chains lying beside Cara. A frown wrinkled her forehead.

"Well, that seems like a bad idea," she murmured.

Without saying anything further, she moved to the fire and sat. The cooking pot lay nearby and Maisie reached for it, moving as though to place it over the flames once more, before pausing. Turning, she scowled at the two of them.

"Someone want to explain what happened to my dinner?"

Erika blinked, then glanced at Cara. The Goddess's eyes widened and she adapted an innocent look. "I think the Archivist ate it," she said. "Terribly greedy, that one."

She crossed to the fire and sat herself by the flames. Beyond, the soldiers still sat gaping at her, but Cara ignored them, turning her eyes to Maisie instead.

"If you *are* going to cook more, though, count me in." A rumble came from the Goddess's stomach. "I'm *starving*."

19

THE FALLEN

The light was fading as Yasin directed their ship ashore, the sun dipping towards the mountains towering to the west. Watching the peaks turn scarlet, Romaine couldn't help but think how strange it was to find himself this side of the mythical mountains. They stretched up overhead, at once the familiar points he had known all his life, yet also different, the stark slopes and escarpments leading to a snowline that was unfamiliar to him.

And how different they were. Where in Calafe, pine and fir trees would have stretched from the river almost to the snow, here in Gemaho the foothills were practically bare, rolling and elongated where those in his homeland were jagged.

Aboard the ship, the sailors hurried to prepare for their disembarking, eager to be rid of Yasin and his soldiers. Throughout the journey, it had become clear their presence did not sit well with all the crew. Romaine couldn't blame them—just a few days ago, Flumeer had declared war on their kingdom. The queen's power could only buy so much loyalty. He wondered whether these sailors would report their passage to the king when they reached the next port—or if prudence would win out. After all, every Gemaho sailor on the ship had committed treason by granting them passage. Romaine doubted Nguyen was the kind of king to forgive such a transgression, however hard they might try to redeem themselves.

Shouldering his pack and readjusting the sword on his belt, Romaine followed the others down the gangplank. The weight hung heavy on his shoulders and there was still an ache in his chest, but three days of rest on the ship had helped to ease the pain. His injuries were healing.

Romaine hesitated as he reached the shore, taking a moment to look around. Why had they chosen here to come ashore? There had been no obvious signs of another ship disembarking here, and in the dying light it was impossible to tell whether others had passed this way recently.

He looked up as the crunch of footsteps announced Yasin's approach. "I won't be able to track them in the darkness," Romaine said softly. The moon had been growing larger these last nights, but it would not be enough to find footprints in the rocky earth. "Even if this is the right place…"

Yasin laughed. "Don't sweat it, Calafe," he said, slapping Romaine on the shoulder. "I know where we're going."

Romaine frowned, but at a gesture from Yasin, the others in their group were already forming up. Anger touched him at being so easily dismissed, but he said nothing. Lorene came alongside him as the leader took his place at the front.

"What do you make of that?" he asked quietly, eyes on the man.

Clenching his fists, one phantom, the other real, Romaine tried to repress his rage. "I told the queen back in camp that Erika would eventually seek out the home of the

Gods." His gaze lifted to the mountains, where the last of the day still lit the icy peaks. "Could she have another copy of the map after all?"

A grimace touched the scout's face. "You know, I signed up to *save* a Goddess—not trespass in their homeland." He hesitated, eyes flickering in Romaine's direction. "You sure about this, Romaine?"

Romaine sighed. "Amina's the only one who gives a Fall whether Cara lives," he said. "I trust her…" He glanced at the smaller man. "I have to."

The scout hesitated, then gave a quick nod. "Better hurry up then, before they leave us behind."

Without another word, the two started up the valley after Yasin's crew. Now that they were off the ship and deep in enemy territory, Romaine had strapped the queen's shield to his arm and kept his hand close to the pommel of his sword. Each evening when the ship had pulled ashore, he and Lorene had practiced with the blade, and despite his injuries, he was beginning to feel more confident with the weapon. He might be of use to Cara yet.

Even so, he was surprised by how quickly his body began to ache as they started up the valley. The daylong climb through the mountains around the Illmoor Fortress had been a trial in the extreme, the sheer slopes they had scaled to reach the goat track requiring short, sharp bursts of exertion. Here though, the long valleys of Gemaho provided a different kind of challenge. The ground might be less steep, but the slow, endless rise of the earth beneath their feet was no less draining. And the darkness made it all the worse.

Without vegetation to bind the soil, the loose rocks were a constant threat. Thankfully his leather boots protected him from twisting an ankle, but more than once the treacherous stones almost sent him crashing to the ground. Lighter on his feet, Lorene seemed to be having a better time of it, but several amongst Yasin's men were even larger than Romaine. Their grunts of discomfort kept the two company through the night, but otherwise the soldiers paid them little attention.

Romaine was happy with the silence. He had grown to enjoy it over the last ten years, to welcome the whistling of the wind through branches, to cherish the gentle bubbling of a stream, the hoot of a distant owl. The Perfugians had offered him companionship, a break from the stillness, but in truth he enjoyed it.

Eventually, however, the silence led his mind to thoughts of Cara. If they were truly on her trail, the Goddess could be as little as a day ahead of them. His heart raced at the thought and for the next half hour, the way felt a little easier.

They continued up the valley, shadowing the stream as it wound its way between the stones. Their quarry had no doubt followed its path for the ready source of water—it must be scarce in these parched hills. Just breathing the air this side of the mountains left Romaine's mouth as dry as the dusty stones.

Yasin led them on through the night, undaunted by the gloom. After three days on the ship, his men were reckless, eager to be on their way. Like their dark-eyed leader, these were fighting men, killers in search of prey.

Romaine still couldn't understand how they were able to track Cara and her captors in the darkness. The moonlight was enough to pick out the largest of the rocks on the valley floor, but Romaine struggled to make out the footprints of even his companions. How could Yasin track the passage of those who had passed hours, or even days, before?

Picking up his pace, Romaine overtook several of his companions, leaving Lorene to trail behind as he sought

Yasin. He found the man still in the lead, picking his way up a slope dotted by ragged boulders the size of small dogs. Coming alongside the man in the gloom, he nodded a greeting.

"How far behind are we?" he asked, trying to find some clue as to how they were tracking their quarry.

"What am I, Calafe, a magician?" Yasin asked with a laugh.

Romaine scowled. "You seem to know where they're heading."

Yasin grinned at that. "Curious about Amina's secret, are you?" he murmured. Then he flicked Romaine a glance, and his eyes narrowed in the moonlight. "Or is it the Goddess that's got you so worked up?"

"Just professional curiosity," Romaine said with a shrug. "I grew up near these mountains, though on the other side. Even in daylight I would have struggled to follow a trail on these stones."

"You Calafe are far too practical, you know that?" Yasin replied with a shake of his head. "So focused on what's in front of your face that you miss the bigger picture." He snorted. "Maybe that's why you're basically extinct."

Romaine scowled, grinding his teeth together in an effort to keep the curses from tumbling from his mouth. Instead, he swallowed his anger and shrugged. Let the brute mock, so long as he led them to Cara.

"Perhaps you can show me the error of my ways," he replied, though he failed to keep the hard note from his voice.

Yasin only grinned. "Nah, where's the fun in that?" he chuckled, then returning his eyes to the path, he strode ahead. "Relax, big man. We can't be more than half a day behind the bastards."

Romaine frowned and was about to press the matter

further when they topped the rise and found themselves on the shores of a small lake. Yasin hesitated, his eyes sweeping their surroundings, and the faint scent of smoke carried to Romaine's nostrils. The breath caught in his throat and his hand dropped to the hilt of his blade, but there was no sign of movement in the nearby boulders.

Yasin was still searching for something, but focusing on the ashen smell. Though the wind was only blowing lightly at that moment, he knew how violent mountain gales could turn. If he'd been making camp on these shores, those boulders would have provided the perfect shelter.

The stench of smoke grew stronger with each step, and fist tensed, Romaine entered the cluster of rocks. Lorene found him there a few minutes later, crouched alongside the remains of a fire.

"So we're on the right track," the scout said as he approached, looking grim. "Suppose that almost makes the trespassing acceptable, right?"

Romaine only grunted, his mind on the discovery. Whoever was accompanying Cara obviously had not suspected they were being followed, for they'd made no attempt to hide their campsite. What were they doing here anyway? Why would Nguyen have taken Cara hostage, only to send her into these mountains with his soldiers?

It had to be the Archivist's doing. Had she promised the king God magic, as she had all those weeks ago to Queen Amina? Perhaps that was why the man had so easily yielded the gauntlet—if Nguyen thought he would soon have the full power of the Gods at his back, its magic must seem trivial.

But no, it still made no sense that he would surrender it to an enemy. And it left unexplained how Erika planned to win the magic of the Gods. Did she expect them to greet her with open arms when she turned up on their doorstep with one of their own in chains?

He touched a palm to the ashes. They were cold, and given their quarry's apparent lack of concern for their pursuit, it seemed unlikely they would have marched through the night.

"More than a day," he muttered to Lorene.

"What?" the scout asked with a frown.

Romaine shook his head and rose as Yasin stepped into the ring of boulders. "They're further ahead than you thought."

A scowl crossed the man's face, though he shrugged off the criticism. "It'll be less by the time the sun rises," he countered.

A few grumbles came from the shadows behind the man, but they cut off as Yasin flashed a glare over his shoulder. Romaine made to join them, when a glint of moonlight reflected off something lying amongst the boulders nearby. Turning from Lorene and the others, he crossed to the gap between the stones and lifted a pair of shackles.

"What have you got there, Calafe?" Yasin questioned. When Romaine did not immediately reply, he shouldered past Lorene to get a closer look.

Romaine's attention was fixed on the chains, and he ignored Yasin as the warrior stepped up alongside him. Unless Erika had dragged more than one prisoner into these remote mountains, they could only have belonged to Cara. But there was no sign of a breakage in the steel. Someone had unlocked them, had freed the Goddess. What did that mean?

He passed a quick eye over the campsite, seeking signs of disturbance, for some indication that Cara had fought her way to freedom. There was nothing. Finally he shook his head and handed the shackles to the queen's man.

"What do you make of this?" he asked, eyeing Yasin closely.

He turned the shackles in his hands, but the night's gloom hid whatever reaction his eyes might have revealed.

"So your little Goddess got loose," Yasin said finally. A smile tugged at his lips as he glanced around the campsite. "No bodies though. I wonder how Nguyen's soldiers regained control of Her Divinity."

Romaine raised an eyebrow. From what he'd seen of Cara in action, he doubted any number of human soldiers would be able to contain her. But at least the shackles finally confirmed once and for all that the Archivist *had* taken Cara against her will. He clenched his fist at the thought of the hateful woman. Erika would pay for what she'd done.

True to Yasin's word, they pushed hard through the rest of the night, pausing only to pull fresh food from their packs. Weighed down by his injuries, Romaine found himself dropping to the back of the line once more, though Lorene kept him company. His mind continued to return to the chains he'd found, to the Goddess and Erika and the king's soldiers. Was Cara still a prisoner, or had she somehow gained the Archivist's trust?

But there would be no answers, not until they finally caught their adversaries. Only then would the truth be revealed.

Throughout the night, Romaine found no more hint of their quarry's passage, though Yasin still seemed confident in his ability to track Erika and the Gemaho soldiers. Only as the first hint of light appeared on the distant horizon did the man begin to slow. Reaching the top of another slope, he squinted, scanning the rocky ground ahead before finally choosing a direction.

Romaine paused as he reached the spot where Yasin had hesitated, feigning the need to catch his breath—though after the slope they'd just traversed, it wasn't much of an act. Ahead, the others continued along a ridge where the way was gentler, while Lorene came to a stop nearby, a grin breaking through the unkept beard that had appeared on his face over the last weeks.

"Getting old, Romaine?" he asked.

Grunting, Romaine ignored the jibe, his eyes turning instead to the east. Looking back across the plains of Gemaho, he was again reminded of the strangeness of where he found himself. Flat land, perfect for farming, stretched out as far as the eye could see, to that distant rising sun.

Even the sight of the sun on the eastern horizon was a novel sensation. In Calafe, the sun's glow appeared behind the Mountains of the Gods hours before it broke their twisted peaks, leaving the land in shadow for much of the dawn. But here the light was already racing across the land towards them, casting back the last of the dark. Shaking his head, he turned his attention back to the trail...

...and caught a glint of something amidst the rocks. He frowned, hesitating in place, even as Lorene started to move off. The forbidden mountains rose ahead of them, capped by glacial peaks, but it was not those mountains that had drawn his attention.

Stepping from the trail, he knelt beside a boulder. A small X marked the rock, glowing with some phosphorescence in the shadow. But even as he leaned closer, there was a flash as the sun finally reached them, and the X vanished.

"You alright, Romaine?" Lorene called back to him.

Romaine remained kneeling for a moment, staring at the spot where the X had disappeared. Blood thumped in his ears as he turned the discovery over in his mind. It might have been created by some natural phenomenon, an algae or fungus that grew here in the mountains, yet…then surely it would have been elsewhere?

No, it had been no natural marking. This was the same spot where Yasin had hesitated, as though looking for something. Something to mark the way for them, perhaps?

Swallowing, Romaine returned to his feet and waved a hand to Lorene that he was okay. Ahead, the light of the rising sun had reached Yasin and the others, who appeared to be downing packs and setting camp for the day.

The sight confirmed Romaine's suspicions. Someone was leaving markers for them to follow, ones that could only be seen in darkness. They couldn't continue now, for Yasin would not be able to track their quarry. There was a spy in Erika's party.

20

THE SOLDIER

Stepping from the darkness of the basilica, Lukys squinted as the sudden brilliance of sunlight greeted his freedom. After so long beneath the ground it was all but blinding. Within moments, tears were streaming down his face. He embraced them.

A warm breeze touched his cheeks. Though winter had hardly just past, it was warmer in the south and the taste of spring was already in the air.

Finally his vision began to clear and he found himself staring across the plaza, empty now, his companions long since taken to their new…homes? He glanced sidelong at Sophia, wondering what had become of his friends, where he was to be taken now. Another day had passed before the Matriarch had granted his freedom and Lukys had spent much of that time wondering at his decision, whether he'd made the right choice. His acceptance had come quickly after the long silence—though of course, he hadn't truly sworn himself to Sophia.

Had he?

Sophia said nothing, only stood watching him, a look of

concern creasing her forehead, as though even now she worried what he might do.

But Lukys had made his decision, down there in the darkness. He had resolved to trust the strange Tangata with her earnest expression, and that was what he would do. For better or worse.

So he offered Sophia a smile and nodded for her to lead the way. A smile of her own appeared on Sophia's face and she started off across the plaza without looking back. Drawing in a deep breath, Lukys followed her into the city.

It was still early, but dozens of Tangata already thronged the streets, moving about their business in the graceful manner in which they completed all tasks. Morning mist clung to the city, making it difficult to spot the humans amongst the wanderers, though if Lukys paid attention he saw them. Assigned humans apparently made up some ten percent of New Nihelm's population.

Despite the presence of his fellow humans, it felt odd to walk so freely amongst the Tangata. There were no guards now, no bonds or watchful eyes. Only Sophia and that gentle smile.

Did the Tangata truly trust their human slaves so easily? What was to keep them from attempting an escape, even after swearing themselves to their assignment? Though even as the thought came to him, Lukys realised the futility of such an action. Where would they go? The Tangata were faster and stronger, better in the wilderness than even the Calafe. It would not take long for the creatures to hunt down an escaped human. Lukys had no doubts as to what would happen then.

The numbers on the street swelled as they made their way deeper into the city, though they still numbered nowhere near the crowds in human cities such as Mildeth or

Ashura. He found himself scanning those who passed them, practicing spotting his human comrades.

His lips twisted into a frown as he glimpsed something strange amongst the crowd. Distracted, his foot caught on a loose cobble and he stumbled, barely catching himself before he fell. Something that sounded distinctly like laughter touched his mind and he scowled to see the eyes of several Tangata upon him. They looked away as he met their gaze, but the whispers continued. These creatures did not know he could hear them.

Shaking himself, Lukys attempted to close his thoughts to the sound and focused on what he'd seen. Sophia had come to a stop nearby, but she said nothing as he searched the pedestrians moving around them. For a moment he thought the group might have already passed on…

There! Lukys stared as the two children wandered past. Their grey eyes were fixed on the curb beneath their feet, arms stretched out wide, and they trailed behind an adult, trying to keep up as they balanced on the stone lip.

"What the hell…" Lukys muttered.

He started after them, but Sophia stepped between him and the youngsters.

What are you doing?

I've never seen Tangatan children before, he admitted.

The sight shattered the last remnants of the lie he'd been taught his entire life. Watching the boy and girl wander past, playing on the street as any human child might have done…it was impossible to resolve with the image of the Tangatan savage, of monsters that sought nothing but the extinction of humanity.

Did you think we grew on trees? Sophia asked, one eyebrow raised.

Lukys shook his head. The two had fallen off the curb and were now leaping from cobble to cobble, obviously trying to keep from stepping on the cracks. Their minder had noticed the delay and turned back to collect them. His eyes were a light blue.

"You trust us with your children?" he whispered.

The amusement vanished from Sophia's face. *Come,* she said, taking him by the arm. *We're almost there.*

Lukys allowed himself to be led away, though not without a sense of confusion at Sophia's reaction. Why did she want him away from the children? He kept an eye out for others as they continued, but after a few more turns, they found themselves in quieter streets. Here, the vibrant colours of the buildings did not change—or rather, they continued to change with every building they passed, and Lukys found himself wondering again at the beauty created by Calafe's spirit of individuality.

Where exactly are we going? Lukys asked finally.

There was a strange look about Sophia as she glanced at him. *Our new home.*

Before he could question her further, she came to a stop in the street. Lukys paused beside her, realising they stood before a set of open wooden gates. A narrow corridor beyond led into what appeared to be small courtyard. The buildings here were only two stories high and even with the day still young, he could see the space was lit by sun.

"Here?" he asked.

Sophia nodded and took his hand. He flinched at the intimate touch, though her hand was surprisingly warm, and flashed her a sharp look.

Together, remember? she murmured.

Lukys detected a sad undertone to her voice, as though his resistance to her touch hurt her. But she was right. The Matriarch, the Tangata, everyone in this city believed he had sworn himself to her. He needed to play the part. Swallowing, he accepted her hand and he gave her fingers a squeeze, trying to reassure her. Sophia seemed to take the action as acceptance, and led the way through the open gates.

Inside the courtyard, a single tree stretched up above the low roofs, its wiry branches brightened by the same pink blossoms that had lined the main avenue through the city. Someone must sweep the cobbles within the court regularly though, for the stones were free of both blossoms and dirt. To their right a set of polished wooden stairs led up to a terrace that ringed the courtyard. Doors to inner rooms led from both the terrace and the lower floors, and Lukys guessed each must belong to a different household.

Wooden tables and benches had been placed out in the courtyard and several figures were already seated there, steaming mugs lifted to their lips. A sharp pressure tightened around Lukys's chest as he caught the distinct northern twang of Perfugian accents amidst the group's chatter. He let out a heavy breath as he recognised several faces, his last reservations fading. Sophia hadn't been lying. His friends were alive.

Heart racing, he started towards them. Several spotted Lukys as he approached and soon the entire group were clapping him on the back and welcoming him to the yard. Despite himself, Lukys found himself laughing, grinning alongside his friends. Travis appeared, dragging him into another bearhug, then Dale was gripping his hand.

After so long alone in the darkness, it felt surreal to suddenly be surrounded by people, by his friends. Somehow he'd expected them to be changed somehow, broken by their own time in isolation, their wills crushed by Tangatan captors. But the smiles on his fellow recruits' faces seemed... genuine. They were happy, just as Sophia had said. It was more than any of them had experienced in Fogmore.

He spotted Sophia standing at the edge of the group,

her arms folded, watching him. Their eyes met and he offered a tentative smile. She nodded back, and her voice whispered in his mind.

I told you.

"So you finally decided to join us!" Travis said, drawing Lukys's attention back to the bulky recruit.

"I…guess so," Lukys said, managing a smile. Despite his friends' apparent happiness, it was overwhelming, being amongst them again.

"Glad you finally saw the light," Dale said with an approving nod.

"Yeah…"

Lukys was surprised to find Dale in such a bright mood. In a way, he'd expected that of Travis, as he always seemed to find the silver lining in any given situation. But Dale…he was a true noble born, proud and aloof. It had taken him weeks just to accept Lukys as his equal. And he had loathed the Tangata. Now he smiled and laughed while one stood watching from just a few feet away?

"Care for a coffee?" Travis offered, gesturing to the tables. "I'm sure Isabella can rustle you up a mug. She does tend to burn it, unfortunately, but it's still better than that river water they used to feed us in Fogmore."

"Coffee?" Lukys frowned. Where had the creatures gotten coffee? "Isabella?"

Dale gave Travis a punch in the shoulder. "Slow your boots, the man's just walked in." He grinned at Lukys. "Relax, Lukys. You look like you're about to have an aneurysm. Why don't you take your lass upstairs? She was here last night, she knows which door is yours. We can swap stories later…" For a moment, Dale faltered. "I…already told them what happened in the north."

Still in a bit of a daze, Lukys nodded, finding Sophia still standing nearby. It didn't seem like she was going to join them, so he took Dale's advice and bid his comrades good-bye. There was obviously more he needed to know about their situation—best he find out from Sophia rather than being caught in a lie by his own friends.

They seem happy, he noted as he re-joined her.

She raised her eyebrows. *You seem surprised.*

Lukys shrugged, deciding it was best not to explain himself. He watched as the recruits returned to their table.

Why keep us together? he asked.

This new life can be…difficult for new assignments, Sophia replied. *The Matriarch has found your kind are able to make the adjustment easier with company from their former lives. It gives them a sense of normality.*

Lukys nodded. *And what of their Tangata?* he asked. *Shouldn't they be here with their new…assignments?*

They have already bonded, Sophia said, looking away.

Again he sensed the sadness in her words. What was the importance of these assignments that the Tangata seemed to covet? His resistance was clearly a source of disappointment, if not pain, for Sophia. He wished he could understand why.

When he didn't respond, Sophia started towards the stairwell, leading them up onto the terrace. It felt surreal to walk along the squeaking boards, listening to the voices of his comrades whispering up from below, to feel the sun upon his face. Ahead, Sophia stopped at a door and turned the copper doorknob. It opened without resistance—apparently there was no need for locks here.

She disappeared inside, but Lukys hesitated in the doorway. This all seemed so *normal*, as though he had somehow stepped into another world, one where the war between Tangata and humanity had never existed.

But it was a lie. He could feel it in his soul, a wrongness about it all, even in the way Sophia looked at him—as though she were looking for something in his eyes. He lingered on the terrace, watching as she turned back to him, and for a moment he wondered if he should run. Sure, he wouldn't make the front gates, and yet…

…wouldn't that be better than betraying his people?

A shiver ran down his spine as he remembered the Tangatan children. There'd been no children in Fogmore— they'd all fled with their families, heading north in search of safety. Only the soldiers and those who supplied them had remained. Yet here…the children played freely in the streets, and humans and Tangata mingled openly, without hatred or strife. Could it really be so easy?

Are you coming? Sophia's voice whispered in his mind.

Lukys swallowed as he looked into those grey eyes. Then he nodded and stepped into the house.

For some reason, he'd expected to find the inside somehow different, as though everything before had only been an illusion to get him here. But it wasn't like the Tangata needed to scheme—Sophia could have forced him here with one arm tied behind her back. So he shouldn't have been surprised to find the inside of the house as normal as the courtyard outside.

He stood in a small, undecorated foyer that opened out into a plain dining room. Sophia had paused in the foyer to remove her boots and after a moment's hesitation, Lukys did the same. In Fogmore, the mud had been so bad most had given up keeping it from their dwellings. Strange that the Tangata should have a greater sense of cleanliness than the militaristic Flumeerens.

Now in socks, Lukys moved into the dining room. A mahogany table was in the centre, while a cabinet of fine porcelain plates stood in the corner. Silver cutlery glinted from a shorter cabinet, and there was no small amount of other finery, lamps and carved wooden animals and teapots.

The sight made Lukys lift his eyebrows—were they to have dinner parties in the future?

But no, it had probably belonged to the place's former owner. No doubt they had left in a rush—or perhaps they'd been killed when the Tangata had taken the city.

The thought shook Lukys from his stupor. Hardening his heart, he allowed Sophia to lead him through the rest of the apartment. They passed from the dining room through a second living space, this time furnished with a plain sofa and coffee table, an unlit fireplace stacked with wood in the corner.

A rich scent hung in the air, and as they passed through the room, Lukys spied the kitchen through another door. He hesitated, then diverted from Sophia's tour. In the kitchen he found an iron coal stove and a simple dining table. Warmth radiated from the stove, as though it had been recently used. His eyes were drawn to the wooden board set on the table, where a loaf of bread was cooling.

Lukys… Sophia's voice called to him.

He turned in the doorway, finding her standing behind him. "Did you…bake that?" he asked.

To his surprise, the Tangata's cheeks turned red. *It was…an experiment.*

Lukys couldn't help it—he laughed. A grin split his face as he watched the inhuman creature that had haunted his nightmares for so long grow brighter. Had he *actually* found himself in some parallel reality? It seemed the only explanation.

Finally he managed to catch his breath, though his smile remained. *It smells good,* he offered. *Can I try some?*

The Tangata's eyebrows lifted in surprise and she seemed to hesitate. Then she swallowed, glancing away. *Yes…but not yet. There's something you need to see…first.*

Lukys frowned at the tone of her voice, but she was

already moving away. There was only one other door that adjoined the second living room. Sophia crossed to stand before it, then hesitated, glancing at him one last time.

Come.

She disappeared within.

Letting out a sigh, Lukys followed. He stepped into the last room and found her standing in the far corner, eyes on the floor, feet scuffing the wooden boards. His frown deepened as he crossed to her, but he only made it a few feet before the contents of the room drew his attention. He froze.

Stumbling to a stop, Lukys stared at the bed. A duvet of white silk shone in the light from the windows and half a dozen pillows had been stacked against the oaken headboard. There was not a hint of straw on the floor as was common in the dormitories of Perfugia and Flumeer, suggesting a mattress stuffed of fur or feathers. It was far more luxurious than any bed he had ever seen in his life.

There was also only one.

I'm sorry, Sophia's voice spoke into his mind. Her cheeks were even brighter than a few moments earlier.

Lukys could only stand there gaping, the wheels of his mind still churning, struggling to place the pieces of the puzzle together.

"What is this?" he whispered.

There was a long silence before Sophia answered.

You trusted me with your life, she said softly. He was surprised to see her eyes were shining. *Now I must trust you with a secret the Tangata have kept from your people for generations.*

🐍 21 🐍

THE FALLEN

A fire glowed in the valley below.

Crouched amongst the rocks, Romaine looked down at the campsite. The light had appeared suddenly as they marched through the night, appearing beyond the boulders that filled the valley floor. Yasin had called a halt immediately and they had backtracked far enough to ensure they would not run afoul of any scouts that might be patrolling the area. Then they had scaled the escarpment at the edge of the valley to gain a vantage point over Erika's people.

Now looking down at the flickering fire, Romaine could hardly believe the chase was at an end. It had taken another two nights—longer perhaps than Yasin would have preferred—but finally Cara's rescue was at hand. Shadows flickered close to the flames and he found himself wondering which was the Goddess, which was Erika. The gloom made it impossible to discern one person from another.

In truth, the queen's spy had made their task easy. Romaine had said nothing of his discovery to the others, but the following nights he'd paid greater attention to Yasin's actions, and had soon begun to spot more of the phosphorescent X's himself. He wondered at the person who dared to commit such treason against his kingdom, to gift his loyalty to a foreign sovereign.

Or perhaps their unknown benefactor was simply one of the few believers amongst the Gemaho, one who renounced their king's blasphemy.

Regardless, it wouldn't be long now before the spy's identity was revealed and Cara freed. A lump rose in his throat at the thought of seeing the little Goddess again. They had hardly spoken a word to each other after the disaster on the Illmoor. It had been too much, the pain of his injuries, of their loss. Lukys and Travis and all the other Perfugians, gone in an instant. The two of them left alone to grieve. Even then, at least they might have had each other, if not for Erika...

"We'll make camp here," Yasin said, interrupting his train of thought. The warrior rose and retreated from the edge of the valley.

"Why not take them now?" Romaine questioned. "There can't be more than twenty." Yasin's own fighters numbered some thirty. "If we attack under the cover of darkness, by surprise, they're like to surrender with barely a fight."

"Is that so, Calafe?" Yasin asked as the others gathered close. A smile tugged at the man's face as he glanced at Romaine's hand and raised an eyebrow. "Suppose you'll be leading the charge?"

Romaine scowled. The queen's man had grown progressively more dismissive of Romaine and Lorene over the past days, as though he blamed them for their quarry's continuing evasiveness. That was at an end now though, and grinding his teeth, Romaine gestured back towards the valley.

"Did you have a better plan?"

The warrior smirked. "I prefer not to go barrelling into a fight blind, Calafe," he replied with a smirk. "First I'm going to scout their camp and see what we're up against."

"And risk stumbling into one of their scouts in the dark?" Romaine argued.

Yasin stepped in close and narrowed his eyes. "What's your rush, man?" he asked softly. "Are you so eager to rescue your precious Goddess? These are Nguyen's soldiers we're talking about. He might not have our queen's nuance, but the man's not a fool. I won't throw my men's lives away by rushing into a trap, though I'm starting to see what went wrong with those sorry Perfugians you led into Calafe."

Romaine almost struck the man. Red flashed across his vision and he dropped a hand to the hilt of his sword. Yasin didn't react. Dark eyes regarded Romaine and a smile touched the warrior's lips. There was no hint of fear in his posture, no concern for the man he faced, though Romaine towered over him.

Swallowing his anger, Romaine shook his head. "You're right," he admitted finally. "Scouting won't hurt—if we're careful. I'll come with you—"

"No," Yasin cut him off. "You and your friend will stay here."

Romaine stared at the man for a long moment. "Yasin, I know the mountains," he argued, trying to keep an even temper. "In the dark, on these slopes, even a single rock knocked loose could ruin everything."

"Then I guess I'd better not knock over any rocks," Yasin said. Dismissing Romaine with a wave, he turned to his followers. "Set the camp. I'll be back within the hour."

He disappeared in the direction of the valley. Romaine watched him go, still smouldering. If the man alerted Erika and her soldiers to their presence it would ruin everything. They had the Gemaho outnumbered, but their quarry could even that advantage if they had time to reach defensible terrain.

"You know, I'm beginning to think he doesn't like us," Lorene commented as the other men began unpacking their sleeping rolls.

Romaine grunted. "There's something more to this," he said, then glanced in the direction of Yasin's followers. They were out of earshot now, engaged in their own conversations. He looked back at Lorene. "I think he has a spy in the Gemaho camp."

Lorene raised his eyebrows. "And how do you know that?"

"They've been leaving markers for us," Romaine replied. "That's why Yasin was only able to track them at night."

"And you didn't think to tell me this earlier?" Lorene scowled, gesturing in the direction Yasin had taken. "Here I was beginning to think the man must have some secret magic!" He hesitated. "You think he's gone to meet his contact then?"

"Could be," Romaine mused. "Though that would risk alerting the others." He shook his head. "The excuse he gave doesn't make any sense either—if this was all a trap set by Nguyen, surely the spy would have warned us."

Lorene sighed. "You know, I'm beginning to miss the days when all I had to worry about were superhuman creatures thirsty for my blood. Simpler times, you know?"

Romaine rolled his eyes. "No one forced you to come."

"Yeah, I'm seriously beginning to question my past self's decision-making abilities." He paused, then shrugged. "Ah well. We going after him then?"

A grin crossed Romaine's lips as he glanced at the others. Just like the past few days when they'd set camp, Yasin's men paid them no attention. He gave a short nod and silently the two of them slipped away into the darkness. Together they crept back to where they'd spied on the Gemaho.

"How do we find him?" Lorene whispered as they paused at the edge of the valley.

"Not sure," Romaine replied, looking down at the burning fire.

He felt a sudden urge to ignore Yasin entirely and head for those flames, to draw his sword and rush the camp, to free Cara from whatever bondage Erika had placed her under. His fist tightened on the hilt of his sword and he drew in a breath. Pain dug at his chest, less now but still there. No, he couldn't rescue Cara alone. But he could at least find out what Yasin was up to.

Exhaling, he started down into the valley, heart beating hard against his ribs. In the darkness, they had to take extra care of the uneven ground, but over the past few nights both had come to perfect the art of stealth. The earth was steep, but there were sections where sheer rock rather than gravel allowed them to move without sound, though having only one hand made it difficult for Romaine to grip the stone.

The light below grew brighter as they continued down the slope, but Romaine had a feeling Yasin would not go too close to the camp. There had to be a reason he was out here. Maybe Lorene was right and he was meeting with their spy. Romaine was still trying to work out the why.

Straining his ears, Romaine caught the first murmur of voices from ahead. The Gemaho were still awake despite the late hour and the cold, though with a fire to warm them they would be far more comfortable than the queen's men.

"What was that?" Lorene whispered, reaching out to catch Romaine by the arm.

Romaine frowned, but before he could reply, he caught another set of whispers—from their left this time. Away from the Gemaho camp, farther up the valley. Following his instincts, Romaine diverted towards the sound. As they moved, the sound of the camp fell away, but the other whispers rose and Romaine slowed, struggling to make out the words over the soft whistling of the wind.

Finally a flicker of movement came from ahead, revealed by the growing moon. Romaine froze, lifting a hand for Lorene to do the same, before crouching and slinking forward into the shelter of a nearby boulder.

"…didn't tell me she was a *God!*" an unfamiliar voice hissed in the night.

"Enough," Yasin replied. "You already wasted enough time responding to my signal."

"Shouldn't have come at all," the spy hissed. "She's a *God—*"

There was an audible *thump* as something hard connected with flesh, followed by strained gasping. Romaine imagined the spy bent in two, struggling to breathe through winded lungs. Why he objected to Cara being a Goddess was still not clear. Romaine shared a glance with Lorene, and carefully they crept closer.

"Listen here, you little bastard," Yasin's voice came again. "Queen Amina doesn't care about your superstitions. You'll do what you're told."

The wheezing continued for another moment before the voice rose in soft defiance. "Please…"

The crunch of stones beneath boots followed as one of the men shifted his feet, though this time there was no sound of blows being exchanged.

"Look, lad," Yasin said, sounding reasonable again. "I

understand. You've found yourself caught up in the workings of monarchs and Gods. I'm trying to help you, but you
need to do your part."

"But I don't *want* any part of this!" the spy gasped.

An audible sigh came from Yasin. "You should try not to
think so much, you could catch your death." There was a
long pause at the threat. Romaine glanced at Lorene, but
Yasin went on before either could speak. "Or perhaps you
think the Goddess will save you?" Yasin chuckled. "She is
not all-powerful, my friend, nor all-knowing. Perhaps she
could save you from me, if I chose to spare your life just
now. But if I do not return, things will go poorly for your
wife and daughter. I hear the queen sent old Skheller to
accompany em. Just between you and me, the man's not
particularly sane. Certainly not someone *I* would like
minding my loved ones."

Romaine's blood turned to ice at Yasin's words. Their
spy was not loyal to the queen at all. Her people had gotten
to his family, were threatening to harm them if he didn't
obey. Images flickered in his mind, of his wife's face, pale in
death, of his son lying frozen in the snow. Slowly his hand
dropped to his sword hilt. Steel hissed on leather as he
dragged the blade free.

"*Romaine*," Lorene hissed as he stepped from the boulders, "Romaine, wait!"

It was already too late. At the movement, Yasin had
spun to face them. His eyes narrowed as he saw the blade in
Romaine's hand.

"That's enough, Yasin," he said quietly. Footsteps came
from behind him as Lorene followed, though Romaine
didn't risk a glance back. Yasin had his crossbow in hand, a
steel bolt loaded in place. A second man dressed in the dull
yellow of Gemaho stood beside the queen's man, eyes wide
in fright. The two stood close together on the slope, though

behind them the earth abruptly fell away, the moonlight rocks turning to empty darkness.

"Calafe," Yasin said softly. "What are you doing out here?"

"Let the man go," Romaine said coldly, hand tight around his sword hilt. "He's done his part."

Stones crunched as Lorene moved alongside him. He too held naked steel in his hand. Yasin's eyes flickered to the scout before returning to Romaine.

"Relax, the both of you," Yasin replied, gesturing with the crossbow. "Our good friend here is just helping us out with your little Goddess. He's going make sure she doesn't get hurt amidst all the bloodshed."

Beside him, the spy seemed to pale at Yasin's words. Romaine took another step towards them.

"I said, *let him go*," he repeated. "I'll not work with anyone who threatens a child." He lifted the shield strapped to his left arm and slid into a fighting stance.

"Just do what he says, Yasin," Lorene said softly. "No one needs to get hurt here."

The queen's man chuckled at that. "Is that so?" he asked. Then the smile slid from his lips. "And by what right do you command me to do anything, Flumeeren? I am here on the orders of Queen Amina. *Your* queen, last I checked. Or are you declaring yourself a traitor, soldier?"

Lorene faltered, then bared his teeth. "I stand with Romaine."

A strained silence followed as the three of them stood facing one another. The helpless spy shrank away from the conflict, but Romaine only tightened his grip on the sword. He knew Yasin's kind. The man was a killer—he would not back down from a fight—

"Oh, very well," Yasin said suddenly. Letting out a sigh, he lowered the crossbow. "Have it your way."

Romaine blinked, still staring at the man, unable to understand his sudden capitulation. He glanced at Lorene, but the scout seemed just as confused by the sudden turn of events.

Twang.

Before either of them could react, a crossbow bolt materialised in Lorene's chest. The man staggered slightly at the impact, his eyes falling to the projectile. A frown crossed his forehead and belatedly he lifted a hand to the arrow, as though confused as to how it had gotten there. Before he could touch it, though, the strength fled his legs and he crumpled to the ground without a sound.

For a second, Romaine stood staring at the body of his friend. Lorene didn't move, didn't speak, didn't even groan. He just lay against the stone, sword still clutched in a pale hand.

Laughter carried across the slope to Romaine. "You just going to stand there for me, Calafe?" The question was followed by the slow racketing sound of the crossbow being reloaded.

A scream tore from Romaine's throat and suddenly he was rushing across the broken stones, sword raised, eyes fixed on the killer. He might have lost his hand, but he was still Calafe. He would not allow his friend to die unavenged.

Yasin grinned as Romaine rushed towards him. Without time to finish reloading the crossbow, he tossed it aside and dragged his sword from its scabbard.

"That a boy," he hissed. "Let's see whether the last soldier of Calafe has any fight left in him."

Romaine's answer was to attack. Muscles rippling across his shoulders, he sent a wild swing slashing for his foe's face. Laughing, Yasin leapt aside, landing easily on the loose stone. His own blade flashed out and Romaine recoiled—

though not before the sharp steel opened a cut on his forearm.

"You know, I told the queen," Yasin murmured, stalking sideways, putting himself on even footing above Romaine. "I told her you were the wrong man for this job. Too sentimental, I said. She was hopeful, though, seemed to think you could bring the Goddess to our side."

Romaine barely heard him. His mind was on Lorene, lying dead on the mountainside, slain because he'd cared, because he'd wanted to help a friend. Grief swamped Romaine but he pressed it down. On the slope above, Yasin snared down at him, but Romaine fought to calm his rage. He no longer had his axe, was no longer the warrior he'd once been. If he was to defeat the queen's personal killer, he needed to be smart.

"It's a shame really…" Yasin was still talking. He slid sideways on the slope, seeking an advantage over Romaine. The Calafe retreated a step, eyeing his foe's feet. On the treacherous ground, a single misstep could gift him the opening he needed. "Our inside man here tells me your Goddess friend has gotten right and cosy with the Gemaho. Just as Amina feared."

The words cut through Romaine's rage. "What?"

The man grinned. "Your little Goddess has betrayed us, Calafe," he sneered. "No choice now but to put her down. Best thing for everyone, if you ask me. Can't have Gods going around pretending they're people. Especially if they side with our enemies."

Romaine tightened his grip around the hilt of his sword and tried to ignore Yasin's words. The man could do nothing to harm Cara. She was a God, beyond his power to touch. Wasn't she? Despite his faith, doubt assailed him. Hadn't she suffered beneath Erika's gauntlet, hadn't the

Tangata bruised her, stopped her? What would a crossbow bolt, delivered from the darkness, do to Cara?

He gritted his teeth, forcing himself to focus on the battle at hand. Yasin would never have the chance to harm his friend. Drawing in a breath, Romaine sought calm, allowing the man's words to wash over him.

Yasin sighed when his taunts failed to bring a response, then without warning he surged forward, sword lancing for Romaine's throat. Moonlight flashed from the blade as Romaine skipped back, his shield barely lifting in time to deflect the blow.

Overhead, a cloud slipped across the moon, and Romaine cursed as the world was plunged into darkness. Pain radiated from the slice on his arm and he retreated another step, swinging wildly to deter any attack. To his surprise, the blade connected with a soft *thud*, though he hadn't put much power behind the blow.

Light returned as the cloud passed and he watched as Yasin staggered back, clutching his arm. Blood seeped through his jacket, but it didn't appear to be a bad cut. Cursing, the queen's man released the wound and hefted his sword.

"You'll pay for that one."

Yasin leapt to the attack and Romaine gasped as a blow slipped beneath his guard. The short sword slammed across his chest and only his chainmail prevented it from penetrating. Even so, agony exploded from his injured ribs, and groaning, he staggered back, trying to lift his shield to deflect another blow.

To his surprise, Yasin did not follow. Instead, he smiled. "I'll admit, you put up a better fight than I expected, Calafe. But it's time for this to end."

Before Romaine could respond, Yasin lurched forward.

Lifting his blade, Romaine tried to counter the attack, but the warrior's blow was only a feint, and instead Yasin lashed out with his boot. The kick caught Romaine square in the chest and he cried out as the pain redoubled. He staggered backwards, but his foot slipped as the gravel began to give way beneath him.

Too late Romaine realised he'd been manipulated. In his rage at Lorene's death and in the darkness cast by the cloud, he'd allowed Yasin to direct the battle, swapping their positions. Now he stood at the edge of the ravine he'd spotted earlier. A cry on his lips, he struggled to regain his balance, to claw his way back from the edge.

Laughing, Yasin stepped forward and shoved him hard in the chest.

And Romaine fell into the darkness.

22

THE SOLDIER

The sun dropped below the rooftop, casting the courtyard into shadow. Lukys snarled as he spun the stave, slashing it down into the face of an invisible enemy, then stepping back and throwing up a block to deflect a riposte. Air hissed around the wooden staff with each thrust. Had there really been anyone in the path of his blows they would have broken bones. As it was, Lukys only spun, continuing through the drill Romaine had taught him back in Fogmore.

He had asked Sophia for the stave after their conversation. It had been a surprise when she'd actually brought one, though the guilt in her eyes told him why. It had no spear tip, of course, making it useless as a weapon against the Tangata. But that wasn't the point.

He needed a distraction, something to take his mind off their conversation, about the truth…

The Tangata are nearly infertile.

Memory of Sophia's words whispered in his mind and gasping, Lukys leapt, launching an attack that would have impaled his enemy. His feet shifted smoothly through the stances his mentor had spent so long drilling into him. It felt good to be moving through the patterns again, to feel his body fall into the familiar rhythms.

Less and less of our pairings can produce children.

He fought on, teeth bared, spinning and slicing, desperate to fend off the unseen enemies, to forget the words that whispered in his mind. A thrust stabbed one foe through the heart, a kick hurled his corpse away, freeing the imaginary blade.

The Tangata are a dying race, Lukys.

A growl slipped from his lips as he moved forward in a series of thrusts, overhand blows, and blocks.

That is why we must take human partners. The pairings are more…favourable. Without them, our species would have died out a generation ago.

Now Lukys began to retreat, his hands moving farther apart on the stave and lifting high, then low, driving his opponent's blade into the cobbles. A kick from his boot sent the imaginary assailant flying backwards.

Zachariah and I, we were a fifth-generation pair—that is, there are five human ancestors in each of our lines.

Grinding his teeth, Lukys's hands tightened on the spear, his knuckles turning white. His breath came in gasps as he paused, spear held parallel to the ground, elbows bent. Slowly he straightened his arms upwards, as though straining to push away an enemy blade.

Sometimes, a child is possible in such couplings. But after five years…

Despite the cool evening breeze, sweat soaked his back. His heart thundered in his ears. Panting, he staggered to a stop. The staff slipped from his fingers, clattering to the cobbles. He blinked drops of perspiration from his eyes, slowly becoming aware of the crowd that had gathered around him. A sigh slipped from his lips as he struggled to recover his breath.

I can sleep in the living room.

The conversation had ended there. Still in a state of shock, he'd asked her for the staff not long afterward. She'd left the compound then, off to hunt deer or maybe pick coffee beans, or whatever she and the other Tangata did during the day. It was his fellow Perfugian recruits who watched him now. Talking to them was the last thing he wanted to do right now, but it didn't look like he was going to have the option not to. He had to keep up the pretence of happiness.

"What was that all about?" Travis asked as he approached, Dale just a step behind.

The other Perfugians wandered over to the tables, most taking seats while a few fetched drinks from their houses. With night falling over the city, coffee looked to have been swapped for ale.

Lukys focused on his two friends. "Felt like I needed to move after all that time in the cell," he offered. "Besides, it's good to practice. No point forgetting everything Romaine taught us."

A grin twisted at Travis's lips. "I suppose. Seems a bit much like hard work to me."

Lukys only shrugged. "Doesn't hurt to be prepared though, right?"

Dale frowned, then clapped Lukys on the shoulder. "I know it's hard to let go. We gave so much of ourselves to the cause. But we're safe here, Lukys. No one's sending us to our deaths, ordering us into the frontlines. I doubt we'll have to ever fight again."

"And thank the Gods for that," Travis added with emphasis. He shivered. "I especially don't miss the cold!"

Eyeing his friends, Lukys found himself nodding to their

words. He might not understand the speed at which their attitudes had changed, but he could appreciate their reasoning. Flumeer and Perfugia both had betrayed them, treating them like playthings, to be cast away when their entertainment ran out. Yet amongst the Tangata they had found acceptance, even appreciation, for their presence.

Though…looking at Travis, he wanted to ask him about Cara. Travis had fallen hard for the Goddess, and while he hadn't known her true identity at the time, she…had seemed to reciprocate the feeling. Had he so quickly given up on the object of his desire?

Movement came from the street beyond the open gates and Lukys watched several Tangata entering the courtyard.

"I suppose it *is* good exercise, though," Travis said. He grinned, though his eyes were on the approaching Tangata. "Gods know, I need to keep up my strength."

That is why we must take human partners.

Lukys's cheeks burned as two females broke off from the group and approached them. Smiles lit Dale and Travis's faces. No words passed between them—they still could not hear the Tangata apparently—but soon they were wandering away with their assignments. Swallowing, Lukys tried to dismiss the nausea in his stomach.

Footsteps sounded behind him. *Lukys…*

Ice spread through his veins as he found Sophia standing behind him. He opened his mouth, then closed it again. What could he say to her after their conversation that morning?

Maybe we'd better go inside? she murmured, looking surprisingly hesitant as she stood there.

Swallowing, he nodded, and together they crossed to the stairwell. Laughter carried up from the courtyard as they slipped into their apartment and Lukys's cheeks warmed again. They found themselves standing in the living room, staring at one another from across the coffee table.

I'll make some tea, Sophia said abruptly, then spun and disappeared into the kitchen.

Closing his eyes for a moment, Lukys slumped onto the sofa. What was he going to do? He had agreed to this arrangement to escape his cell, but he had not accepted this new life as the others had. How could he? Despite all the revelations, the realisation that the Tangata were not so different…it was still wrong. Wasn't it?

Movement came from the doorway to the kitchen as Sophia reappeared holding two steaming mugs. She hesitated, then crossed quickly and placed one of the teas on the table before Lukys.

Peppermint, she said, stepping aside. *For the anxiety.* She paused. *May I sit?*

Letting out a sigh, Lukys nodded. The sofa was big enough for the two of them. Picking up the cup, he breathed in the steam, then took a sip. The pounding in his head retreated a little and he managed a smile.

"Thank you," he murmured, eyes in his mug.

An uncomfortable silence fell over the living room. Lukys watched as a few pieces of green leaves bobbed to the surface of his cup. It was one of the ceramics from the cabinet that stood nearby. He noticed the teapot was missing from the set as well. When had she taken them?

"Sophia, I don't know what to think of any of this," he said at last.

I'm sorry, she replied, and he noticed she didn't seem able to look at him either.

The others, my friends, they don't know…the real reason they're here?

Sophia shook her head, and Lukys let out a sigh. He'd

thought as much, but it was best to be sure before he accidentally blurted out any secrets. It meant he was likely the only human alive who knew the Tangata's secret.

What is it that you want, Lukys? Sophia's voice whispered in his mind. *What is it you fight for?*

Lukys looked at her sharply. "For humanity…" He trailed off, a lump lodging in his throat and he slumped into the sofa. Absently he took another sip of the tea, wondering at the question. How could he *not* fight for humanity?

And yet, what had his fellow man ever done for him? Other than Romaine, the only friends he'd ever had in this world were sitting outside enjoying the cool evening air. And they had sided with the Tangata.

"I don't know what I fight for anymore," he said finally. "I've only ever known what they taught us in the academy, but that was all lies. I'm lost."

They were silent for a while then, though it was pensive. There was a depth to Sophia's expression now, her eyes lost in the distance, as though she were contemplating the secrets of the universe.

I never wanted to be a warrior, Sophia said at last. *I did it for my people, to protect the weaker amongst us. But I am tired of killing for duty.*

Lukys nodded. He recalled the last Tangata he had slain on the banks of the Illmoor. It had hardly been older than himself. Lukys recalled the fear he'd glimpsed in the creature's eyes before the final blow. Maybe that had been Zachariah. He would never ask.

I want children, Lukys. His heart clenched and he struggled to look at her as she continued: *To bring life to this world, instead of death.*

The truth shone from her eyes, could be seen in the earnestness of her smile. For just a second he wondered what that would be like, to give himself to this strange creature. A shiver ran down his spine and he stood up suddenly.

"I can't," he gasped, heart suddenly racing.

Sophia stared at him for just a moment, those solid grey eyes wide, then looked away.

I think you must have Tangatan blood, you know.

Lukys started at her words. "What?"

She still couldn't look at him, but was instead inspecting the blue flower pattern on her cup. *It's the only explanation for your talent. It's why I chose you.*

That's impossible! he shouted in his mind, but still she did not look at him.

It's not...unheard of, she murmured. *Those of the seventh and younger generations, many are born with human eyes. They practically are human. They sometimes went to live amongst the Calafe, before the war.*

He shook his head. "How would they have gotten to Perfugia?"

Sophia shrugged, but there were no answers this time. Lukys swallowed, his mind turning over her words. It wasn't possible, was it? Perfugia was hundreds of miles away from the Tangatan homeland. How would one of the creatures, even one who appeared human, have reached the distant island? And yet...if not the Tangata, where *had* his ability come from?

There were still so many questions, but he wouldn't find the answers this night. Letting out a long breath, he looked towards the bedroom.

"I'm...going to sleep," he said, his voice strained.

Still Sophia did not look at him. *I'll sleep here.*

There was no missing the sadness in her voice. It tugged at Lukys, but he steeled his heart and nodded. *Goodnight.*

He strode through the open door and closed it softly

behind him. Then he was alone, looking down at that soft bed, the empty covers, the pillows plumped and stacked lovingly against the headboard. Tears stung his eyes and he slumped onto the cushioned mattress.

It was just all too strange.

✺ 23 ✺

THE TANGATA

Adonis stood in the unnatural glow of the magic lights and gazed upon the Old One. His heart was racing, fear setting his every sense on edge, images of blood and gore flashing through his mind.

The Matriarch had been right. They had found one, alive, still slumbering in a magic sleep. The creature hung before them in the giant glass cylinder, suspended by the liquids within, her bare body cast in a red glow by the illumination rising from below. A slight hum filled the room, like the distant buzzing of bees, but otherwise the Birthing Ground was silent, as though the very earth held its breath, waiting for what came next.

A shiver ran through Adonis as he looked upon his ancestor. The red light felt almost a warning, as though whoever had left the creature here had feared someone might one day try to wake her, and was sending him a warning.

But Adonis could not heed their council. The female hanging suspended before him represented the hope of his entire race, their last chance to restore strength to future generations. From her would spring a new first generation of Tangata, their powers, their strength restored. Then humanity would quiver before the might of his people.

If she was sane.

His skin crawled but Adonis fought to suppress the sensation and held out his hand for a hammer. There was no point lingering, delaying that which must be done. Breath held, he stepped forward and hefted the tool. But as he approached the cylinder, his doubt came rushing back, and he hesitated, hammer raised to strike.

Was this the right thing to do, the right decision for his people, for the world?

What do I care about the world if it belongs to humanity?

He brought the hammer down.

A *crash* shattered the peace of the Birthing Ground as the glass caved outwards, the pressure of the liquid within sending the cylinder's contents spilling across the ground. Adonis leapt aside as the body followed. Not the most dignified reawakening for his ancestor, but the Tangata did not know enough about the magic of this place to free her any other way.

Retreating to stand with his sisters and brothers, Adonis watched as the Old One slowly woke. He kept the hammer clutched tight at his side as he waited, watching for the first hint of madness, for a clue that the endless passage of time had stolen her sanity. If he struck fast enough, perhaps he could avert disaster…

A hiss whispered through the chamber as the Old One took her first breath. Lying naked amidst the broken glass and strangely gelatinous liquid, blonde hair plastered against her skull, she sucked in great lungfuls of air. Her skin was drained, turned an unhealthy grey, almost translucent, though as Adonis watched, colour reappeared in her cheeks, life returning. The hammer shook in his hands; the window to act was quickly closing. But he did nothing. Slowly the Old One's head lifted, and her eyes fell upon them.

A soft growl rasped from her throat as she rose, and despite himself, Adonis took a step backwards. The terrible eyes flickered in his direction. They were the eyes of the Tangata, pure grey, pupils dilated by the light, but in those depths he saw none of the intelligence of his people. The madness was upon this creature, the berserker rage that sometimes came upon them in battle.

He tensed, sensing what the creature was about to do, and lifted the hammer.

There was a rush of movement, a harsh *thud*. Beside Adonis, his brother Tangata died.

A cry echoed through the chamber as the Tangata leapt back from their companion, weapons held at the ready, but the female did not pay them any attention. Instead, she held their dying brother by the top of his skull, his feet an inch above the floor. Blood still pulsed from his throat, but as Adonis watched, it slowed to a trickle, the last of his brother's life fled.

Lips curled back in a snarl, the Old One leaned in close, as though to inspect her victim. Whatever she'd expected to find, apparently their brother was found wanting. With a flick of her wrist, she sent him toppling sideways. And the grey eyes turned once more to the living.

A cry escaped Adonis's throat, one of rage and frustration, of the knowledge that he and his comrades had made a terrible mistake. Hammer clutched in one hand, he moved towards the Old One.

She was faster. Another of his Tangata cried out and Adonis watched, helpless, as his sister crumpled, a terrible hole torn through her chest. Laughter whispered from the

Old One as she stood over the body, blood dripping from her fingers.

Stop her! Adonis screamed, and his brethren charged.

They died one by one, the Old One dancing between them like a fox amongst the chickens, dropping them at will. Adonis's hammer blows failed to touch her and even his enhanced vision struggled to follow the speed of her movements.

Aghast, Adonis found himself retreating from the carnage. He watched in horror as the best of the fourth generation were butchered like humans. It took the Old One just moments to finish his warrior pairs, though the last she lingered with, feinting, toying, as though she enjoyed watching his fear, his pain. Finally, with a cry of defiance, the Tangata leapt, hammer raised in a desperate strike. She struck him with a backhanded blow so powerful he was flung backwards into the broken cylinder, impaling him on the giant shards of glass.

Then she turned her insane eyes on Adonis. Something in their icy depths seemed to understand he would not fight her, and a smile touched her lips.

Adonis shivered as she approached him, her naked figure covered in the blood of his companions. He knew now how great their error had been. This creature cared not for the Tangata. It cared only for death. This creature would see the world burn.

Death, death, death.

The words pounded in his skull and Adonis found himself taking a step back. Faster than thought, the Old One was there, her fingers closing upon his throat like an iron vice. He cried out, but a squeeze stole the sound away as her fingernails clamped upon his windpipe. Desperately he tried to break her hold, to tear himself loose, but for the first time in his life, Adonis's strength failed him in the face of a greater foe. The hammer was still in his hand and awkwardly he tried to swing it for her face. She caught him with her spare hand.

Death, death, death.

The fist tightened around his throat, but through his agony, Adonis finally recognised the whispers for what they were. Gasping, he thrust out with his mind.

Stop, please!

The Old One let out a cry, and releasing him, she leapt back, teeth bared, eyes wide. Adonis collapsed to the ground and gasped in great breaths of the stale air. The creature's scent was strong now that she was free of her liquid cocoon and he found his head swirling. But eventually fresh oxygen restored strength to his failing body and his mind cleared.

Slowly, Adonis drew himself back to his feet. His eyes were drawn to the bodies of his brethren. They lay all about him, their blood staining the cold stone. He quickly looked away, looking at the Old One once more. Why had she stopped? She hadn't hesitated to strike a mortal blow against the others.

She made no move to attack now, only stood watching, as though she were waiting for something…

What…are…you?

Adonis leapt back as the words reverberated in his skull. The Old One's voice was so loud she was practically screaming into his mind.

So strong!

He drew in a breath, then sent his thoughts out towards the creature.

We are your descendants, Old One, he said, his gaze drawn again to the dead. His heart twisted at the loss, but he forced his mind to focus. The grey eyes still watched him. *Centuries have passed since you began your slumber. We came to wake you, to free you from your chains.*

The Old One regarded him in silence. The strange liquid still dripped from her naked body, mingling with the blood of his brethren. Adonis clenched his fists as he suffered her gaze, wondering what it must have been like, to slumber for so long, to wake in a foreign world. No wonder she was insane…

Show me. She spoke in a softer tone this time, with more control, though the words still pierced Adonis to his very core.

He bowed in response, and silently he summoned memories of these past years—of the terrible force of humanity that had invaded their homeland, slaughtering children and innocents, of the Tangatan counterattack, the years of battle and death as wave upon wave of humanity came against them. Each time the Tangata had emerged victorious, yet still the enemy fought on, and all the while the Tangatan numbers dwindled, their strength fading.

Finally he saw again that last battle on the banks of the Illmoor, the humans they had taken—and the Anahera that had come against them, wings spread in the wind. The Old One started at this image, a frown creasing her forehead.

Adonis let the images fade. *You see?*

There was a long pause before the Old One replied: *These…Anahera, they are your enemy?*

Adonis hesitated. The Anahera had not been seen in centuries—a single one did not mean they had joined the war on the side of humanity. And yet…there was a glow in the Old One's eyes as she watched him, and swallowing, he nodded.

So it would seem.

The Old One took a step towards him and Adonis flinched, still expecting to be struck down. But she only reached out a hand, gentle now, as though fearing she might harm him unintentionally.

What is your name, child?

A shiver ran down his spine at the creature's words and for a second he felt an inexplicable desire to flee. He could feel the weight of her mind pressing against his, the power behind her words. It was almost like…

He shook his head as the thought trailed away to nothing. *I am Adonis.*

The Old One nodded. *You may call me…Maya.* Her smile grew as she traced a finger down the curve of his jaw. *Fear not, child. I will see our enemies burn like the forest before an inferno.*

✿ 24 ✿

THE FUGITIVE

It was a few days before the soldiers finally began adjusting to the sight of Cara and her wings. To her credit, the Goddess hadn't taken to the skies in that time, though Erika sensed this was more to assuage her worries than their companions' benefit. Even so, Cara's actions still felt incomprehensible. The Goddess had still made her disapproval about their destination clear, refusing to give the slightest hint as to whether they were on the right path. Yet she had also kept her word.

If Erika had been in the Goddess's shoes, with wings and the freedom of the sky beckoning, she would have fled at the first opportunity. But then, that was the point, wasn't it? Erika was only human, not a fifty-year-old Goddess in the body of a twenty-year-old with wings. She couldn't possibly hope to understand the forces that bound the Anahera.

At least the Gemaho had not been *completely* struck dumb by Cara's wings, unlike their Flumeeren counterparts. Nguyen's soldiers might have been stunned by the sight, but they hadn't fallen to their knees in awe, and their shock had mostly passed quickly. There were only a few now who still lost their ability to speak in Cara's presence.

Which was fortunate, as the going had become progressively more difficult with each passing day. While the snow line seemed higher this side of the mountains, the valleys they traversed had become progressively steeper, the terrain more and more difficult. And as they neared the soaring peaks, Erika found each inhalation brought less energy, as though however hard she tried, she could not quite fill her lungs. By the end of each day, her temples were pounding, and despite the warmth of the sun overhead, she found herself trembling whenever they stopped for more than a few minutes.

Dawn, on their fifth day since disembarking the ship, found them waking in a broad, U-shaped valley, snow-capped peaks towering all around them. Despite the cold, Erika rose from her sleeping bag touched by excitement. If her guess was correct, the home of the Anahera was close.

Shadow still clung to the valley as she pushed aside the canvas tent flap and stepped into the open. Several of the soldiers were already up and busy repacking their tents for the day's journey. Erika was relieved their presence had spared her from carrying the heavy things.

A moan came from inside her tent and a few moments later Cara's face appeared, tangled copper hair hanging across her face. Erika might have trusted the Goddess not to harm them, but it had still seemed prudent to keep her close in the night.

"Arg, Erika, the sun's not even up," Cara muttered as she crawled through the flap. "You know, if you're going to drag me back to my parents, you could at least let me sleep in a little."

One of her wings caught in the canvas and the Goddess cursed and had to contract the limb before she could pass.

The movement dislodged several of her feathers and a gust of wind sent them swirling away. Absently, Erika snatched one from the air. The things still amazed her, their length, the depth of their colour. Shaking her head, she released it again. Despite her growing familiarity with the Goddess, the sight of those wings still sent a shiver down her spine at times.

Ignoring Cara's complaints, she turned towards the remains of last night's fire, only to find another of the soldiers standing there, eyes wide as he watched Cara finish clambering from the tent. Erika sighed—this was one of the few Gemaho who still hadn't overcome his awe for the Goddess. Knowing it would be some time before he recovered his wits, she stepped around him and approached the ring of stones they'd placed there for seating.

Lowering herself onto her rock from the night before, Erika was relieved to see someone had already lit the fire for the morning. Stretching out her hands, she let the heat wash over her. Her eyes drifted to the way ahead.

Gravel slopes rose away from them, turning to sheer cliffs a few hundred yards up the valley, becoming a narrowing gorge that twisted out of sight. There was no way of telling whether the canyon would end in a dead end. Where they sat, they could still climb from the valley and continue along the ridge instead, but Erika didn't relish the thought of climbing those treacherous slopes. If only Cara had been willing to take to the skies and scout the way ahead, she could have told them which was the best option.

Still muttering to herself, Cara lowered herself onto a rock nearby. Apparently recovered from his shock, the soldier stepped past her to attend to the fire, before pulling a pot from a nearby pack and placing it over the flames. Oats and a generous helping of water from an oilskin followed with a soft *hiss*.

Erika watched the man with amusement—he seemed to be studiously trying not to stare at Cara. Across the flames, the Goddess wrinkled her nose as she watched him, then rose and crossed to where the soldier was working, her footsteps silent on the loose stones.

"Arg, is there a reason for humanity's obsession with oatmeal?" she asked, pouting slightly. Beside her, the soldier yelped as he finally noticed her presence at his shoulder, but Cara only went on: "I can't imagine why you find it so appealing, it's basically just grey mush."

"I…I…sorry, Your Divinity!" the improvised cook gasped. He fumbled at the pot and almost dropped it into the flames.

"You should be!" Cara exclaimed, leaning forward and fixing him with a glare.

The man yelped and almost tripped over himself. Erika rolled her eyes. Just as the soldiers had become accustomed to her presence, the Goddess had grown used to their staring. In fact, now she seemed to take a certain amount of amusement from their awe.

"Oatmeal is perfectly acceptable, soldier," Erika said before Cara made the poor man any more mortified. She turned her gaze on the Goddess. "If you'd ever made it to Mildeth, I'd have shown you a real breakfast."

Erika immediately regretted opening her mouth as Cara's face darkened.

"A shame," was all the Goddess said, but the conversation died after that, and they waited in silence for the soldier to finish preparing the breakfast.

"Here, Archivist," the man said finally, offering her a bowl of freshly poured oatmeal.

Nodding her thanks, Erika accepted the offering. She held her tongue when she saw it was just as unappetising as Cara had claimed. The man collected another bowl and turned his back from them to scoop another portion from the pot—or probably two, knowing Cara's appetite—before bowing low and passing it to Cara. She took it with a smile.

"Thank you."

The man hesitated, still looking nervous, before he finally blurted out: "Are you really a God?"

A smile touched Cara's lips and she crooked her head to the side, eyeing the man. "What do *you* think?"

"I…" The man swallowed visibly. "You…you have wings."

Cara glanced over her shoulders and gasped. "You're right!" The feathered limbs lifted slightly with her mock surprise. "What does it mean?!"

The soldier swallowed again, shaking his head, looking at the ground. "I don't know. We…I…didn't believe…not like they do in the west. I don't…know what to think."

Erika chuckled to herself as she watched the exchange, but at the man's last words Cara's shoulders drooped and she looked away.

"Maybe I'm not sure what I am either," she said at last.

The soldier stared at her for a moment, then finally he nodded, seemingly satisfied. He let out a long breath. "Enjoy your meal."

He moved away at that, and Erika returned her attention to her oatmeal. To the man's credit, he'd added dried apple and raisins. They gave a little flavour to her first bite. She ate slowly as the soldiers moved about, preparing for the day's march, until Maisie finally appeared from her tent. Erika waved the spy over.

"Enjoying the meal?" Maisie asked as she approached, nodding a greeting to Cara.

Her mouth full of oatmeal, the Goddess didn't reply, and the spy chuckled. Turning to Erika, she raised an eyebrow in question. The spy didn't need to speak for Erika to understand her question.

"I think we're in the right place," she said, then reached into her satchel and drew out her map. "See these," she said, pointing to the twin white spots on either side of the red star marking what they thought was the home of the Gods. She nodded to the peaks rising either on side of the valley.

The spy leaned closer, eyes wide. "We're almost there?" she asked, scanning the map. Then her head whipped around to focus on Cara and she repeated the question: "We're almost there?"

Cara looked up from her meal, scowled, but said nothing. Silently she scooped the last morsel from the wooden bowl and placed it in her mouth, then exaggerated chewing motions.

Erika rolled her eyes. "Ignore her," she replied. "She won't tell us anything useful."

Maisie nodded. "But you're sure?"

"I am."

"Excellent!" Maisie exclaimed. "Then what are we sitting here for? Let's go find the city of your Gods!"

Despite herself, Erika's heart throbbed at the thought. Stifling a groan, she levered herself to her feet and looked at Cara. "Well, are you going to sulk? Or join us?"

Cara rolled her eyes, but after a moment she set aside her bowl and made to stand. She managed to rise halfway to her feet, but suddenly seemed to lose her balance and pitched forward. Erika's hand snatched out and caught the Goddess by the arm, steadying her.

"Are you alright?" she asked with a frown.

Cara nodded. She released Erika's arm and tried to take a step, but immediately swung off-balance and staggered sideways instead. This time Erika wasn't fast enough to catch her, and the Goddess slumped to her hands and knees beside the fire. Her wings flared outwards, the twelve feet of feathered limbs forcing everyone back.

"Cara?" Erika hissed, suddenly concerned. "What's wrong?"

A moan rumbled from the Goddess. "I…don't feel so well," Cara croaked, even as she tried to push herself back to her feet.

This time her legs gave way completely and she pitched face-first into the rocks. Pale fingers clawed at the stones as Cara twisted on her side. Her eyes were wide, pupils dilated, becoming huge black circles amidst the amber depths. They darted around in her skull as she looked up at Erika.

"Why is it getting dark?" Cara whispered.

Heart clenched, Erika reached for the Goddess, but before she could reassure her, Cara's back suddenly arched, a scream tearing from her throat. She started to thrash, arms and legs and wings hurling stones, forcing everyone back. Another cry rattled from her throat before she stilled, on hands and knees now, sucking in great mouthfuls of air.

"Erika…" Cara's voice was barely a whisper now. "Something's…not right."

The Goddess's face was a terrible grey when she looked up and sweat beaded her brow. Erika moved quickly, kneeling beside Cara and placing a hand on her shoulder, but the act seemed to offer little reassurance. With a final moan, Cara crumpled back to the stones.

"What's happening to her?" Maisie whispered.

Swallowing, Erika glanced at the spy. She was about to say that she had no idea, when her eyes alighted on the breakfast bowl lying nearby. A sudden suspicion touched Erika and she swung around, searching the faces of the gathered soldiers. All stared at the Goddess with looks of confusion—all except one.

The young man that had served their breakfast stood at the rear of the soldiers, eyes wide, his face pale. He stared in horror at where the Goddess had fallen, a soft keening sounding from the back of his throat.

Without thinking, Erika leapt to her feet and rushed the man. The man cried out and tried to flee, but her hand was already coming up, the gauntlet bursting into life. Her victim screamed as his legs crumpled beneath him.

Enraged, Erika stalked towards the fallen man, palm extending, magic still pulsing from her gauntlet. On the ground, the soldier thrashed, mouth wide, veins bulging from the flesh of his throat. Reaching the thrashing body, Erika did not relent. Teeth bared, vision stained red, she thrilled in his suffering. He must have slipped poison into Cara's food when they hadn't been looking. Now he would pay…

"Erika!" Maisie snapped, catching her by the arm and dragging it away from her victim.

The soldier collapsed to the stones, gasping as though his lungs had just been released from a vice. Shaking herself free of her anger, Erika looked at Maisie, then the soldier. Blood ran from his nose, ears, and nostrils, turning his face to a scarlet mess. He lay on the ground moaning, unable to move, to see, probably even to hear. A few moments longer, and he would have succumbed to her magic.

A lump lodged in Erika's throat as a sudden horror touched her. It had been so long since she'd used the magic, she'd almost forgotten the thrill of its power, the call to use it against her enemies.

"I'm sorry." A whisper rasped from the man's throat. "I'm sorry, I'm sorry, I'm sorry. Please!"

Looking at his pitiful form, listening to his pleas, Erika felt her anger rising again, but Maisie moved faster. A knife appeared in her hand and she crouched beside the soldier and placed the dagger against this throat.

"What did you do?" she hissed.

"I'm sorry," the man repeated. He blinked, as though struggling to clear something from his vision, but the whites of his eyes had been stained red with blood. He would likely never see again. "The queen…she made me."

Erika's heart turned to ice at the man's words. The queen? She couldn't possibly be here, could she?

Before any of them could question the man further, a horn sounded from above. Swinging around, Erika watched as thirty men leapt over the ridge above and raced down the slope towards them.

❦ 25 ❦

THE SOLDIER

Lukys sat in the courtyard looking up at the starless sky, a pint of ale before him, the laughter of his friends all around. He joined in with them every now and then, if only to keep up appearances. Watching their merriment, it occurred to him that he was no longer their leader, that the authority he'd built as Romaine's right-hand man had slipped away as he sat alone in the darkness. Lukys found he did not miss it.

A week had fled like the snow before the breath of spring. He and the other recruits had been put to work, though that was often no more than sitting on the river-banks with a fishing pole.

The most strenuous of activity came when they cleared the buildings yet to be occupied by the Tangata. Thankfully any dead had been removed from the city long ago, but many houses were worse for wear after close to a year of unoccupancy. Coal stoves had cracked with the invasion of winter's cold and had to be removed, while vines were busy invading through cracks and windows. At times the Perfugians were even asked to attempt basic repairs on shutters and rooftops. Then they would be joined by groups of Tangata who watched their actions with interest, Lukys assumed to learn from their human captives.

If that was the case, though, they were sorely disappointed, as the recruits had few such skills. They hadn't been sent to the frontline to die because they'd been useful to Perfugian society.

Maybe that was why his friends laughed now, why their smiles seemed so genuine—they had finally found a place in society, even if it was amongst the strangest of people. They even seemed able to communicate with their Tangata through notes and actions, despite their obvious limitations.

Watching his friends embrace their new life, their new lovers, it left Lukys feeling excluded, as if there was something wrong with his resistance to Sophia. It wasn't that he did not find her attractive, in a lithe, Tangatan manner, or even that he did not like her. She had surprised him with her sweetness. The image of her baking bread each morning was such a sharp contrast to the monsters he'd always imagined the Tangata to be...

...perhaps that was the source of his reservations—not that he did not find her attractive, but that he *did*. She had taken him captive, stolen away his freedom. Human or Tangata, he should *loathe* her.

Instead, he found himself lying awake each night, tossing and turning in the giant bed, thinking of Sophia sleeping alone on the sofa. Of the pain he glimpsed in her eyes each morning when he found her with her bread.

It was galling.

"You're looking grim."

Lukys looked up as Travis sat across the table from him. Most of the others had been washing up after their afternoon on the riverbanks and Lukys had been enjoying the peace in the courtyard. He forced a smile.

"Didn't catch anything today."

His friend chuckled. "Fish not biting? Ah well, rest day tomorrow, no point stewing over it." He lifted his mug and clinked it against Lukys's.

They drank and Travis laughed again, then gestured around the courtyard. "Who knew our damned Sovereigns were hiding this from us all this time?"

"You think they knew?" Lukys asked, surprised.

Travis's eyebrows lifted into his mop of light brown hair —there were certainly no barbers in New Nihelm. "You think they didn't?"

Lukys's eyes drifted over the groups of Tangata standing nearby. "I don't know what to think anymore," he mused.

His friend said nothing at that, and when he looked back at Travis, he found the other man's gaze fixed on him. He swallowed, worried he might have given away his secret, but after a moment the Perfugian waved a hand.

"Ain't that the truth," he said, then leaned across the table. "So, what's it like?"

"Huh?" Lukys asked, mug halfway to his lips.

"Being able to hear them," Travis explained.

Lukys quickly dropped his eyes to the table. That was one secret he had been unable to keep. The other Tangata had soon learned of his ability from Sophia, and often came to him when they wanted to convey something to their partners. It seemed a novelty to them, to be able to communicate with Travis and the others without using notes. For Lukys, it was slightly mortifying.

"I…" he stammered, unsure how to progress. "It's…different."

"I bet." Travis wore a grin from ear to ear. "Especially at night. I can only imagine the thoughts running through Isabella's mind sometimes."

Warmth flushed Lukys's face but thankfully he was

spared any further conversation about his love life by the arrival of voices at the gates of the compound. He frowned, turning in his seat to see several men and women approaching, carrying straw baskets.

"Hello to the compound!" the first of the new arrivals called, the southern twang in his accent announcing him as Calafe. "We heard there were some new arrivals, how are y'all settling in?"

The Perfugians stood around the courtyard as the group approached, frowns revealing their confusion. So far they hadn't had much interaction with the other humans in the city. But the frowns soon turned to grins as the newcomers revealed the contents of their baskets.

"Y'all hungry?" A woman asked, approaching their table.

"Damn right!" Travis exclaimed, rising to look into the basket. He jabbed a thumb in Lukys's direction. "This one didn't catch us anything for dinner."

Lukys flashed Travis a scowl, but nodded his thanks as the woman passed him something wrapped in a cloth. She took a seat alongside Travis as Lukys unwrapped the offering, revealing a small pastry pie within.

"It's venison," the woman explained, taking out one of her own. Uncovering the pie as Lukys had done, she proceeded to take a bite while holding the bottom half in the cloth.

Raising an eyebrow, Lukys shared a glance with Travis, then attempted to mimic their new companion's actions. The pastry was still hot, and taking a bite, he was surprised to find chunks of meat and gravy inside. It dripped down the side of the flaking pastry, but thankfully the cloth kept it from scalding his fingers.

"So Perfugians, right?" the woman asked as they ate.

"We don't get many of your kind here. Must be quite the story."

Lukys glanced at the woman, thinking it must be the same with her. These were Calafe—this had been their city, before the Tangata had come. He wanted to ask her what they thought about this new life, their new masters. But that would have given him away.

"You're dammed right about that," Dale said, interrupting Lukys's thoughts as he appeared alongside them.

He'd gotten a pie of his own from another of the Calafe, and sitting beside Lukys, he started to tell the tale of how they'd found themselves captives of the Tangata. Travis interrupted now and then with his own witty remarks, but Lukys found himself tuning out their words.

Their expedition with the Archivist seemed like another life now, a different reality. Had he met Sophia back then, he would have run her through with his spear. Now, though…

Lukys started as a single note of music rang through the courtyard. Swinging around, he saw that one of the newcomers had taken out a lute. Eyes fixed on the instrument, the woman paid the rest of the courtyard no attention, only strummed the instrument again, starting into a song—soft at first, but quickly building in volume. Each strum of the strings reverberated from the wooden walls of the courtyard.

A harmonica soon joined her, then a violin, as others took instruments from their baskets and began to play. The Perfugians remained at their benches, a look of wonder in their eyes as voices rose to greet the night. It was an old song, beginning in the darkness of The Fall, when death had stalked the land and even the Tangata had hidden far beneath the earth.

Then the pace increased. Hope appeared in the tone of

the singers, as light returned to the world. Swept away by the music, Lukys sat with his eyes closed, imagining those ancient days when the only worries of mankind had been their own follies. The early tribes had warred upon one another, until finally alliances had been formed. Kingdoms had risen from the ashes, binding the people together and restoring civilisation. But even then, the wars had continued, as each kingdom strove for supremacy.

Only the threat of the Tangata had finally united them.

What was left of that alliance now? Calafe had fallen and Gemaho had retreated, seeking refuge behind the mountains. Even Perfugia shirked its responsibilities, sending only their rejects, their unwanted to fight against the Tangata. Flumeer alone fought on.

Lukys opened his eyes as he sensed movement nearby. A female Tangata now stood beside Travis—Isabella. Her grey eyes shone in the lanternlight as she ran a hand through his friend's long hair. Lukys noticed then that the others had returned as well. He found himself looking around for Sophia.

Lukys.

Lukys started as a voice spoke into his mind. He looked back at Isabella, finding her eyes on him.

Yes? he asked tentatively.

She glanced at Travis. *Could you tell him I would like to dance?*

Oh! Lukys lifted his eyebrows, surprised by the request. He hadn't realised the creatures even knew what dancing was. Smiling, he shifted his gaze to Travis. *She wants to dance.*

Travis grinned and standing, he offered a hand to Isabella. "Hey, would you like to dance?"

Isabella was still watching Lukys, a frown creasing her forehead, but after a moment she smiled. The two moved into the open space in the middle of the courtyard. Lukys watched as Travis drew his partner close.

They began to dance, cautiously at first, moving slowly in time with the music. The bulky recruit appeared clumsy beside the Tangata's fluid grace, yet the smile Isabella wore seemed genuine. The music washed over the two, carrying them away across the cobbles.

Lukys found himself wondering where the Tangata had learned such things. Legends claimed they'd been little more than animals when they'd first emerged from beneath the earth. Had those too been lies? Or had their species evolved through the centuries?

"I wonder where Travis got that idea," Dale commented.

Frowning, Lukys turned to his companion, but at that moment the man's partner appeared. He rose without prompting and the two followed Travis and Isabella out into the middle of the courtyard. The couple danced freely now, in tune with one another's bodies, sliding through the steps with a refinement the recruits had never managed with Romaine's drills.

One by one, others rose to join the dancers, bringing the courtyard to life. The Calafe woman that had given them the pies rose to join one of the guitarists, leaving Lukys alone on his bench. Sitting there, he could almost begin to see the magic of the place, the peace his friends had found with these strange creatures. Some struggled more than others, moving through the steps with difficulty, but their Tangatan partners didn't seem to mind; indeed, they wore patient smiles on their faces.

Lukys shook his head as he watched the dancers. Then he frowned, his thoughts drawn back to what Dale had said. Why had the man been confused about Travis's actions?

Lukys had told his friend that Isabella wanted to dance…hadn't he?

They seem happy.

Lukys looked around as Sophia's voice interrupted his thoughts, finding the Tangata standing beside him. For once, her arrival did not startle him. It seemed right that she was here, and at first he did not reply, only sat looking at her.

Sophia's eyes were dark in the starlight, her hair cascading down around her shoulders, sharp cheekbones adding an elegance to her face that Lukys had rarely seen amongst humans. She had changed into a satin dress, the fabric of purest black, clinging to her athletic frame, high-lighting her slim waist, and…other things.

Suddenly Lukys's throat was dry. Heart pounding, he felt as though he were seeing Sophia for the first time. He had treated her poorly these past days, ignoring her for the most part, staying away. Now though…

Rising, Lukys offered his hand. *Would you like to dance?*

Sophia's eyes grew wide and to his surprise, she dropped her gaze. *You don't have to do that.*

I want to.

He took her hand before she could argue further. She didn't resist as he drew her towards the other dancers, though he sensed her trepidation.

Are you sure? she asked as the music picked up pace, sending the dancers spiralling around them.

Lukys nodded, and the hint of a smile touched her lips. Silently, she stepped closer and Lukys placed his hand on her hip, so that their bodies were just inches apart. A spark shot through his body, a thrilling, surging sensation that set his every nerve alight.

I'm dancing with a Tangata.

Sophia's smile broadened and he realised she'd heard

him. Silently she placed a hand on his chest. He shivered at the touch. They began moving to the music. Lukys was no dancer, but he found the steps came more easily to him now than during his days at the academy, and he realised this wasn't much different from the fighting patterns Romaine had taught him atop the walls of Fogmore. His feet, accustomed to maintaining his balance now, moved naturally through the steps.

With their minds in tune, he found Sophia moving almost before he did, matching him stride for stride. Together they spun through the courtyard, bodies pressed close, breaths mingling, the rest of the couples forgotten, until Lukys felt it was just the two of them, alone in the courtyard. For just a moment, he allowed himself to be carried away by the music, drawn in by the shimmer in Sophia's eyes, the magic of the moonlight shining down from overhead.

His mind pounded with a distant beat, matching the pulse of the music. Belatedly, he realised it was the voices of the other Tangata, the racing of their minds, the murmurs of their silent voices to the music of the Calafe.

How can I hear you all? Lukys asked, looking at Sophia.

Her eyes were only an inch from his, her lips so close he could feel the warmth of her breath on his cheek.

I told you, her reply came hesitantly, *or perhaps...perhaps humanity is evolving?*

Perhaps...

Concern showed in Sophia's eyes as she watched him. It pained Lukys to see it, and without thinking he pressed his lips to hers. She flinched in his arms, but a moment later he felt her relax, and then she was kissing him back, her lips parting, the warmth of her mouth mingling with his.

Lukys found himself grinning as he drew back and saw the shock on Sophia's face.

That was…unexpected, she murmured.

He didn't reply, only held her in his arms, turning her through the steps of the waltz. She was right—he'd surprised even himself. But maybe he was done ignoring his own logic, done fighting the inevitable. The music was fading now, and he realised belatedly that they were the last couple in the courtyard. The others had vanished into their apartments, to their rooms…

Lukys's heart started to race as he looked into Sophia's eyes. His hand tightened around hers as he found himself imagining what it would be like to share that grand bed with this strange woman, to look into those strange eyes as they…

The thought was interrupted as a distant thumping sounded in his mind. It began like the distant whispers of the Tangata, but quickly rose in pitch, until it seemed it would force all other thoughts from his mind. The smile fell from Sophia's lips, and he knew she was hearing the chanting too. Slowly the words took shape.

Death, death, death.

The hairs on his neck tingled as though a cold breeze had blown through the courtyard. The chant was already growing to a crescendo, the words practically shouted now, like the banging of drums, a call to war. And he knew then that he'd heard this same chant before, deep in the tunnels under the earth, in the Birthing Grounds of the Tangata.

The Old Ones.

His blood ran cold as he looked at Sophia. "They're here."

❧ 26 ❧

THE FALLEN

Pain engulfed Romaine as he reached out with his one hand and gripped the rock.

One, two, three.

Groaning, he heaved himself halfway onto the ledge, then using his injured arm to lodge himself there, then shifted his hand so he could push himself up the rest of the way. His feet found fresh purchase and gasping, he looked up, seeking his next handhold.

The brightening sky still seemed so far away. The crack that marked the mouth of the ravine might as well have been a hundred miles off. He would never make it, certainly not before Yasin…

One step at a time.

Determined, Romaine reached out again, hauling himself up, planting himself in place with his elbow, then pushing up the rest of the way. He was lucky—the ravine was not as steep as it had looked from above. The ground sloped at maybe a sixty degree angle. With his body pressed to the stone, he had just enough purchase to hold himself in place. If it had been a sheer cliff, he'd never have climbed out.

But then, the fall probably would have killed him, and he wouldn't have been around to worry about whether he could escape. He wouldn't still feel the pain of his loss, of seeing yet another friend murdered, wouldn't have felt the agony of his own failures. Despair hung around his shoulders like an anchor, threatening to drag him back into the depths, whispering for him to let go, to surrender.

Just a little farther.

He would not give up. He would not let Cara down. She was all he had left.

Hours before, Romaine had awoken in darkness, surprised to find himself alive, though his body ached as though he'd taken a dozen beatings. Thankfully his sword had been lying nearby, and while the shield Amina had gifted him was dented, its strappings had survived the fall. If he made it out of this hole, Romaine would need both. Yasin would not go quietly.

He'll kill you anyway.

Thrusting aside thoughts of defeat, Romaine continued, climbing up and up, until finally he found himself rolling over the lip of the ravine, free. Sunlight touched his face, searing his eyes, waking him from his despair. Romaine blinked, then pushed himself up. A familiar collection of boulders dotted the site around him.

Lorene still lay where he had fallen. A groan tearing from his lips, Romaine crawled to his friend. Blood stained the dirt beneath him, but otherwise Lorene could have been sleeping. There was a peacefulness to his face, if one ignored the bolt still embedded in his chest.

Romaine scrunched his eyes closed, struggling to contain his grief. Only one thing kept him from lying down beside his friend and waiting for death to find him.

Cara.

He came to his feet. His legs felt weak, unsteady, but at least he hadn't broken anything in the fall. His eyes were drawn to the sky and he saw that the sun was still low on the distant horizon. Erika and the others would just be preparing to depart. If Yasin had not ordered an attack in the night, there might yet be hope to warn them

Fist clenched, Romaine started towards the campsite, but as he cleared the ring of boulders, a distant sound carried to his ears. He hesitated, heart hammering in his chest. It sounded almost like...

Romaine started to run. The clashing of steel and the screams of men grew louder as he cleared the last of the boulders and started down the slope. The valley twisted away from him, hiding the Gemaho campsite from view, but they couldn't be far. Pushing beyond his pain, Romaine increased his pace.

Ahead, the basin twisted and at last he spotted movement, still a few hundred yards away. Men swarmed around across the valley floor, where flashes of yellow revealed the Gemaho soldiers, desperately trying to defend themselves.

Gathering his strength, Romaine drew his sword. Pain swamped him. He knew he could not change the outcome of the battle. Yet still he pushed on, past the doubt, past the agony. In that moment, it didn't matter if he succeeded, only that he tried, just as Cara had tried to save their friends, back on the shores of the Illmoor.

Stones crunched beneath his boots but none of Yasin's men noticed his approach above the roar of battle. He saw one of the defenders go down, then another, and pressed on. The Gemaho seemed to be gathered around a cluster of boulders, but there was no sign of Cara, or even Erika. Had something happened to them?

There was no turning back now. The remaining

Gemaho were outnumbered, but where Yasin's men attacked with cold fury, they met them with a cool proficiency. Even so, the thugs that had accompanied Romaine on the journey from Flumeer were taking a heavy toll. The Gemaho would not last much longer.

Then Romaine noticed something strange. As one of the Flumeeren warriors attacked, he staggered as though struck by something invisible. Before he could recover, a Gemaho sword took him in the throat. Narrowing his eyes, Romaine saw it happen again to another soldier. Realisation followed and he searched the thrashing bodies for a glimpse of Erika. There was still no sign of her amongst the defenders, but he was sure it had to be her magic. It gave him a flash of hope, though he couldn't understand how she had tricked the queen. Had Nguyen given her an imitation gauntlet?

Romaine was growing close now, and as the bodies of Yasin's fighters piled up, he finally caught a glimpse of the man himself. Yasin stood at the rear of his soldiers, crossbow in hand. As Romaine watched, he calmly fired over the heads of his men into the Gemaho ranks, taking a man in the shoulder. Drawing another bolt from the quiver at his side, he began to reload.

Rage touched Romaine and for a moment he longed to throw himself at the cursed warrior. But what would that achieve? He had already failed to defeat Yasin once. In his injured state, he wouldn't stand a chance now. No, he had to find Cara, to protect her. She was all that mattered.

Where would she be? He had expected to see her somewhere below, but there was no sign of the winged Goddess. Could it be that she'd never been with the group in the first place? Romaine's stride faltered and he almost crumpled at the thought. But no, Yasin's spy had talked about the Goddess. So where was she?

Ahead, one of the Flumeerens glanced back and finally saw Romaine approaching. His eyes widened in shock and gritting his teeth, Romaine put on a burst of speed. Caught between the Gemaho soldiers and Romaine, the man hesitated. It was enough, and dropping his shoulder, Romaine slammed into the man's chest, hurling him back into his fellows.

The Flumeerens staggered away from their comrade while on the hillside above Yasin himself cried out in rage. Ignoring them all, Romaine waved his sword and leapt past the Flumeerens, making for the Gemaho line. The yellow garbed soldiers drew together, weapons raised; but before they could strike a voice called out from somewhere behind them.

"*Don't!*"

Erika appeared—not from the boulders but seemingly thin air. Romaine started, so shocked by her materialisation he almost forgot about the armed men around him. But instinct carried him forward and as the Gemaho responded to the Archivist's orders and parted, he joined them in the line. Spinning, he raised sword and shield, prepared for the inevitable charge.

Steel shrieked on steel as a crossbow bolt struck his shield and embedded there. Thankfully, its razor tip missed the flesh of his arm. Romaine's eyes were drawn to the hillside where Yasin still stood, calmly reloading the weapon. Gritting his teeth, Romaine prayed for the ability to strike the man down, but already the Flumeerens he'd scattered were forming up again.

The Gemaho gathered to either side of Romaine, more than one flicking him bewildered glances, but he ignored them, his attention fixed on the Flumeeren, on Yasin above. Their eyes met and the man sneered, but then the Flumeer were upon him and Romaine had time only for the battle.

A shudder jarred his arm as his shield deflected a sword. Pain tore at his chest and Romaine's knees buckled. Silently he reached within, drawing on his last reserve of strength, and surged forward, short sword stabbing low. Trapped between his fellow Flumeerens, his foe had no room to manoeuvre and Romaine's blow took him in the stomach. Blood burst from the wound as Romaine tore back his blade and retreated to his position amongst the Gemaho.

Another of Yasin's men stepped in to fill the gap and the battle raged on. Despite his early success, Romaine found the others who came against him far more wily, and slowed by his wounds, he struggled to fend them off. Luckily, blows that would have killed him were diverted as attackers stumbled—due to Erika's magic no doubt, though the woman had vanished again.

Yet even with the Archivist's magic, the Gemaho were being pressed back, their numbers whittled down by the relentless assault of Yasin's warriors. Caught off-guard, the ground they defended offered no advantages, and too many had fallen in the first minutes. And Yasin's arrows continued to do their damage, though he hadn't managed to strike at Romaine again.

"Romaine!" Erika's voice rose above the clash of weapons, drawing Romaine's attention. "We need you."

Unable to turn his back from the enemy, Romaine stepped back from the frontline, allowing the Gemaho to close ranks around him. Only then did he glance back, though he kept an eye out for more of Yasin's arrows. There was no sign of the Archivist though, and puffing, he was about to return to the fight when something grasped him by the arm.

"Quickly!"

Romaine flinched as Erika's voice spoke from empty air.

The pressure on his arm tugged him towards the boulders, and still shocked by whatever new magic she was wielding, he allowed himself to be drawn away.

There was a flash of light, and then suddenly the Archivist was standing before him. Despite their inherent danger, the rage Romaine had been nurturing over the past weeks boiled to the surface. This was the woman who had betrayed him who had kidnapped Cara and sold her loyalty to a foreign nation. His fist tightened around the hilt of his sword and he clenched his jaw, fighting the urge to drive the blade through her chest.

"Cara needs you," the Archivist hissed.

The words cut through Romaine's anger like a knife. He lowered his sword, heart racing. Erika's lips were pursed and there was fear in her eyes. Blood was beginning to seep through a bandage wrapped around her upper arm, though she didn't seem to notice. Light glowed from the gauntlet she wore on her arm, and Romaine frowned, still wondering how she had fooled the queen. But there was no time for questions now. Only one thing mattered.

"Where is she?" he growled.

Erika glanced at him, and she hesitated as their eyes met. Romaine wondered if it was guilt he saw in her eyes, but she quickly broke away, nodding towards the cluster of boulders the soldiers were protecting.

"In there," she said.

Movement came from the shadows and a second woman stepped out from behind a boulder. She held a globe of brilliant white in one hand, though there was no source of fire. Magic, like Erika's, he presumed. For the first time, he looked around, noticing the dome that enclosed the area before the boulders. Beyond, the soldiers still fought, but they looked indistinct now, as though viewed through a film.

Putting the connections together in his mind, he faced the newcomer.

"How are you doing that?" he asked.

The woman only raised an eyebrow. "Is that really what you want to talk about right now?"

Romaine shook his head, and stepping past him, Erika gestured into the boulders. "Come on, Maisie is hiding us, but she won't last much longer." She hesitated, looking over her shoulder. "And neither will they."

With that Erika slipped into the shadows. Casting a final glance at the Gemaho soldiers himself, Romaine followed. He felt a pang of guilt at abandoning them, but there was nothing he could do to save them.

The Archivist didn't ask how he'd come to be there. She had probably guessed he'd come with the Flumeerens. Nor did Romaine hurl accusations. There seemed little point when they might all be just minutes from death.

They didn't have to go far before Erika came to a stop again. Romaine froze as he saw the figure lying propped against a nearby boulder. Cara's auburn wings lay limp in the dust and her copper hair stood out in stark relief against her pallid skin. With each inhalation, her eyelids fluttered. She appeared to be unconscious, but as he took a step towards her, she spoke:

"Romaine…" Her voice was like sandpaper, and his name was followed by a soft groan, lines wrinkling her forehead. "I thought…I smelt you."

A sob tore from Romaine and in a second he was at her side, drawing her into a hug. "I thought I'd lost you," he murmured.

Pained laughter rasped from the Goddess. "How…?"

"We'll talk about it later, lass," Romaine murmured.

He'd never seen her like this, not even when he'd found

her injured and alone in Calafe, when the pain of her broken bones had caused her to pass out. Swallowing, he looked at Erika.

"What happened to her?"

Erika shook her head. "She was poisoned."

✺ 27 ✺

THE TANGATA

New Nihelm.

For some reason, Adonis was surprised to find himself looking down upon the city. When he'd left, a part of him had been convinced he would never return, that the Old Ones would slay him when they woke. Looking at Maya standing beside him, he could hardly remember why he'd feared such a thing.

Wearing the clothing of Adonis's fallen sister, Maya's slender figure was covered now, though he had come to know it in intimate detail this last week. She had invited him to lie with her their first night, pinning him to the stone. She seemed to delight in his weakness, in her power over his body...his mind.

He could feel her touch on his consciousness now, like the constant beating of a drum, though he could never quite make out the words she whispered. It no longer seemed important.

New Nihelm lay spread out beneath them, its lights glittering on the surrounding waters, waiting. It had taken them just a week to return. They had moved faster without his fallen brethren, and Adonis had found himself the slower of the pair. It did not bother him. He was only thankful she had chosen him.

Maya's long blonde hair swirled in the breeze as she turned to look on him, dark grey eyes aglow by the rising moon. *Your city reeks of humanity, Adonis.*

Adonis bowed his head. *Yes,* he replied deferentially, *we have spoken of the Tangata's weakness. We need them.*

No longer, Maya whispered, running a hand across his cheek. *Come, it is time your Matriarch and I spoke.*

Her gaze returned to the city and despite himself, Adonis shivered. Maya was everything the Matriarch had hoped for—powerful, intelligent, *sane.* An opportunity to sever themselves from the humans altogether.

Silently, he followed her down the hillside. The southern bridge beckoned and Maya strode across without hesitation, unchallenged. Only as they approached the island did two shadows appear to bar the way.

Who goes there?

The words seemed mere whispers in Adonis's mind after so many days spent with Maya. The Old One advanced on them, her stride unchecked by their warning, and Adonis hurried to catch her before blood was spilt.

Adonis, he called. He didn't recognise the guards, but they would know him. There weren't many of the third generation left now. *We have returned from the south.*

Confusion shone on the guards' faces as Maya finally drew to a stop before them. Their eyes flickered from her to Adonis.

Where are the others?

Adonis shook his head. *They were lost.*

How—

You guard these shores, child? Maya's voice interrupted, so strong each of the guards leapt back half a foot.

A long silence followed as they stood staring at the Old One. Understanding seemed to dawn in their eyes and they straightened, bowing their heads in respect.

Yes...Old One, the one who had been speaking replied.

Good, Maya rasped. Her gaze lifted to stare down the broad avenue that stretched across the island. *And there are others...to the north?* When the two nodded, she stepped closer, placing a hand on the first's chest. *Better. Go to your brethren in the north. Tell them that none may leave the city this night. Then return to your post.*

I... the Tangata's eyes flickered in Adonis's direction. He gave a slight nod, and the Tangata repeated the gesture to the Old One.

Releasing him, Maya stepped back. The guard seemed to take a moment to gather his composure, then he spun and started down the avenue, running with the long, bounding stride of the Tangata. Maya turned her gaze upon the second of the guards.

You know your duty, child? she whispered.

The Tangata nodded eagerly. Maya left him as he was and with Adonis they started down the avenue after the first of the guards, though they soon turned onto lesser streets. They made their way quickly through the moonlit avenues, over bridges and between the blossoming trees, making for the grand basilica the humans had raised to honour their so-called Gods.

The thought sparked an image in Adonis's mind and he saw again the Anahera as it soared towards him, wings flared, teeth bared. With the memory came anger. The Anahera could have aided the Tangata, could have stood alongside them against the disease that was humanity. Instead, they had sided with the enemy.

He shook his head. The Anahera would pay dearly for their betrayal, but that revenge would have to wait. The

creatures were too powerful—first the Tangata must regain
their strength.

The sound of voices came from some of the buildings
they passed, and at these Maya would pause, eyes shimmering in the lanternlight. Adonis could sense her anger,
that her descendants had fallen so low. But she never made
a move towards the revellers, and finally they neared to the
basilica.

Crossing the open plaza, they found the great doors of
the temple barred. Guards of the fourth generation stood to
either side, eyeing their approach, though they bowed their
heads in respect when they recognised Adonis.

We must see the Matriarch, he called to them. *Our greatest
hope has been realised.*

Grey eyes turned to inspect Maya. She said nothing
beneath their appraisal but met their gaze with a soft smile.
To Adonis's inner ears, it seemed the pounding in his skull
increased in notch. A flicker crossed the guards' faces.

Old One, they whispered, any hints of defiance evaporating beneath her piercing stare.

The Matriarch, Maya's voice all but thundered in the
silent square.

The guards leapt to obey, thrusting open the great doors
to admit them. Maya strode through, once again leaving
Adonis scrambling to keep up. The familiar darkness
greeted him within, though it made little difference to his
vision. An aged figure moved upon the dais as the Old One
strode across the chamber.

Adonis, my child, what have you brought me? The Matriarch
rasped into his mind as they came to a stop before the pool
that surrounded the upper dais. He was surprised at its soft-
ness—always before her voice had rung with power. Now it
seemed but a whisper beside the thundering of Maya's
words.

He fell to his knees all the same. *Matriarch,* he called, *I bring you Maya, of the Old Ones.*

Whispers spread through Adonis's mind as movement flickered at the edges of the chamber. Beside him, Maya said nothing, though her eyes flickered towards the unseen guards.

So it's true. Clothing rustled as the Matriarch leapt from the dais to land before them. She inclined her head to Maya. *Welcome to New Nihelm, Old One. You have no idea my joy at your emergence.*

Maya leaned her head to the side, regarding the Matriarch with those deep, dark eyes. *And how* did *you find my prison?*

The Matriarch smiled. *A human who came to us. He bore a map of the Birthing Grounds from which the Tangata sprung. Yours was the last.*

Silence answered the Matriarch's words as Maya paced. *And why did you seek me?*

Our people are dying, unable to produce offspring without a human partner, the Matriarch responded. *And so our powers fade with each generation. But if we were to merge our line with yours, we could begin to rebuild, to create a new generation of Tangata.*

Maya did not immediately reply to the Matriarch's words. Her gaze fell upon Adonis, still knelt upon the floor beside them. A frown touched her face.

Why does he kneel? she murmured, though even at a whisper her words had the strength to make the lesser generations flinch.

The lines on the Matriarch's face deepened as she frowned. *Kneel?* She glanced at Adonis, then gestured for him to rise. *It is a gesture of respect, Old One.*

I see. There was a long pause as she regarded the Matriarch. *Then...kneel.*

Shock registered on the Matriarch's face and even Adonis lifted his head in surprise.

I am the Matriarch. The response was slow in coming. *This is my city, the Tangata my people. I bow to no one.*

Cold grey eyes watched her for a long moment, then Maya smiled. *Of course.*

Turning away, she paced to the edge of the chamber where the guards stood watching. She started her way around the circumference of the chamber, eyes on the dark alcoves in which the Tangata hid. Adonis and the Matriarch watched as she disappeared behind the dais.

Such grandeur, Maya's words carried to their minds. *All of it, crafted by the strength of your Tangata?*

She reappeared, rounding the chamber, drawing the eyes of the guards. Doubt showed in the Matriarch's face as she watched the Old One's return.

Crafted by humanity, she admitted hesitantly as Maya returned to stand before her. *Taken from them as spoils of war. It will be the foundation on which we build our own civilisation.*

*Civilisation…*Maya seemed to roll the word in her mind as she appraised the Matriarch. *And…what of the humans who live amongst you?*

To Adonis, the Matriarch seemed to shrink before Maya's presence. *The assigned are carefully controlled.*

A frown touched Adonis's forehead and he stared at the leader that had guided the Tangata for so many decades. Her power, her cunning and strength of resolve had held his people together when the threat of humanity might otherwise have broken them. They owed her for that, honoured her for it, and yet…

…Adonis saw none of that strength now. Instead, a creature withered by age stood in place of the Matriarch, her will crushed by the endless warring, the relentless threat of the enemy. Where before there had been awe, now Adonis felt only disdain.

Controlled? Maya smiled and looked around the hall. To Adonis, it seemed her eyes fell upon every one of the guards. *Their stench is everywhere, even in this place that you claim as your seat of power.* Her eyes returned to the Matriarch. *I ask you, do you seek to defeat your enemy…or* become *them?*

A snarl crossed the Matriarch's lips and she stepped in close to Maya. Her eyes burned as they faced one another, and for a moment the strength of the Matriarch's voice matched that of the Old One.

Everything I have ever done was for the survival of my people!

Maya did not react to the words, though a flicker of movement went around the chamber as the Tangatan guards flinched at the force of her voice.

Survival? Adonis found himself replying, his voice taking on a bitter tone. *Is that what you call this? Living amongst the hovels of our enemy, forced into bondship with them, to breed with them?*

There was no choice! the Matriarch spat back. She turned her strength on him now, but bolstered by the rhythmic pounding of Maya in his mind, Adonis endured. Faced by his defiance, she seemed to wither and her voice took on a desperate tone. *Please, Adonis, my child, you were ever my champion.*

Adonis shuddered as he felt two minds pressing upon his consciousness. But in the end there was no contest. He stepped up to Maya's side.

He is your champion no longer, Maya replied.

The Matriarch retreated a step, her pale eyes taking on a panicked look. She swung around, searching the shadows, her movements betraying her desperation.

My children, guard yourselves! she cried to the guards hidden in the wings. *Before—*

One by one, the guards emerged from the shadows. Their eyes were focused not on the Matriarch, but Maya. Advancing until they stood in a circle around the three of them, the Tangata fell to their knees.

For a long moment the Matriarch stared at them, shoulders slumped, one hand extended as though to lift them back to their feet. Then slowly she faced Maya, and for the first time, fear registered in her eyes. Adonis watched on, impassive, as Maya laid a hand on the Matriarch's shoulder.

You have allowed humanity to claim this world, the Old One said softly, almost apologetically. *Allowed them to infect our own people, to bring the Tangata to the brink of extinction.*

A tremor shook the Matriarch and her pure white eyes fixed on Maya's face. A single tear slid down the lines of her cheek, but she did not retreat from the Old One's gaze.

It is you who will lead my children to extinction, Old One, she replied, her voice little more than a croak now.

A heavy silence hung over the chamber; and then Maya spoke: "Your time has come to an end, Matriarch."

With a sharp, jerking movement, she snapped the Matriarch's neck. The *crack* of breaking bones sounded like a klaxon in the empty basilica, so loud that even Adonis flinched. He watched as the light faded from her eyes, and felt an inexplicable thrill of terror. This was the leader who his people had followed for decades, who had led them to victory after victory against humanity. Without thinking, he took a step towards her.

But already she was falling, crumpling to the ground, lying still against the stones. Her pale eyes stared up at him and for a second, guilt clamped around his heart, stilling his breath.

Then he turned and found Maya watching him, and the feeling receded, replaced by the glory of victory. Maya smiled, then turned to his brother and sister Tangata.

Rise, my children. Her words lifted them back to their feet, reborn beneath the power of the Old Ones. *No longer will you go quietly to your destruction. Today, a new age dawns for the Tangata.*

What do you wish of us, Old One? the guards called back. There was desperation in their eyes. They were of the fourth generation, eager to please, subservient to one so far above them.

A smile crept across Maya's lips as she looked towards the doors, her grey eyes seeming to take in the city beyond.

Bring me the humans, she commanded. *It is time for a cleansing.*

❧ 28 ❧

THE SOLDIER

*B*ring me the humans, the Old One's mental voice carried from across the plaza. *It is time for a cleansing.*

Lukys's heart thundered in his ears as he listened to the words. At his urging, he and Sophia had tracked the pounding of the Old One's thoughts across the city. Even hidden in the shadows on the other side of the plaza from the basilica, they had easily heard her from within—though the others' voices had been fainter.

Now they stood beside the river and watched as silhouettes raced past—the Matriarch's guards, off to do their new master's bidding. Thankfully they did not look left or right as they disappeared into the streets of New Nihelm. Silence returned to the night. It would not last. Whatever safety he and his friends had found here, it was at an end.

His whole body trembling, he looked at Sophia. *What are we going to do?*

Run! she hissed.

There was fear in Sophia's eyes, bordering on panic. Lukys could hardly blame her. He had felt the Matriarch's power, her strength. And the Old One had slaughtered her, had claimed her guards, even Adonis, as her champions. The thought gave him pause and he wondered at the creature's power. But there was no time to linger.

I can't leave the others, Lukys replied, taking her hand in his. *Please, you have to help us, Sophia.*

Sophia's grey eyes were large in the moonlight, but after a moment, she nodded. In silence they turned and raced away, desperate to reach the compound before the Tangata did. As they ran, Lukys scanned the way ahead, fearful they would encounter the Matriarch's guards—but the streets remained dark, empty.

After several blocks, though, he began to hear sounds behind them. Doors slammed and masses of boots struck pavements as the city woke. A distant buzz touched his mind and he felt the tingle of annoyance broadcasted by the collective minds of the Tangata. The odd voice carried through the night as well. Lukys did not look back, though in his mind he pictured Tangata and their human partners forced from their houses, corralled into the streets.

Shame touched Lukys as he contemplated the fate of his fellow humans. But there was nothing he could do for them. It was already too late. He couldn't fight the Old One; he couldn't even fight the Tangata—at least not unarmed.

Sophia! he cried, his stride slowing. *We need weapons.*

His partner glanced over her shoulder, then drew to a stop. Concern showed on her face.

Lukys…

Please, Sophia, he insisted. *We don't stand a chance without them.*

Still Sophia hesitated. He could sense her doubt. What he asked was a betrayal of her people, to arm the very enemies they had waged war against for a decade. And yet…he had seen the Tangata's affection for their human partners. Looking at Sophia…Lukys thought he could almost understand his friends' decision, almost accept.

"We're not your enemies, Sophia," he whispered. He looked back then, eyes lifting to the spire of the basilica. "That thing…that thing is the enemy of all of us."

He looked back at Sophia, wanting to say more, but the words didn't come. Still, he was surprised to find a smile on her lips. She nodded.

This way. There's an old storage building close by, many of the weapons found in the city after its fall were placed there.

Weaving through unfamiliar streets, it took them only minutes to reach their new destination. Unlike most buildings in New Nihelm, this one was of stone, though thankfully the door was still wood. It gave way beneath a single blow from Sophia, unleashing a wave of dust and forcing Lukys to stifle a sneeze.

Pulling his shirt over his face, he moved with Sophia into the darkness. It took several long minutes before he found what he wanted—a bundle of spears tied together by twine. He took one from the pile and immediately his heart began to calm. It felt good to hold a weapon again, to feel like his fate was in his own hands again.

Unfortunately, there was no armour—and time was quickly evaporating. If the Tangatan guards arrived at the compound before they did, this would all be for nothing. He reached for the bundle, but Sophia was faster. Hefting the spears onto her shoulder as though they weighed no more than a sack of feathers, she nodded for the door.

Outside, he let her take the lead again, still unsure of himself in the dark streets of New Nihelm. The moon had shifted overhead, the night stretching on, and he swallowed. Even if they escaped the city, the Tangata would come for them. What then? They could not outrun these creatures.

Despair touched him, but he forced it down. One step at

a time. First, he needed to convince his companions that they must flee. After the comfortable weeks they'd spent in New Nihelm, even that task could prove difficult, even with Sophia's support.

They found the doors to the compound standing open, though where they'd left the courtyard empty, now dozens of tired faces stood around the tables. It was clear from their faces that they'd heard the sounds of alarm from elsewhere in the city.

"Lukys?" Frowning, Travis stepped up to greet him. "Where have you been?" The recruit's eyes were immediately drawn to the spear in Lukys's hands. "Where did you get *that?*"

Sister, several of the Tangata present spoke at the same time, moving toward Sophia. *Why is your human armed?*

Lukys and Sophia shared a glance. "The Matriarch is dead," Lukys said to them all. Whispers assailed his mind as the Tangata cried out, demanding answers, but he pressed them down and continued: "She was slain by an Old One. She calls herself Maya. Adonis is with her. The creature intends to rule over the Tangata." His eyes slid to Travis and the others. "And cleanse the humans from amongst them."

Silence fell suddenly over the group and Lukys nodded, gesturing to Sophia. "Quickly, take a spear and gather supplies for the road. We need to be gone before the creature's followers reach us…" He trailed off as he saw the group was no longer watching him.

Their eyes were on the gate to the compound. His stomach twisted as a voice whispered into his mind.

My dear human, Adonis said softly. *I hope you aren't trying to leave us. Maya was so looking forward to meeting you. There is so much you could tell us of our enemies.*

Heart hammering in his chest, Lukys turned to face the Tangata. Adonis stood in the entrance to the compound, arms clasped behind his back. His eyes narrowed as he stepped into the courtyard, taking in the gathered recruits and their Tangatan partners, before settling on Lukys and Sophia. A tightness crossed Adonis's face as he saw the spear in Lukys's hands.

Sister, he murmured, turning to Sophia. *Have you betrayed us?*

Sophia wilted beneath that terrible gaze. *I—*

Adonis surged forward before she could finish speaking, his hand flashing out, catching her by the throat. A cry sounded in Lukys's mind and he raised his spear, but a back-handed blow from Adonis sent him staggering backwards. A silence settled over the courtyard as the others shrank back from the Tangata's rage.

Teeth bared, Adonis lifted Sophia into the air. *You would betray your own kind for these...these swine?*

Terror swept over Lukys as he watched his partner struggling to break Adonis's grip, but she was as helpless in his grasp as any human would be. Her mouth opened and closed, gasping for breath, but no sound came out. With a sneer of contempt, Adonis tossed her aside, sending her crashing into one of the tables. The heavy wood cracked beneath the impact and she slumped amongst the ruins, unmoving.

"No!" Lukys screamed.

Smiling, Adonis faced him. Their eyes met and Lukys froze. Death reflected from those icy depths, its promise pounding against his mind, assaulting his consciousness. A gasp escaped his throat but words, thought, abandoned him. Tears burned in his eyes as he sank to his knees, but still he could not look away, not even to seek out where Sophia had fallen. Whispers of movement came from around the court-yard as the others followed, Tangata and human alike.

Brothers, sisters, Adonis called, arms spread as he turned those terrible eyes on the Tangata. *The Old Ones have returned. They have cast down our tyrannous Matriarch. No longer will we bow to humanity, allowing them to live among us as equals.*

Out from under his direct gaze, Lukys felt as though he could breathe again. His heart pounded in his ears as he watched the Tangatan leader. Anger touched him, but it was like a spark amongst damp tinder, unable to catch. How could he go up against this creature if even Sophia could not match him? He was like a fly, trapped in the spider's web. Nowhere to hide, nowhere to run; he could only wait for death to finally find him...

His gaze travelled to the other Tangata. They bowed their heads to Adonis's words. The spark in his core flickered, burning brighter. How could they kneel there and accept the death of their leader so easily? How could they sit and do nothing when this creature would condemn their human partners to death? Had Lukys only imagined the fondness he'd seen in their eyes, the love?

Then he frowned as he noticed how Travis and Isabella held hands as they knelt. Tears shone on the Tangata's face. Looking past them, he saw the same grief in the eyes of others. He ground his teeth. Why did they not act? There were a dozen of them—surely Adonis could not defeat so many at once, whatever his generational advantages...

Lukys's frown deepened as the despair swelled once again. What did it matter if they fought? They were doomed regardless. They would never escape the city now, never make it to safety, make it home...

The thought trailed away as Lukys's gaze settled on his spear tip. In that moment, he was transported back to that desperate battle beside the Illmoor. He had been terrified then as well. There'd been no denying the death that awaited them, no escaping it. And yet he had stood strong and faced the Tangata with courage. He had not lost heart then.

So why would he now?

His head lifted as the pieces of the puzzle clicked into place. Movement came from the corner of his eyes. His heart throbbed as he saw Sophia on her knees. Blood streaked a trail from her lip and a bruise swelled on her forehead, but she was alive.

Hope.

Lukys clutched at the thought as he fixed his gaze on Adonis. Here was the reason the other Tangata did not act. Somehow, Adonis controlled them, controlled his despair. He had noticed Sophia now and his laughter whispered on the breeze.

Still alive then, sister?

You can't do this, she whispered, seemingly unable to regain her feet. *It's forbidden.*

Forbidden by your treacherous Matriarch. Adonis shook his head, sweeping a hand across those gathered in the courtyard. *But no longer. All will have a part to play in the coming conquest, but no longer will we constrain ourselves on behalf of the weak. A new age dawns for the Tangata, one ruled by the strong!*

Lukys's heart was pounding so hard against his ribs he feared it might explode. The fear returned as Adonis turned on him once more, but now he knew its source. Closing his eyes, he endured, clinging to that memory beside the Illmoor, to the feel of the spear in his hands, to the presence of his friends at his side, to the sight of Cara soaring across the swirling waters.

"Adonis," he found himself saying.

Silence fell across the courtyard and opening his eyes, he found the Tangata watching him. His breath caught in his throat and for a moment he could not think, could do nothing but stare into those deadly eyes.

Hope.

Lukys swallowed. "You said the Old One wants me?" he rasped. A frown twisted the Tangata's features. When he did not reply, Lukys continued: "I will…go freely," he choked out. "If you spare them."

Lukys, no! Sophia's voice shouted in his mind. Sobbing, she tried to stand, but could not seem to gather her feet.

Adonis laughed. *You think you have a choice, human?*

The cold eyes bored into Lukys and he gasped as his entire body began to tremble. The spear slipped from his fingers, clattering to the cobbles. Desperately, he tried to stand, but wave upon wave of emotion broke upon him, of desolation, of anguish, cast at him by the creature he faced. His gaze fell to the bricks beneath his knees.

Hope.

Footsteps approached, soft in the darkness. *No, human, your weakness betrays you, betrays all your kind. Betrays even our lesser generation. No wonder so many of the fifth fell to your blade. No wonder they wilted before the Anahera. But no longer.*

Lukys gasped, hardly able to breathe, to think. All he could hear were the words, that pounding in his skull, the awful doom approaching on soft feet. He could not fight this thing, could not endure. He could only fall.

Hope.

With Maya, we will forge a new world. The Tangata will be restored in all their glory. None can prevent it, not humanity, not even the Anahera.

The footsteps stopped beside him and Lukys looked up. A silhouette towered overhead, blacking out the stars, the moon—though beyond he could see Sophia struggling, arm outstretched, a desperate grief in her eyes.

Hope.

Lukys met Adonis's steely gaze.

Are you ready to meet your doom, human?

His fingers closed around the wooden haft lying beside him.

"My name is Lukys," he hissed.

Adonis's eyes widened as the spear tip slammed into his chest. His hands came up, but Lukys did not relent, driving the blade deeper, screaming his rage, until the point burst from his enemy's back. A growl came from Adonis's throat and the terrible eyes fixed on Lukys, but skewered by the spear, they no longer seemed to hold any power.

A cry bubbling from his throat, Adonis stumbled back, tearing the weapon from Lukys's hands. Gasping, he clutched at the spear, fingers curling around the wooden haft. Another scream echoed through the courtyard as he began to pull.

Heart pounding in his chest, Lukys watched as the Tangata drew the bloody spear from his body and tossed it aside. Grey eyes fixed again on Lukys, but as Adonis took a step, his knees buckled and he crumpled face-first to the cobbles.

A groan slipped from Lukys's lips as he looked at the fallen Tangata. His own legs shook as he tried to take a step. A wave of exhaustion swept over him then, and suddenly he found himself slumped against the bricks. Whispers came from the others and a moment later a hand touched his shoulder.

Lukys.

He flinched away from the voice, looking up to find the bruised and battered Sophia crouching beside him. His insides twisted as he looked into her eyes. How could such honest eyes have lied so easily? All this time, she'd hidden the true secret of the Tangata, of the power they possessed. The power that Adonis had used so easily to subdue them.

She reached for him again, but he shrank away, and a

frown creased her purpled forehead. "Lukys, what's wrong?"

Tears burned in his eyes as he looked at her, seeing her pain, and a lump lodged in his throat. He swallowed it down, forcing himself to speak the words.

"Stay away from me."

❧ 29 ❧

THE FUGITIVE

"There was a spy," Erika said.

"He was a pawn," Romaine replied. The Calafe was still crouched beside Cara. "The queen had his family abducted, forced him to leave markers for us to follow you. Where is he?"

Erika's heart twisted and she looked away, her eyes falling to the soft glow of the gauntlet. "Dead," she whispered. He'd passed before they could drag him into the shelter of the rocks, succumbing to whatever internal damage her magic had done.

Romaine cursed, but Maisie spoke before he could reprimand them. "He didn't know what kind of poison it was anyway."

"Didn't you hear me?" Romaine snapped. "He didn't want to be here."

"None of us *want* to be here, Calafe," Maisie replied coolly. "But we each made our choices."

Romaine fell silent at the Gemaho's words and Erika did not miss the grimace that touched the warrior's face. She glanced towards the sounds of fighting. The men that had attacked might not be wearing Flumeeren colours, but the archer who led them had been with Amina back at the Illmoor Fortress. The same man she'd found so familiar, though she still could not remember from where.

"Can't you stop them with your magic?" Romaine asked from the ground.

Erika shook herself from her stupor and scowled. "Oh yes, I hadn't thought of that," she hissed. The anger left her as quickly as it had come. "I've done what I can, using Maisie's magic to hide me, but your *friend* with the crossbow figured us out." She lifted a hand to the bandage Maisie had wrapped around her arm. Thankfully, the arrow had only grazed her.

"Then what's the plan?" the warrior growled.

Erika and Maisie exchanged a glance, before looking back at the warrior. "The city of the Gods is close, we think," Erika whispered, gesturing at Cara. "If anyone can save her, surely it's her people."

Romaine was silent for a moment. "What about those men out there?"

"I can conceal us long enough to get away," Maisie replied.

"I wasn't talking about Yasin's men," Romaine said, glaring at the spy.

Maisie sighed. "We cannot save them, Calafe. At least they will die knowing they were protecting a Goddess. Maybe that will give them some comfort."

"I'm sure they'd prefer not to die at all," the Calafe snapped, but Erika could see the defeat in his eyes.

Silently, she looked Romaine up and down, noting the bruises on his face, the wounds and his missing hand. He'd fought well against the Flumeerens, but…

"Can you carry Cara?" she asked softly. "She's…heavier than she looks."

"I heard that," muttered Cara. But even as Erika smiled, the whisper turned to a moan and she coughed, sending blood splattering across the rocks.

Romaine nodded, but he hesitated as he reached for the Goddess. "Can you…do something about your wings, Cara?" he asked. "I don't want to damage them."

The Goddess didn't reply, but her face tightened, and the auburn wings contracted slightly. She only managed to half fold them before her strength gave out.

Erika swallowed, tears springing to her eyes at the sight of Cara in such pain. She moved alongside Romaine and they shared a look. Something passed between them, and together they rolled the Goddess onto her side.

It was the first time Erika had taken a closer look at her wings. They sprouted from either side of Cara's spine, though lower on her back than she'd thought, stretching upwards then folding back down to allow them to fold flat. At some point Cara had cut an extra hole in her shirt, almost like a third sleeve, to allow them freedom.

"Her jacket," Romaine grunted.

Erika nodded. Her jacket could cover her wings and hold them in place while they carried her. She looked to Maisie, and taking a breath, the woman vanished. Erika hadn't even realised she'd let the illusion drop, though it made sense. Amongst the boulders they couldn't be seen from the outside, and the Gemaho spy needed to conserve her strength.

Romaine still crouched beside her, but neither spoke as they waited, their eyes on the way leading back to the battle. The clash of distant weapons and the screams of the dying filled the silence, and Erika wondered how much time they had now. Without her magic, how much longer could the brave men and women of Gemaho last?

The thought made her shiver and her eyes fell again to

the gauntlet. It had felt good to use its power again, to strike down men who came to kill her. And yet…she shuddered as she recalled the young man groaning at her feet. He'd betrayed them, had left breadcrumbs for the queen's soldiers to follow, had poisoned Cara.

Now Romaine claimed that he'd only done it all to save his family.

She clenched her fist, watching as the light of her gauntlet pulsed. Had he truly deserved death? A shudder ran through her, but before she could consider the matter further, Maisie sprung from empty air beside them. Romaine flinched but Maisie only tossed them the jacket.

"Quickly," she hissed. "Nguyen's soldiers won't last much longer."

Erika nodded, and as Romaine held Cara on her side, she carefully folded the auburn wings tighter against the Anahera's back. Cara whimpered at the movement, a trickle of blood running from her mouth, but she no longer spoke. Surely it was sacrilege to touch such talismans of the Divine, but Erika had already done much worse. If the Gods intended to condemn her, this would be the least of her crimes. With Romaine's help, she managed to get Cara's arms into the jacket, covering the wings and holding them in place.

Then she looked at the Calafe. "Can you do this?"

Romaine only grunted. Sheathing his sword, he scooped his one good hand around Cara and hefted her onto his shoulder. When they were sure the Goddess was secure, Erika drew in a breath and raised her gauntlet. She no longer trusted its power, but there was no choice now. They would need every advantage they had to survive what was to come.

She turned to Maisie. "You ready?"

The woman nodded grimly and raised her sphere,

unleashing a flash of brilliance. A moment later they were cast into that odd light again, the outside reduced to a shimmering other world.

"Stay close," Maisie said as she turned towards the battle. "The area of influence needs to be small if we're to sneak past the soldiers."

Together they crept back towards the battle. Light shone through from the outside, but it seemed unnatural, changed by whatever magic Maisie's talisman cast. Ahead, they could see the soldiers that had travelled with them all this way.

Suddenly, Erika was struck by a terrible sense of déjà vu. She staggered, and the others glanced at her. She ignored them, a moan building in her throat. There were less than ten of the Gemaho left now. So many dead. As she watched, another fell, his head almost severed from his shoulders by the vicious swing of an enemy axe. The others retreated another step, seeking to plug the gap left by his death, but the Flumeeren men continued to press forward.

She scrunched her eyes closed, overwhelmed. It was happening again—innocent men dying because of her folly. She shuddered, faces running through her mind, of the men and women she had failed, too many to name.

The last was a face she had tried hard to forget, to push from her mind, his loss too painful to remember. Her father, the man that had raised Erika to be a princess, who had shielded her from the evils of the world, who had protected her. If only she could have protected him in return.

"*Erika!*" Romaine's voice cut through her pain. Their eyes met and understanding passed between them. "You can't save them," the Calafe said softly. "But you can still save *her*."

She nodded, forcing her grief to the side. Space had appeared to either side of the defenders now, but the enemy had been enraged by their defiance, and rather than seeking to encircle the Gemaho soldiers, they continued to attack from the front, determined to destroy them.

But this also created space for Erika and the others to escape. Staying close to Maisie, they snuck past the battling soldiers. Erika felt a coward, watching those brave souls fight to the death while she fled. But then, wasn't that what she had always been, ever since that day she and her mother had fled Flumeer?

A coward.

Never again.

Clearing the line of soldiers, they started away from the battle. Looking back, Erika was shocked by the toll the Gemaho had taken on their attackers. Half the Flumeeren number had fallen, and while only a handful of Gemaho fought on, the battle had been far closer than she'd thought. Even the Flumeeren archer seemed to have disappeared. Maybe if they'd stayed…

Another Gemaho soldier fell, run through by a long sword. His comrades tried to retreat, but the Flumeeren men fell upon them, forcing them back against the boulders, though not before yet another died screaming.

Quickly Erika looked away. It was over. The remaining few might fight on a little longer, but there would be no victory. Erika could only hope the Flumeerens would be unable to track them, now they'd lost their spy. She hurried after Romaine, heading up the slope, up the narrow canyon, and prayed it led to salvation.

Slowly the canyon twisted away from the campsite, hiding them from sight of the soldiers below. There was a soft *pop* as Maisie released the magic, and the globe that had covered them vanished. Suddenly the sun was shining full upon them. The return of its heat was so shocking that Erika swung around, half-expecting a fresh wave of soldiers to fall upon them. There was no one, though. Hopefully their pursuers would take a long time to figure out how they'd escaped.

Facing ahead again, Erika found Maisie slumped on her hands and knees. The spy's face was pale as she looked at them.

"Might have...pushed myself a little too far," she murmured, looking down the valley. "Think I bought you enough time."

Anger touched Erika as she saw the defeat in the woman's eyes. She strode forward, stones crunching beneath her boots. "Get up," she snapped.

Maisie shook her head. "Don't have the—"

She broke off as Erika slapped her across the face. "No," she said, then offered her hand. "We're going on together, got it?"

The spy's eyes had widened at the blow and now she stared up at Erika, as though not quite sure what to do.

"I'd do what she says," Romaine grunted from beside them. "She's a princess, after all—used to getting what she wants."

Maisie looked at the Calafe, still looking dazed, but finally she took Erika's offered hand and allowed herself to be pulled back to her feet. Looping the woman's arm across her shoulder, Erika took some of her weight, then nodded her thanks to Romaine.

The warrior said nothing, only started up the slope once more, Cara still hung across his back. The Goddess's eyes remained closed, and her face was grey as death. Erika's heart twisted at the sight. Would they make it in time? Could Cara's people even help with her ailment?

Of course they can, they're Gods!

But there was a voice whispering to her, her Archivist's mind, asking if that was really true. Being weak to magic or the Tangata was one thing—both came from the Gods. But poison? She looked at Cara again, heart twisting, stomach in knots. Surely a God should be immune to something as benign as poison?

She thrust the thought away. It did her no good now, not while danger still lurked, while they were still so far from help or rescue. One thing was without doubt—Cara's people *were* out here. Gods or no, they would help Cara. They would protect them from the queen's soldiers.

If they let you in…

Erika cursed and started after Romaine, dragging Maisie with her. They continued up the gorge, though its walls grew narrower with each bend in its winding depths. Erika began to wonder if they'd chosen the wrong path after all—if the canyon did not open out soon, they risked striking a dead end. Yet the ground was still lifting beneath their feet, and looking around she thought that the cliffs looked shorter. Or perhaps that was just hopeful thinking. There was no going back now.

After a time Maisie seemed to recover some of her strength and was able to walk unaided—much to Erika's relief. Romaine, on the other hand, lagged farther and farther behind, struggling with his burden. Erika wished she could aid him, but there was nothing either of them could do besides rely on the big Calafe's strength—they'd already tried.

Eventually though, Erika saw that she'd been right. The cliffs were shortening as they climbed, until finally they were barely twice their height. In places they might have even climbed free. They were so close now, Erika could sense it, could almost feel the secret calling to her, waiting to be uncovered. The city of the Gods was here somewhere.

The crunch of footsteps from ahead suddenly ceased and Erika looked up, surprised that Maisie had come to a halt. Then she realised the spy had stopped because the mountain had come to an end. While the cliffs still rose to either side of them, the slope beyond Maisie vanished, starting back down into a fresh valley. Could this be it?

Blood pounded in Erika's ears as she staggered towards the spy. Maisie hadn't said a word, but her eyes were fixed on the land beyond, as though…as though there was something *there!*

Romaine reached the crest a second before Erika, but he too remained silent, only came to a stop, eyes fixed on the unknown beyond. Erika scrambled her way up the last few feet and straightened at the top. Holding her breath, she looked down at the valley beyond…

And frowned.

An empty scree slope stretched away beyond them, down into a broad valley between the icy peaks. But that was not what the others were looking at. There in the centre of the valley, a squat, square building rose from the barren mountainside. Shaped of the same smooth grey rock she'd encountered in other sacred sites, it was massive, ringing a large yard in its centre. But other than its size, it seemed so…plain.

Erika didn't know what she'd been expecting from this sacred place hidden away in the forbidden Mountains of the Gods, but the structure below certainly hadn't been it.

"Welcome to my home." Cara's voice was bitter as she laughed into Romaine's shoulder.

Erika turned to the Goddess, but a movement from across the slope drew her attention instead. Stones came crashing down from above, then a dark figure dropped from the cliff, striking the ground with a crash. The man straightened, a smile on his lips, crossbow pointed at Erika's chest.

"If you'd be so good as to lower the gauntlet, Archivist," the man said, "I think it's about time we had a little chat."

30

THE SOLDIER

Racing through the streets of New Nihelm, Lukys wondered how he could have ever been so blind. The others ran around him, Tangata loping along in stride with their human partners. Travis, Dale, all the others, they didn't know, couldn't see.

But then, how could they?

The Tangata were playing with their minds.

His stomach twisted as memories flickered before his eyes—of the Matriarch towering over him, drawing the map from his mind; of Sophia's daily visits, the slow whittling down of his will. No wonder his friends had given in so quickly. They couldn't distinguish the creatures' whispers from their own thoughts, couldn't resist as he had.

They had been brainwashed, their minds manipulated until they thought they loved the creatures who ran alongside them.

How could he not have seen it sooner?

Grinding his teeth, Lukys forced his mind to the task at hand. Sophia's betrayal would have to wait—now he needed to concentrate on escaping the city. Ahead, the others had slowed as they approached a corner. Beyond, lanterns lit the main avenue across the city. So far they had kept to backroads, avoiding the whispers of Tangata and humans heading through the city, making for the basilica. Guilt touched Lukys as he thought of his fellow humans, prisoner to their Tangatan partners, being led to their deaths. There was nothing he could do for those poor souls.

But he might yet save his friends.

If they'd reached the main avenue, they must be near the bridge. He slunk forward, ignoring Sophia as he passed her and coming to a stop just before the corner where Travis stood waiting.

"Guards," the recruit hissed.

Lukys cursed. They were at the southern edge of the city. He'd thought they might outthink the Tangata's new leader by taking the least likely escape route, but apparently the Old One was taking no chances in letting anyone out of the city. He leaned out for a glimpse of his own and spotted the two guards watching the entrance to the bridge.

There was no way their group of thirty-odd humans and Tangata were leaving unnoticed. They might have fought their way past, but the noise would attract attention and point their eventual pursuers in the direction they'd taken. They needed to escape without anyone knowing which way they had gone.

Dozens of eyes watched him as he glanced back, some frightened, others simply confused. The Perfugian recruits had gathered what food and clothing they could from the compound and now carried them in bundles they'd made of sheets from their apartments. With spring beginning, Lukys hoped they could scavenge more on the road, or perhaps bring down a deer with one of their spears, but first they had to escape.

His gaze switched to the unreadable eyes of the

Tangata. A shudder ran down his spine and he wondered how he could have ever come to trust these creatures. He didn't want them with him, but there'd been no choice, not with the others still convinced of their love for their Tangatan partners.

"What now?" Dale asked, creeping forward.

He held his spear tight in one hand. Most of the recruits were similarly armed, and Lukys was momentarily tempted to cast caution aside and rush the bridge. Night was passing quickly and it was only a matter of time before Adonis's body was found. Then the pursuit would begin in earnest. They needed to be a long way from New Nihelm by then.

Lukys pushed down the temptation to attack. The others were looking at him to save them. How quickly he had become their leader again. He couldn't let them down now.

There were only two ways out of the city, two bridges. If there were guards here, there would be others at the northern bridge. There had to be another way.

Could they swim? The river was broad and the current swift, but coming from an island nation, Perfugians were decent swimmers—and used to the cold. It would be dangerous in the darkness. He eyed the others, wondering if anyone had ideas to offer. Instead, he glimpsed Sophia moving towards him.

"We swim," he said quickly. He looked at Travis but the recruit only raised an eyebrow. Lukys sighed. "We need somewhere we can enter the water without being seen."

Travis only raised an eyebrow.

"Trust me," Lukys said.

I know a place, Sophia offered, coming to a stop beside them.

A bolt of rage struck Lukys as he looked at her. Their dance, their kiss…they seemed a million years ago already, a lifetime. Silently he pushed his anger down. At least she could be trusted to help them escape. After Adonis's death, none of these Tangata had a place in New Nihelm any longer. He gave her a curt nod.

There was no missing the hurt in Sophia's eyes as she looked at him. Lukys still hadn't told her he knew. How would she react? Would she try to control him again, to manipulate him, to wash away his doubts with her power?

"Show us," he said shortly.

Sophia's jaw tightened and without a word she turned away, striding back the way they had come. Lukys gestured for his friends to follow her, even as he felt a flare of distrust. He pushed it down. She and the others had tried to fight Adonis; they could at least be trusted this far. Couldn't they?

They retreated several blocks before cutting into an alleyway leading back towards the river. Lukys frowned as he realised they were upriver of the bridge. There was no way they could fight the current. That meant they would be washed straight back to where the guards were waiting…

…except the guards weren't watching the water. An idea started to form in his head.

The place Sophia knew turned out to have been an old waterfront restaurant. By the polished mahogany furnishings and crystal chandeliers, Lukys thought it had probably been an expensive place to eat once, frequented by the wealthy of Calafe society. Apparently, the Tangata hadn't been so easily impressed, for a thick layer of dust now covered every surface.

Sophia led them through a room stacked with dining tables waiting for patrons that would never return, to where a small jetty stretched out into the river. Lukys was relieved to see the nearby buildings were dark, leaving the river to reflect the faint glint of moonlight.

Boards creaked as Dale stepped onto the jetty. He froze, but no movement came from the surrounding buildings, and they were a good quarter mile upriver from the bridge now. Not even Tangatan guards would hear the noise from such a distance.

Beneath the planks, the dark waters of the Shelman River swept past, shimmering in the starlight. Lukys glanced back at the others, wondering how they would cope with such a crossing. There was no way any of them could fight the current, but if his plan worked, that wouldn't matter.

Exhaling, he looked out across the river, but even by the light of the half moon, he could barely see beyond the jetty. In those currents, there would be no knowing whether they were making progress. They could be ten feet from the other side and not know it until their feet struck rock. And the icy waters would quickly drain their strength. It would be a dangerous crossing, even for the best of swimmers.

Hopefully they wouldn't need to swim the entire crossing.

"We're going to use the bridge," he said, his words carrying in the silence of the night. "Once you're in the water, kick out as far as you can, but don't fight the current. Eventually the river will carry you beneath the bridge. When that happens, grab for the support pillars. Use them to cross the rest of the way. Hopefully we'll be far enough out into the river that the guards won't hear us.

The Perfugians stared back at him, fear shining in their eyes. He cursed inwardly, suddenly doubting himself. Could they do this? Surely there was another way to escape, some plan that didn't risk them all perishing in the icy waters…

Travis stepped forward and clapped Lukys on the shoulder. "Let's do it."

Moving past Lukys, he took hold of a ladder at the end of the jetty and slid over the side. Isabella followed him, her eyes catching Lukys's. He suppressed a shudder, but said nothing. The Tangata were powerful swimmers, capable of crossing even the broad expanse of the Illmoor. Perhaps they could help their partners survive what was to come.

"Hurry The Fall up." Travis's voice came from below. "The water's bloody freezing."

"Go," Lukys whispered. "Wait for us on the other side."

His words seemed to break some spell that had been cast over the rest of the recruits. Dale followed and one by one they stepped past him, jaws clenched, eyes fixed on that distant, invisible shore. Freedom. Finally only Lukys stood on the jetty—until a figure stepped from the shadows, and he realised Sophia had not yet entered the water. A lump lodged in his throat as the Tangata approached.

Lukys, she whispered. He tried to turn away, but she caught him by the arm. *Lukys, please, what's wrong?*

He looked at her and saw the pain in those pure grey eyes, the fear. He swallowed, seeing again their dance, the soft music whispering in his ears, their kiss. His heart throbbed and he could almost taste her lips, feel her breath against his cheek…

His stomach twisted as another image came to him, of Adonis towering over them, his mind crushing them down. Anger returned and he tore his arm loose.

"You know," he spat.

Her eyes slid closed and he could see the truth on her face, so much more open than the other Tangata, as though she could not help but reveal her true emotions to him. He ground his teeth, fists clenched, wishing…for what?

I can explain, she whispered, reaching out an arm.

He stepped back. "Explain what, Sophia?" he asked, voice bitter. "That you've been manipulating us all along, controlling us? Is that what you can explain?"

No! she cried, a tear streaking her cheek. *That's not how it works, not how we use our Voices!*

"No?" Lukys growled. "Are you telling me you and your

brethren were *happy* to bow to him, to allow him to murder us?"

I… Sophia trailed off, her eyes wide. Then she hung her head, and Lukys sensed shame rolling off her. *What Adonis did, feeding our despair, using our fears to subdue us, it was forbidden.*

And yet each of you has done the same to us.

We haven't, Sophia hissed, matching his gaze now. *At least, not as he did. We can only…encourage what is already there—trust, appreciation, happiness, joy. That is why not all assignments are…successful.*

Encourage? Lukys asked. He looked away. *And what have you encouraged in me?*

Nothing, Sophia murmured. She stepped towards him, placing her hand on his arm again. He shuddered, but this time he did not pull away. *Don't you see, Lukys? Your Voice, it's… stronger than mine. That was why you could resist Adonis, why the humans follow you. I could never have encouraged you, nor manipulated you as you claim. I could only wait for you to see me as I truly am—rather than the monsters from your history books.*

Lukys's heart throbbed at her words, and yet…how could he believe them? After everything she had lied about, everything the Tangata had concealed from them, the trust was gone. He looked at her, at the woman he had spent so much time with these last weeks, and felt only a coldness in his core.

And the others? Lukys asked, his inner voice bitter.

Sophia shook her head. *What they feel is real, Lukys,* the Tangata replied. *Their partners only helped them see the truth… faster. Please, Lukys…you have to see—*

"No," Lukys whispered. He swallowed, glancing back at her. "I don't. I'm sorry, Sophia. You're right, I can see you're not the monsters we thought. But…this is wrong. I can't trust you."

With that he turned and stepped to the edge of the

dock. The dark waters rushed past below, silent, the others disappeared into the night. He let out a long breath, blood thundering in his ears, and fought the urge to turn back, to embrace the warmth he had found in this strange city. Clenching his fists, he leapt.

And plunged into the icy depths.

31

THE FALLEN

Romaine froze as Yasin's voice whispered across the pass. Cara weighed heavily on his shoulders and exhaustion had wormed its way deep into his soul. His legs ached from the ascent and his head was pounding. He was at the end of his endurance, but he turned to face the man who had tried to kill him.

Wearing a smug grin, the Flumeeren pointed his crossbow at Erika. He was obviously well aware of the powers contained in her gauntlet.

"Take it off," Yasin growled, his finger wrapped around the trigger. "Now, like old Nguyen did before."

Breath held, Romaine glanced at Erika. He had seen her down Tangata from as far away as Yasin stood from her. She could do it now—if she had the courage. It was almost certain that Yasin would be able to fire before the magic incapacitated him, but at least then he and Maisie would have a chance to stop the queen's man.

No, even without the crossbow, he's more than my match.

Romaine's shoulders fell as he realised they would all die here. Erika must have known it as well, for she reached up and pressed her thumb to the gauntlet around her wrist. There was a soft *hiss* as the relic released, before it dropped to the ground with a gentle ring of metal chains.

"Good, good," the rogue laughed. His beady eyes turned on Romaine. "Why don't you put the Goddess down now, Calafe? I'm sure the burden couldn't have been easy, carrying her all this way."

The hairs on Romaine's neck stood on end as he stared Yasin down. In his mind, he saw again and again the image of Lorene falling, crossbow bolt in his chest. He clenched his fist, straining for something—anything—that might allow him to fight back. But there was nothing.

Cara whimpered as he lowered her slowly to the stones. Then he rose and stepped in front of her.

"Why are you doing this?" he growled.

"Why, *I* haven't done anything." Yasin laughed and spread his hands. Romaine tensed as the bow was lowered, but on the uneven slope he would never reach the man fast enough. "It was the villainous Gemaho who kidnapped the daughter of the Gods. The noble queen of Flumeer tried to save her, but alas, we only arrived in time to take vengeance."

Romaine bared his teeth. "I won't let you harm her."

"Yasin…" A murmur from Erika drew their attention. She still stood beside her fallen gauntlet, but now her eyes narrowed as she stared at the man. "Why do I know that name?"

"You can't stop me, Calafe," Yasin continued, ignoring the Archivist. "I do as Amina commands. I'm sure you would have done the same for your king, if the fool hadn't gotten himself killed."

A sharp intake of breath came from Erika, but this time Yasin kept his attention fixed on Romaine. The man seemed to have decided he was the most dangerous of the three. If only he knew how Romaine's entire body ached, he might have reconsidered.

"You're one of Amina's spies," Maisie said. Stones shifted as she moved to the side, as though trying to divert his attention.

Yasin laughed at that. "Spy, soldier, cutthroat." He shrugged. "I have the honour of being whatever my queen requires of me." He flicked a knowing glance at the woman. "I hear you have some experience in that regard…it's Maisie, no?"

Maisie sneered. "You're little more than a common thug, Yasin."

"No, no, no," Erika staggered forward a step, breaking into the conversation. She pointed an accusing finger at Yasin. "I *know* you!"

The smile slipped from the cutthroat's face. "Ah, so you finally recognise me, Princess."

"You were a friend of my father."

"For a learned woman, you took a long time to make that connection." Yasin smirked. "I guess gullibility runs in the family."

Romaine's blood ran cold at the man's words. "What is he saying?" he asked, looking from Yasin to Erika in disbelief.

She shook her head. "It's not possible," she whispered. "You…you rode south with him. You're…dead!"

"Ay." Yasin turned the crossbow on Erika. "Now I can see the resemblance. That open-mouth surprise, that disbelief. Your father looked much the same when I drove my blade through his chest."

"*No!*" Erika screamed.

A ringing sounded in Romaine's ears as he stared at Yasin, trying to understand, to pry meaning from his words. He had killed Erika's father, the Calafe king. *His king.* But that wasn't possible. King Micah had ridden south with the allied armies, to destroy the threat of the Tangata once and for all. It had been the beasts that had slain him…

…but then why would the queen's own cutthroat have been friends to the Calafe king? Not unless…

"She betrayed us," Romaine whispered, but Erika drowned out his words.

"*You killed my father!*" Erika screamed. She started towards the killer, but Yasin lifted the crossbow and she froze.

"Now, now, Princess." He tisked. "I'd rather not have to kill you. The queen was rather excited by the prospect of welcoming you back to her court."

Fists clenched, Erika's entire body was trembling. "Why?" she hissed.

The rogue raised an eyebrow. "Why? Why else?" he asked, looking from the Archivist to Romaine. "Calafe lies shattered, Gemaho grasps at empty straws for its survival, and Perfugia withdraws more and more from the workings of the continent. Meanwhile, Flumeer is resurgent. All because of that disastrous campaign."

"But the Tangata," Romaine growled, clenching his fist. In that moment he wanted nothing more than to reach out and throttle the man. "Surely the queen couldn't have thought…" He trailed off, unable to complete the sentence.

"The thoughts of the lion rarely make sense to the sheep," Yasin replied. "Who would think the death of a king could lead to the fall of his nation. Yet here we are."

"She cannot hope to fight the Tangata alone."

Yasin's face hardened. "The beasts are cursed by the Gods. They are destined for extinction." There was a coldness to his eyes as he glanced at Maisie. "As are the Gemaho, when the Gods learn of the depravity that took place here."

The three of them fell silent, staring into the eyes of the

killer. Then to Romaine's surprise, stones crunched behind him. He glanced back, and watched in horror as Cara pulled herself to her feet. Her face a motley grey, she took a trembling step towards Yasin.

"The Anahera will not help you," she croaked, her voice barely audible above the wind whistling through the pass.

"Of course they will," Yasin said easily. "They just need the proper motivation."

The crossbow came up. A gasp came from Maisie. Erika screamed.

Romaine was already moving.

The bolt took him full in the chest, just as it had for Lorene. For the briefest of seconds, he felt nothing, only a rush of triumph, that he had stopped the arrow meant for Cara, that he had succeeded.

Then the pain struck, a searing, burning agony. It blossomed in his lungs and spread outwards like the tendrils of a rose, tearing and rending through his body, through his very being.

He staggered, then slumped to one knee as the strength went from his legs. Somewhere, someone was screaming, but he could barely hear them over the pounding in his ears. His vision swam and suddenly he was lying on the cold stones, staring up at Yasin. The man looked surprised, as though he couldn't quite believe what Romaine had done. Before he could reload his crossbow, a blurred figure attacked with sword in hand, and the two danced out of Romaine's field of vision.

The tear-streaked face of Cara replaced them as she fell to her knees beside him. She reached out a hand and her lips moved, but Romaine could no longer hear what she said. The agony was still growing, threatening to sweep him away on its irresistible tide. But he couldn't let go yet—not until he knew she was safe.

"Run!" he tried to gasp, though he couldn't know whether the word actually left his mouth.

Romaine! Inexplicably, Cara's voice spoke into his mind, a keening, howling sound that pained him beyond even the arrow in his chest. *Romaine, please, no!*

Tears burned in Romaine's eyes and somehow he lifted a hand, grasping at her jacket, desperate for her to flee, but his lips no longer seemed to work. He spoke them in his mind instead, a desperate prayer to the Goddess crouched beside him.

Cara, please, you have to run!

32

THE SOLDIER

Lukys gasped as his head broke the surface. A pounding began in his skull and he struggled to inhale, the sheer cold pressing on his chest, making each breath a battle. He swung around, trying to find his bearings. Lights drifted past him, away to his right—houses occupied by the Tangata. The currents were carrying him downriver fast. He needed to make it farther from the shore before he reached the bridge, lest the guards notice his passage.

Turning, he kicked out. His boots slipped on the currents, making the going difficult, and his clothing threatened to drag him down. At least the spear he held helped to keep him afloat. Teeth chattering, he focused on the darkness ahead, seeking some sign of the others, of the distant bank, of the bridge, but there was only the soft glint of the waters around him.

His body grew numb, the icy waters drawing away the last of his heat. Pain stabbed at his calves as he struggled on. At least he didn't carry any of their supplies like the Tangata. How had the creatures managed to cross the Illmoor? Its waters were twice as wide as these. Already he could feel his strength fading, his desperate gasps unable to sustain him.

Time crept by, the moon high above, the whispers of the river the only sound in his world. Soon, Lukys began to wonder if he had somehow missed the bridge. Surely it should not be taking so long to encounter it. Fatigue crept through his limbs, slowing his strokes, and he found himself glancing back, struggling to judge how far he'd come.

Something large loomed in the darkness, blocking out the moonlight. He gasped, realising the bridge was upon him. In the pitch-black, he grabbed desperately for a pillar. But its surface was smooth, cloaked in algae, and his fingers slipped. He cried out as the currents swept him between the pillars. Unable to see, he thrashed out with the spear, hoping to catch it on something, anything that would keep him from being dragged past the bridge—

Lukys lurched to a stop as something caught his spear, almost jolting it from his grasp. Water rushed around him and gritting his teeth, he held desperately to the weapon as he was dragged into a sheltered nook behind one of the columns. A hand went around his waist, pulling him in the rest of the way, until he found himself pressed against a warm body.

Grey eyes glinted in the darkness as Sophia held him close, keeping him from being sucked back into the river. Lukys swallowed, a shiver running through him, though he wasn't sure whether it was from the cold or her closeness. He opened his mouth to thank her, but amidst the shadows she raised a finger to her lips, then pointed to the stones above.

Lukys's heart lurched as he caught the soft tread of feet from overhead. He swallowed back the words he'd been about to speak. The steps grew closer, and he sensed the distant whisper of voices in his mind, still faint, but growing closer. He clutched at Sophia, her warmth bringing him back to life, and prayed the guards hadn't—

I heard something, a voice announced, clear now. *I swear.*

He felt Sophia tense against him, could feel her heart racing in pace with his own. There was no sign of the other recruits—hopefully they were already across, out of sight, free. Lukys closed his eyes and waited. There was nothing else they could do.

There's nothing out here, another replied. *You really think someone got past us?*

You really want to face that Old One if they did?

A pause. *Should we check the other side?*

The whispers in Lukys's mind grew louder as they neared. Beneath the bridge, they could not be seen, but Lukys's heart quickened at their words. If they crossed to the southern banks, there would be no missing the Perfugian recruits that had gone ahead.

He frowned as an idea came to him and he looked again at Sophia, turning her earlier words over in his mind. What had she said…that they could *encourage* emotions in others? Did that include the Tangata? She'd said he was stronger, that his Voice carried more force—could he use that? Had he already?

Silently, Lukys stretched out his mind to the guards, trying to take care not to broadcast his own fear. He was still too new at this, too inexperienced. Surely this was too dangerous…

…but no, he couldn't allow the guards to reach the far shore. One glimpse of the recruits would doom them all.

He touched their minds, gently, softly, brushing against their thoughts. He sensed their worry, their fear of failure, broadcast for the world to hear. But deeper, he sensed the fiery confidence of the Tangata, the belief in their strength.

He mimicked those thoughts himself, trying to augment, to reassure the two creatures there was nothing there.

No, the first said finally. *Nothing got passed us. Come on, I don't want to be caught away from our post.*

Lukys released a breath he hadn't realised he'd been holding as the footsteps retreated, moving quickly back towards the city. Sophia's eyes found him in the darkness, but she said nothing, and after a moment Lukys looked away.

They continued across the river, the cold now so ingrained in Lukys's bones that he could barely feel his extremities. If they spent much longer in the water, he feared discovery would be the least of their worries. He tried to pick up his pace, moving through the currents by pushing off one pillar with his feet and grasping desperately at the next as it came within reach, using the spear to find them in the darkness. In some places, though, the pillars were missing, and here it took all Lukys's energy just to keep from being swept away. On two occasions, Sophia had to grasp his spear and drag him back to safety. He prayed to the Gods that Travis and the others had managed to cross safely.

Lukys's frozen mind barely registered their arrival on the distant shore. He stumbled from the river, water coursing from his clothes. Shadows flickered ahead as first Travis, then Dale stepped from the darkness and embraced him. A tremor shook Lukys, but his friends were just as cold as he was. After a moment they broke apart and Lukys slumped to the sandy shore.

It was the worst thing he could have done. Now that he'd stopped moving, the tremors redoubled until his teeth were chattering so loudly he feared the guards might still hear him all the way from the city. He looked around as

Sophia strode from the water. Their eyes met and he opened his mouth to thank her, but could not get the words out.

Get up, she said, the words a command. *If you don't move, you'll die.*

Lukys hesitated at the coldness to her tone, but finally he nodded and dragged himself off the sand. He almost went to her, but fought the urge. They stood beside the bridge, its shadow stretching away into the dark, only to reappear in the distance where lanterns burned at the entrance of the city. He wondered how long it would take the Old One to discover their absence.

Still shaking, he turned his gaze from the river to the shoreline. His fellow Perfugians stood there in various states of wakefulness. It looked like all had survived the crossing, no doubt aided by their Tangatan partners. The creatures themselves stood alongside the recruits, keeping them moving, keeping them warm. A pang of longing touched him, that he could experience that same closeness, but he shook it off. His friends still didn't know what had been done to them.

That could wait. They needed to be away from this place.

"Where to?" Travis asked as the recruit caught his gaze.

Lukys shook his head, trying to force his frozen mind into action. His gaze lifted to the east. The first hints of morning silhouetted the Mountains of the Gods. He swallowed, images of Cara soaring towards him across the Illmoor appearing in his mind. Somewhere in those peaks, her family lived, their location marked by the map he held in his head. If they could reach that hidden site…

He turned back to his comrades, taking in their sodden state. Half appeared to have lost their spears in the currents, and only the supplies carried by the Tangata had made the crossing. Their clothing thin, suited to the milder climates of the south, and in the endless wilderness of Calafe there would be no finding anything better. Without proper cloaks and furs, they wouldn't last a night in those snow-capped peaks.

His heart sinking, he returned his gaze to the river. The currents swept past, making their endless journey down through lowland Calafe, to the coast, to the ocean. They had made it to the southern shore, the least likely place the Tangata would look for them, but they would need to cross again eventually if they wanted to journey north. But what then? Hundreds of miles lay between here and the questionable safety of Flumeer—and all of it territory claimed by the Tangata.

He shook his head. They would never make it.

"Let's go," he said, trying to keep the despair from his voice. They needed to move or they wouldn't even last the day.

We must walk in the water, Sophia's voice drifted through his thoughts. *The older generations might track us by your scent.*

Lukys gritted his teeth, but nodded. "Back in the water," he said to the recruits. "We go downriver."

Several flashed him strange looks, but they were soon marching west away from the bridge, boots squelching with each step. Thankfully the water was shallow this side of the Shelman, the stones firm beneath their feet. They made good progress, though Lukys could feel the cold eating at his legs. Despite the risk, they would need to light a fire when they finally stopped, or risk frostbite.

They pressed on through the darkness, making it a mile downstream before finally leaving the water. From there they continued west, threading their way through the light shrub that grew along the riverbank.

Despite their progress, Lukys could feel his spirits falling with each step. He still didn't know where they could go, whether they should cross the river again. All he knew was they had to keep moving. But were they only delaying the inevitable? Even if they reached Flumeer, how long could the nation stand? Against the power of the Old One, of the Tangata, the human armies that defended the banks of the Illmoor seemed pitiful by comparison.

A sense of hopelessness crept into his thoughts and he found his shoulders slumping, his steps slowing in the darkness. What was the point of fighting on when all hope was lost?

He started as light appeared in the darkness, illuminating the ground beneath his feet. Stumbling to a stop, he swung around, almost surprised to see the sun lifting out from behind those towering mountains. Again he felt the urge to seek the distant peaks. Perhaps there he would find answers—about Sophia and the other Tangatan partners, about the Old Ones, about his own strange ability.

But that path was barred to him. Yet the sight still lifted him, reminded him there were still greater forces at play in the world, counters to the power of the Old One. Cara would stand against them, Romaine as well. They had already defeated the creatures once, down in the bowels of the earth. They could do it again.

No, Lukys needed to focus on his own survival, on the survival of his Perfugian companions. Let the queens and Gods and the Tangata wage their war; Lukys only needed to save the few brave souls that had dared to follow him this far. He would see them safely home.

His eyes lifted to the river and he thought again of its endless journey, down to the distant ocean, and his heart quickened as a thought came to him. He turned, seeking out Sophia. His heart clenched as he found her nearby, ashy hair lit by the rising sun. She had stayed close, his own personal guardian—

He shook off the thought, concentrating on the task at hand.

Sophia, he murmured, keeping their conversation private for now. She looked around, eyes lifting in surprise, and he quickly went on. *You know these lands. What lies at the mouth of the river?*

The Tangata's eyebrows knitted together and it was a moment before she responded. *Sand,* she replied, *and…there is a small fishing village, I believe.*

Lukys's heart quickened, and nodding to her, he strode ahead. They would stop soon, to rest and recover, to dry out their soaked clothing, but for now a fresh determination set him alight. He knew where they needed to go now, difficult as the journey might be. There was only one place left in the kingdoms of man that might grant them safe harbour, one place that could withstand whatever fate befell the rest of humanity. One place where he might find answers.

We're going home.

🌿 33 🌿

THE FUGITIVE

Erika watched as Romaine slumped to the ground, his eyes fluttering closed. The Goddess clutched desperately at his chest, but the Calafe did not move.

Grief touched Erika as she looked on the dying man, but the loss barely registered beside her anguish, beside her rage at the man Yasin. Nearby, Maisie had drawn her blade and was battling furiously with the Flumeeren cutthroat. Silently Erika crouched, her fingers closing around the gauntlet she'd dropped.

Lifting it to her hand, she made to put it back on, then froze. Blood pounded in her ears as she looked on the source of the magic she had wielded these past months. Fear touched her as she recalled the ecstasy she had felt at its use, the power it had granted her. She longed for that power, and yet…if she put it back on, would she ever have the strength to remove it again?

A *thump* from nearby diverted her attention back to the warring pair in time to see Maisie's blade go skittering across the gravels. The spy herself staggered back clutching her arm. Blood soaked her fingers as she tripped over the uneven ground and collapsed against the stones.

It was now or never. Closing her eyes, she moved her hand towards the gauntlet.

Then she flinched as a terrible keening sound erupted through the pass. Her eyes snapped open and she watched as Cara strode past, her eyes fixed on the Flumeeren killer.

Eyes stained grey, eyes the colour of death.

The keening turned to a terrible growl as auburn wings snapped wide. Cara no longer looked on the verge of death. She looked as she had in the tunnels of the Gods, fighting those ancient creatures.

Like a monster herself, the Tangata reborn.

And her gaze was fixed on Yasin.

"What the…" Yasin began, then broke off as Cara continued towards him.

Realising his danger, the cutthroat leapt for his crossbow. Erika's heart lurched in her chest and she looked at Cara, but the Goddess made no move to stop him. Snatching up the weapon, Yasin hesitated, seeming confused at Cara's hesitation. But he didn't hesitate for long, and quickly he wound back the crossbow and dropped a bolt into place. Looking more confident now, he pointed it at Cara.

"Now, where were we?" He smiled again, though this time it seemed forced.

Cara only tilted her head to the side, as though perplexed by the human's actions. A snarl tore from Yasin and a sharp *twang* followed as the crossbow discharged. Erika cried out as Cara seemed to *shift*, but a blink later, and the winged Goddess was still standing. Only now she held a crossbow bolt in one outstretched hand.

What?

The terrible growl rumbled through the pass again.

Then the Goddess was stalking towards Yasin, and her grey eyes promised death.

Cursing, Yasin threw aside the crossbow and drew his sword. "Come on then, bitch," he hissed. "Let's see if Gods bleed."

A smile spread across Cara's lips. Erika shuddered as she looked into the Goddess's eyes. There was a madness in those grey depths. This was not the woman she had come to know over the last weeks, the Goddess who had spoken of unbreakable promises and peace. Cara had become something else entirely. And all her attention was fixed on Yasin.

Screaming, Yasin leapt at Cara, sword flashing for her throat. The attack came suddenly, without warning, and despite herself Erika flinched. Cara only watched him come, that same sickly smile on her lips, until at the last moment she twisted, becoming a blur, and the sword cut empty air.

Carried forward by his momentum, Yasin found himself standing alongside the Goddess, sword pointing in the wrong direction. Snarling, he swung again, and this time Cara was forced to move, ducking beneath a wild sweep of his blade. She straightened almost instantly as Yasin stumbled past, her cold grey eyes still watching him, mocking him.

Yasin roared as he spun and stabbed out again. This time, Cara's hand flashed down, catching the Flumeeren by the wrist. Cursing, he tried to pull himself free, but Cara didn't seem to notice his efforts. She looked into his eyes, then her grip tightened. And the rogue started to scream.

Erika's hair stood on end as the sharp *crack* of breaking bones carried to her ears. Steel clashed against rock as the sword tumbled from the man's fingers. Then suddenly he was free, released from the Goddess's grip. He stumbled away, hand held up before him, and Erika choked, her stomach roiling.

His wrist was bent where Cara had held him, a shard of bone jabbing from the flesh. A moan rattled from Yasin as he stared at the mangled limb, but adrenaline must have swamped the pain, for as Cara moved again he screamed, and dropping his left hand to his belt, he drew a dagger. Face twisted in agony, he drew back his hand to hurl the blade.

Cara moved faster still, her wings beating down, sending her hurtling forward. Before Yasin knew what was happening she was upon him, his left arm now in her grasp. The cold smile spread as he cried out, a plea on his lips…

…it turned to a shriek as she wrenched. Another *crunch* echoed through the canyon.

Yasin staggered back from Cara, dagger on the ground, mangled arms held before him. His screams were constant now. Erika could hardly bare to watch, though this was the man who had killed her father, who had cast her entire life into the void. The murderer's face was pale and tears ran from his eyes as he retreated from Cara, shaking his head, pleading.

The Goddess stalked after him, and with a mortal cry, Yasin turned to flee.

Like a cat with a mouse, Cara pounced. She moved with a languid confidence now, of a predator that knew its prey could not escape. Her boot flashed out, catching the Flumeeren in the side of his knee. Another *crack* punctuated the blow.

Yasin slammed into the rocks, his cries breaking off as the impact drove the breath from his lungs. Cara stood over him, wings spread, icy eyes watching him. She was still smiling. A desperate moan came from the man as he finally caught his breath. It turned to sobs as he looked up and saw the Goddess.

"Please, Gods, no—"

She broke his other leg.

Unable to bear it any longer, Erika looked away. A shudder ran down her spine as her gaze fell on the gauntlet. It was still in her hand, but the thought of putting it on now turned her insides to liquid. If this was what the magic of the Gods could do to the peaceful, good-humoured woman she had known, what would it do to her?

A sudden silence fell across the canyon as Yasin's final scream was cut off. Erika flinched, and looking up, she noticed Maisie. There was fear in the eyes of the spy. Steeling herself, Erika looked for her friend…and stifled a scream as she found Cara standing just a few feet away.

Blood covered the Goddess's tunic, still dripped from her hands. The scream again built in Erika's throat as she looked into Cara's grey eyes and saw the madness there, the thirst for blood. A snarl rumbled from the Goddess's chest as she bared her teeth and stepped towards her.

"Cara…"

The voice was so soft, Erika barely caught it on the wind, but the Goddess heard. Her head whipped around as though she'd been struck, grey eyes fixing on the crumpled figure in the mouth of the pass. Romaine had not moved from where he'd fallen, and Erika swallowed at the sight of blood staining the rock beneath him.

Glancing at the Goddess, Erika watched as Cara blinked. Once, twice, three times. Then the grey was gone, the amber returned. Tears spilt down her cheeks as she cried out. In a second she was at the Calafe's side, crouching beside him, reaching for the bolt that still protruded from his chest.

"Don't," Romaine breathed.

"Romaine," Cara whispered, hand still outstretched, voice filled with pain.

Erika moved closer, her own vision blurring at the sight of the fallen Calafe warrior.

"Is it…done?" the man croaked, trying to lift his head.

A moan built in Cara's throat as she looked at where the mangled remains of Yasin lay. Erika could see her horror—and something else. Terror at what she'd done? Quickly Erika moved alongside them, crouching on Romaine's other side.

"He's gone, Romaine," she murmured. "We're safe."

"Good," Romaine whispered. "Good."

"Romaine, no…" Cara sobbed, grasping at his shirt, Yasin's blood mingling with the Calafe's. "No, please don't, you saved me, you can't..."

"Ah, little one," Romaine replied. He reached up with a trembling hand, touching it to her face. "Don't cry. I couldn't…let him hurt you. Couldn't fail…anyone else. Ahh…but that hurts…"

"My people, they'll help you," Cara gasped. "We're so close, just don't go, please, promise me."

A smile touched Romaine's face, but his eyes no longer seemed to see them. "No, little one," he whispered. "No, not…this time. They're…waiting for me."

Air whispered from his throat in a long, unending sigh. Erika crouched alongside him, waiting for the next whisper of breath. It never came. The keening sounded in Cara's throat again, but this time she only threw herself against the warrior's chest. Muffled sobs sounded as she hugged him and Erika looked away, grief touching her as well.

She sat back on her haunches, unable to believe the warrior was really gone. They had survived the creatures of the earth together, withstood the assault of the Tangata, escaped the soldiers of Flumeer. After so much, he had seemed invincible, able to overcome any obstacle.

Now he was dead.

The last warrior of Calafe, her final connection with a past she had tried for half her life to bury.

Or perhaps not. Looking down at the face of the warrior, she was reminded of all those lost refugees of Calafe camped outside the Flumeeren capital. She had looked down upon those sorry men and women, condemned them for their weakness, judged them for failing to rise above the destruction of their nation.

But the truth was, Erika was the one who had failed. The queen was a tyrant, had schemed and plotted to murder her father, to see Calafe fall, all so Flumeer could rise from the ashes of their kingdom. And Erika had served her. The thought was like bile in her mouth.

Slowly she rose and turned to look down upon the valley below. The squat building still awaited them. The secrets of the Gods, of her gauntlet. Drawing in a breath, she took a step towards the valley.

A sharp *crack* from overhead brought her to a halt and she swung around, thinking it must be Maisie. But the spy's eyes were on the sky. The hairs on the back of Erika's neck stood on end as she followed the direction of the woman's gaze in time to glimpse a flash of green and blue. Then something solid slammed into the ground nearby, sending a shower of stones flying outwards from the figure that had landed. Two more followed as the first straightened.

The breath caught in Erika's throat as she looked upon the Gods. Two were male with wings of emerald and sapphire feathers, stretched wide for all to see. The last female bore wings of purest white, an angel from the heavens. The sight robbed Erika of her courage and she slumped to her knees, unable to tear her gaze from their glory.

Beside her, finally Cara moved. Releasing Romaine, she rose. A tremor shook her body as she cast one last look at the fallen Calafe, then she stepped past him to face the three Gods.

"Hello, brother," she whispered.

The first of the Gods stepped towards her, emerald wings lifting in response. Eyes the colour of flames inspected the little Goddess, before darting to the bodies of Romaine and Yasin. Upon sighting the fallen cutthroat, his jaw tightened and he returned his gaze to Cara. A look of pain crossed his face as he shook his head.

"Ah, sister," he whispered. "What have you done?"

EPILOGUE
THE TANGATA

A donis gasped as consciousness returned in a sudden flash of agony. He groaned, struggling to suck a breath into lungs that felt as though they were drowning. Tasting blood in his mouth, he rolled onto his side and spat it out. It didn't help. He clenched his fists, struggling against the pain, against the call of unconsciousness.

So you live.

A shiver ran down Adonis's spine and looking around, he found Maya standing nearby. The stony eyes pierced him as she crossed the courtyard and stopped beside him.

Where is the human? she asked, crouching.

Adonis swallowed, trying to draw back his memories. There was a warning in the Old One's voice. She would not tolerate failure. He had to be strong. Gathering himself, he pulled himself to his knees. Agony threatened to swallow him and a trickle of hot liquid ran down his chest. Gritting his teeth, he pressed a hand to his wound to slow the bleeding.

Gone, he replied, meeting her gaze.

Maya did not offer him a hand, though her eyes

remained on him, as though waiting. Clenching his fists, Adonis forced himself to his feet. Pain radiated from the wound. The spear had punctured his left lung, but thankfully missed his spine. Again he felt the drowning sensation and for a second his vision spun. He held on, clinging to consciousness until it cleared. He was of the third generation; he would not allow a mere human to strike him down.

And yet it had. How? Adonis gritted his teeth. He would be sure to ask the human when he caught it.

A smile twisted Maya's lips at the sight of him standing and she reached out to stroke his cheek. Adonis sighed, some of the pain receding at her touch.

It will not get far, he breathed. *I will hunt the human down, bring it back for you.*

No, Maya replied softly.

She took his hand then and led him from the courtyard, out into the street. The sun had risen unnoticed as he slept, and now it shone brightly in a cloudless sky. In the distance, the snow-capped peaks shimmered in the morning light.

Show me again my enemy, Maya's voice whispered into his mind.

Unbidden, Adonis found himself back on the banks of the Illmoor, watching as the Anahera fought her way through his warrior pairs. She had batted them away like mere children at first, wings and feet and fists making short work of the fifth generation Tangata. Yet after each blow, his warriors had risen and come for her again, fighting on until eventually even the Anahera's strength had faded.

She does not kill, Maya's voice whispered over the scene, and Adonis again found himself standing in the streets of New Nihelm. The Old One looked at him, eyes alight with bloodlust. *My enemies have grown soft.*

Adonis swallowed as he found himself trapped in that steely gaze. *What do you wish of me, my love?*

Laughter rasped from Maya's throat as her eyes returned to the mountains.

It is time we brought war to the Gods of man.

———

HERE ENDS BOOK TWO OF
DESCENDANTS OF THE FALL

The story continues in:
Age of Gods

———

Hey folks, just a quick note to say thank you for reading this book! I hope you've enjoyed the journey so far. It would really mean a lot to me if you stopped by Amazon to leave your honest review—even if it's just a few words. Reviews are such an important part of marketing our books to the world and without them I literally would not be able to continue writing these stories! Thank you in advance. You can find the link to the Amazon and Goodreads pages for Wrath of the Forgotten below:
Wrath of the Forgotten Amazon
Wrath of the Forgotten Goodreads

NOTE FROM THE AUTHOR

Well this book had to be written in some of the strangest, scariest circumstances I've ever experienced. Wrath of the Forgotten was started in late March 2020, not long after Buenos Aires went into lockdown. Little did I know at the time that the city would remain in quarantine for three months (and counting), and that I would end up finishing this book while in a quarantine hotel in Auckland, New Zealand. I'm still sad about having to leave my adopted home, but glad I made the decision given how difficult that isolation was becoming. Despite being luckier than most with my job and apartment, I could feel the creativity being crushed out of me day after day. Here's hoping a few months in winter wonderland New Zealand can bring it back!

Anyway, I hope you enjoyed the story. With my newfound freedom, I'm excited to see what the characters discover in Age of Gods!

FOLLOW AARON HODGES...
And receive TWO FREE novels and a short story!
www.aaronhodges.co.nz/newsletter-signup/

LEGENDS OF THE GODS

If you've enjoyed this book, you might want to check out another of my fantasy series!

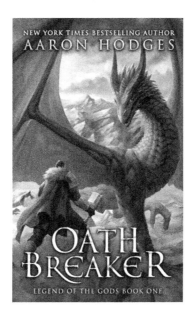

A century since the departure of the Gods, the Three Nations are now united beneath the Tsar. Magic has been outlawed, its power too dangerous to remain unchecked. All Magickers must surrender themselves to the crown, or face imprisonment and death.

Alana's mundane life has just been torn apart by the emergence of her brother's magic. Now they must leave behind everything they've ever known and flee – before the Tsar's Stalkers pick up their trail.

Tasked with hunting down renegade Magickers, the merciless hunters will stop at nothing to bring them before the Tsar's judgement.

THE EVOLUTION GENE

If you've enjoyed this book, you might want to check out my dystopian sci-fi series!

In 2051, the Western Allies States have risen as the new power in North America. But a terrifying plague is sweeping through the nation. Its victims do not die—they change. People call them the *Chead*, and where they walk, destruction follows.

Printed in Great Britain
by Amazon